Praise for Heather Blake's
Wishcraft Mystery Series

"An enchanting and thoroughly likable sleuth."
—*New York Times* bestselling author Denise Swanson

"Magic and murder . . . What could be better? It's exactly the book you've been wishing for!"
—Casey Daniels, author of *Supernatural Born Killers*

"Blake successfully blends crime, magic, romance, and self-discovery in her lively debut." —*Publishers Weekly*

"Wow! Ms. Blake has taken the paranormal mystery to a whole new fun yet intriguing level. . . . This story is . . . mysterious, whimsical, [and] delightful. . . . Heather Blake makes it *work*!" —Once Upon a Romance

"Heather Blake has created a wonderful new spin on witches in Salem that is both lighthearted and serious. An all-around wonderful read." —The Hive

"Heather Blake casts a spell on her audience."
—The Mystery Gazette

"A good quick, breezy read."
—Pagan Newswire Collective

"This stellar, standout serie
Extremely high! . . . Wicked

Other Mysteries by Heather Blake

The Wishcraft Series
It Takes a Witch
A Witch Before Dying
The Good, the Bad, and the Witchy

A Potion to Die For

∾◉ A Magic Potion Mystery ◉∾

HEATHER BLAKE

AN OBSIDIAN MYSTERY

OBSIDIAN
Published by the Penguin Group
Penguin Group (USA) LLC, 375 Hudson Street,
New York, New York 10014

USA | Canada | UK | Ireland | Australia | New Zealand | India | South Africa | China
penguin.com
A Penguin Random House Company

First published by Obsidian, an imprint of New American Library,
a division of Penguin Group (USA) LLC

First Printing, November 2013

ISBN 978-0-451-41630-8

Printed in the United States of America
10 9 8 7 6 5 4 3 2 1

A Potion to Die For

❧ Chapter One ❧

If there were a Wanted poster for witches, I was sure my freckled face would be on it.

Ducking behind a tree to catch my breath, I sucked in a deep lungful of humid air as I listened to the cries of the search party.

I didn't have much time before the frenzied mob would turn the corner and spot me, but I needed to take a rest or risk keeling over in the street.

It was times like these that I wished I were the kind of witch who had a broomstick. Then I could just fly off, safe and sound, and wouldn't be hiding behind a live oak, my hair sticking to its bark while my lungs were on fire.

But *noooo*. I had to be a healing witch from a long line of hoodoo practitioners (and one rogue voodoo-er, but no need to go into that this very moment). I was a love-potion expert, matchmaker, all-around relationship guru, and an unlikely medicine woman.

Fat lot of good all that did me right now.

In fact, my magic potions were why I was in this predicament in the first place.

I'd bet my life savings (which, admittedly, wasn't much) that my archnemesis, Delia Bell Barrows, had a broomstick. And though I had never before been envious of the black witch, I was feeling a stab of jealousy now.

Quickly glancing around, I suddenly hoped Delia lurked somewhere nearby—something she had been doing a lot of lately. I'd been trying my best to avoid a confrontation with her, but if she had a broomstick handy—and was willing to loan it to me—I would be more than willing to talk.

There were some things worth compromising principles for, obviously. Like a rabid mob.

But the brick-paved road, lined on both sides with tall shade trees, was deserted. If Delia was around, she had a good hiding spot. Smart, because there was a witch hunt going on in the streets of Hitching Post, Alabama.

And I was the hunted witch.

Again.

This really had to stop.

Ordinarily I would've ridden my bike, Bessie Blue, to work, but when I saw the crowd gathered on my curb that morning, I snuck out the back door. Unfortunately, someone had spotted mc and the chase was on. I'd cut across to the next block over, then doubled back to my street. And now here I was, trying to catch my breath and hoping for a broomstick, of all things.

Pushing off from the tree, I spared a quick glance behind me as the crowd turned the corner.

"There she is!" someone shouted.

Heart pounding, I made a break for it. I jumped the rotting picket fence surrounding my aunt Marjoram's front yard, skipped over loose stepping-stones, brushed away overgrown shrubs, and then made a dash toward the back gate.

I nearly tripped as I tried to wade through a thigh-high weed patch, and heard the cackle of my aunt's voice.

"Carly Bell Hartwell, get your skinny ass out of my garden!"

Some garden. "Sorry, Aunt Marjie!" I yelled over my shoulder. "But they're after me."

"Again?" she shouted from the steps of her dilapidated deck.

The high-pitched cries of the crowd trying to find me carried easily in the quiet morning. "Mr. Dunwoody made his forecast."

"Land's end!" Marjie shouted. "I'll get my gun."

I didn't bother to try to talk my aunt out of it. The townsfolk would be safe enough—most knew better than to trespass in Marjie's yard. And if they blatantly ignored all the posted No Trespassing signs, they'd get what they deserved.

Just like those Birmingham lawyers who'd been sniffing around Marjie's place the past few weeks.

I didn't think those stuffed-shirt businessmen would be back anytime soon.

Shotgun blasts had that effect on city folk.

Taking a deep breath, I yanked open the wooden gate at the back of Marjie's property. Rusted hinges groaned in agony, and the brambles at my feet didn't want to give the gate an inch of swing, stubbornly digging their thorns into anything they could grab onto. Including my shins, which made me regret my choice of shorts over jeans that morning.

I yanked for all I was worth. The gate swung only a

foot, but it was all I needed. I wiggled through the narrow space. Safe on the sidewalk on the other side, I assessed the damage from the brambles (minimal), and wished I had a cell phone to call for backup.

Unfortunately, I didn't have a cell phone. No one in town did because there was no coverage, thanks to the surrounding mountains and the town's refusal to build an ugly cell-phone tower that would ruin the picturesque landscape. Except for a noisy few, we'd all embraced the quirk as a charming throwback to a simpler time. But right now, a cell would've been handy.

I headed for the town center, not having time to admire the sun-dappled view of the Appalachian foothills in the distance. I had lived in Hitching Post, Alabama—the wedding capital of the South—nearly my whole life, with only one brief, somewhat disastrous foray beyond its borders. I loved this town, but right now, I wished it were smaller. Much smaller. Like, a one-stoplight kind of place—because it seemed as if I'd been hotfooting it down side roads and back alleys for an hour now, even though it had been only ten minutes.

The heart of Hitching Post was made up of a large circle, nicknamed the Ring (very appropriate, considering it was a wedding town). In its charming middle was a grassy picnic park with twisting trails, big shade trees, flowers, and a gazebo smack-dab in its center. A wide cobblestone sidewalk (no roadways inside the Ring) connected the park to dozens of shops, offices, and restaurants.

Splintering outward from the Ring were parking areas, quaint neighborhoods, the scenic river walk, and the bread and butter of Hitching Post: the chapels, inns, and reception venues catering to the marriage crowd. People came from all over for quickie country weddings—more intimate and personal and less tacky than Vegas. Hitching Post looked postcard perfect, too, and was consistently named one of America's most beautiful small towns, which had a lot to do with the mountain backdrop, the river views, and all the effort the beautification committee expended to create the perfect idyllic Southern atmosphere.

Occasionally tossing looks over my shoulder as I stealthily entered the Ring, I zipped down the sidewalk toward Déjà Brew, the local coffee shop. Ordinarily I'd go in and visit with the shop owner, Jessamine Yadkin, pick up a muffin, linger over some coffee.

This morning, however, Jessa waited in the doorway of the shop with a to-go bag dangling from an outstretched arm. I grabbed it—kind of like a marathoner would snatch a cup of water—and kept on going. "Thanks, Jessa!"

"Run faster, Carly!" she yelled in her raspy, used-to-smoke-two-packs-a-day voice. "They're gaining on you!"

Run faster. Easy for her to say.

At this rate, I was going to need a defibrillator by the time I reached the safety of my store, the Little Shop of Potions. The crowd was gaining on me; I needed to pick up my pace.

Unfortunately, my shop was on the opposite side of the Ring from Déjà Brew. A good half mile at least if I followed the walkway; less if I cut diagonally across the picnic park and hurdled some shrubbery. The choice was a no-brainer. Thankfully, I had a head start. A small one, but it was enough.

Sweat dripped from my hairline as I dodged picnic tables and flower beds. Behind me, I heard pounding footsteps, along with hollers of "Carly! Carly!"

I ran at a dead sprint and finally my shop came fully into sight. The storefront was painted a dark purple with lavender trim, and the name of the shop was written in bold curlicue letters on the large picture window. Underneath was the shop's tagline: MIND, BODY, HEART, AND SOUL. Behind the glass, several vignettes featuring antique glass jars, mortars and pestles, apothecary scales, and weights I'd collected over the years filled the big display space.

At this point I should have felt nothing but utter relief. I was almost there. So . . . close.

But instead of relief, a new panic arose.

Because standing in front of my door was none other than Delia Bell Barrows.

I could hardly believe it. *Now* she showed up.

I grabbed the store key from my pocket and held it at the ready. "Out of the way, Delia!"

Delia stood firm, neck to toe in black—from her cape to her toenails, which stuck out from a pair of black patent flip-flops that were decorated with a skull and crossbones. A little black dog, tucked like Toto into the basket that hung from Delia's forearm, barked.

The dog and the basket were new. The cape, all the black, and the skull-and-crossbones fascination were not.

"I need to talk to you, Carly," Delia said. "Right now."

I hip-checked Delia out of the way, and the dog yapped again. Sticking the key into the lock, I said, "You're going to have to wait. Like everyone else." I threw a nod over my shoulder.

The crowd, at least forty strong, was bearing down.

Delia let out a gasp. "Did Mr. Dunwoody give a forecast this morning?"

"Yes." The lock tumbled, and I pushed open the door

and scooted inside. Much to my dismay, Delia snuck in behind me.

I had two options: to kick out the black witch—which would then let in the crowd . . . or keep Delia in and the crowd out.

Delia won.

I slammed the door and threw the lock.

Just in time. Fists pounded the wood frame, and dozens of eyes peered through the window.

I yelled through the leaded glass panel, "I'll be open in half an hour!" but the anxious crowd kept banging on the door.

Trying to catch my breath, I walked over the cash register counter, an old twelve-drawer chestnut filing cabinet. I set down my to-go bag, opened one of the drawers, and grabbed a small roll of numbered paper tickets. Walking back to the door, I shoved them through the wide mail slot. "Take numbers," I shouted at the eager faces. "You know the drill!"

Because, unfortunately, this wasn't the first time this had happened.

Turning my back to the crowd, I leaned against the door and then slid down its frame to the floor. For a second I rested against the wood, breathing in the comforting scents of my shop. The lavender, lemon balm, mint. The hint of peach leaf, sage, cinnamon. All brought back memories of my grandma Adelaide Hartwell, who'd opened the shop more than fifty years before.

"You should probably exercise more," Delia said. Her little dog barked.

My chest felt so tight, I thought any minute it might explode. "I think I just ran a 5K. Second time this month."

"What exactly did Mr. Dunwoody's forecast say?"

"Sunny with a chance of divorce."

Delia peeked out the window. "That explains why there are so many of them. I wonder whose marriage is on the chopping block."

The matrimonial predictions of Mr. Dunwoody, my septuagenarian neighbor, were never wrong. His occasional forecasts foretold of residential current affairs, so to speak. On a beautiful spring Friday in Hitching Post, one might think a wedding—or a few dozen—were on tap. But it had happened, a time or two, that a couple had a sudden change of heart over their recent nuptials (usually after the alcohol wore off the next morning) and set out to get the marriage immediately annulled or file for a quickie, uncontested divorce.

And even though Mr. Dunwoody was never wrong, I often wished he'd keep his forecasts to himself.

Being the owner of the Little Shop of Potions, a magic potion shop that specialized in love potions, was a bit like being a mystical bartender. People talked to me. A lot. About everything. Especially about falling in love and getting married, which was the height of irony, considering my mother's side of the family consisted of confirmed matrimonial cynics. Luckily, the hopeless romanticism on my father's side balanced things out for me. Mostly.

Somehow over the years I had become the town's unofficial relationship expert. It was at times rewarding . . . and a bit exasperating. The weight of responsibility was overwhelming, and I didn't always have the answers, magic potions or not.

Because Southerners embraced crazy like a warm blanket on a chilly night, not many here cared much that I called myself a witch, or that I practiced magic using a touch of hoodoo. But the town did believe I had all the answers—and expected me to find solutions.

My customers cared only about whether I could make their lives better. Be it an upset stomach or a relationship falling apart . . . they wanted healing.

And when there was a divorce forecast, they were relentless until I made them a love potion ensuring their marriage was secure. I had a lot of work to get done today. Work I'd rather not do with Delia around.

"Why are you here?" I asked her.

"You've been ignoring my calls."

If one was especially myopic and viewing us from afar, we might pass as sisters. The blond hair, the same height, the same nose and jawline. Which made sense. Seeing as how we were first cousins. Delia's mother, Neige, was my father's sister.

Delia (Hartwell) Bell Barrows was a snowy-white blonde with shoulder-length hair, ice-blue eyes, and creamy, pale skin. I was a cornfield blonde with golden wheat–colored hair, big milk chocolate–colored eyes, and dozens of freckles. Where I was the very image of a girl next door, Delia was ice-princess striking.

"You've been calling?" I asked, straight-faced.

My cousin was persistent, I'd give her that. I had been ignoring her phone calls for the past two days. I could only imagine what she wanted as she looked around the shop—it was the first time she'd been in here. Just as I'd yet to step foot in her shop, the Till Hex Do Us Part boutique, a mystically themed gift shop that featured her personalized liquid hexes.

"You know I have." She used minimal makeup, and that was the only thing that kept her from looking as though she'd completely lost her mind, with all the black she wore. "It's quite rude of you to make me track you down."

It wasn't the first time I'd been called rude. "Don't you have to get to work?"

Our businesses were yet another thing that set us apart. I used our hoodoo roots to heal people, and Delia used our voodoo roots to create hexes.

It was a divide that had defined our heritage, really, harking back to our great-great-grandparents, Leila Bell and Abraham Leroux. The legend of what happened to them was infamous in Hitching Post as one of those bittersweet stories of star-crossed lovers that was retold over and over again as a warning to young girls as to why they should never, *ever* marry a bad boy.

"Carly," she said, taking hold of an engraved round silver locket, an orb that swung from an extra-long chain around her neck. "This is serious."

The engraving on the locket was of two lilies entwined to form a heart, and inside it held a strand of our great-great-grandmother Leila's golden hair.

I knew, because I had an identical locket around my neck.

Beyond our looks, common middle name, and nail-biting habit, Delia and I also shared one *big* similarity, a trait passed down to all the women on my father's side of the family.

We had all inherited Leila's ability to feel other people's emotions. Their pain, their joy.

The lockets, protective amulets given to us by our grammy Adelaide when we were babies, weren't meant as defense from others. They offered protection from ourselves. From our own abilities. These lockets allowed us to shut off our empathetic gift at will so we could live as normally as possible.

Well, as normally as possible while practicing magic in this crazy Southern town.

My ability was almost always turned off, way off, except when I needed to tap into a client's energy in order to create a perfect potion for him or her. However, there were times, despite my charmed locket, when I was overstressed or tired, that I couldn't control the ability at all and was forced into hibernation until I could handle society again.

My empathetic gift also came with an added bonus that no one else—not even Delia—shared: a sixth sense of sorts that I had no power over whatsoever. Warning signals that all wasn't quite right in my world. My best friend, Ainsley, called them my "witchy senses." It was as good a description as any.

"How serious?" I asked.

"Very."

I was feeling warning twinges now, and had to wonder if they were coming from the crowd outside . . . or Delia's dramatic pronouncement.

"Well, out with it already." I was very wary of Delia, and wondered if she was trying to trick me somehow. As a dabbler in the dark arts, one who used her magic with no concern for its consequences or side effects, Delia's magic was definitely dangerous but not nearly as potent as my magic.

She'd do just about anything to learn my spells and uncover the secret component that made my potions so successful—mostly because she was still in a snit that due to an unfortunate (for her) case of bad timing, I had possession of the secret magical ingredient and she didn't. And essentially, because of that one ingredient, my magic was more powerful than hers would ever be — and that bugged her to no end.

"Rude," she muttered.

"I'm kind of busy, if you can't tell."

Delia was six minutes younger than I — a source of contention that had created a chasm as deep as Alabama's Pisgah Gorge through the Hartwell family, splitting brother and sister apart.

All because I had been born two months prematurely, making *me* the oldest grandchild.

Making *me* the heir to the family grimoire and the keeper of the Leilara bottle and all its magical secrets.

Making *my* abilities superior to Delia's.

The grimoire was basically a recipe book for Leila's hoodoo remedies, folk magic at its most natural. It had been handed down to the oldest child on my father's side of the family ever since Leila and Abraham died tragically. And the Leilara, well, that was pure magic born from their deaths. The way the Leilara drops mixed with specific herbs and minerals in a potion was what made that concoction effective. I couldn't rightly say I understood how it worked, but I firmly believed magic was one of those things to *feel* rather than study.

If my mother hadn't gone into labor two months early, the grimoire and the Leilara would have gone to Delia and the dark side. Aunt Neige had argued for years that gestational age should have taken precedence over actual birth dates, but her outcry had been overruled by Grammy Adelaide.

Currently, the grimoire and the Leilara were safely hidden, tucked inside a specially crafted hidey-hole in my shop's potion-making room. Hidden, because if Delia had her way and got her hands on the book of spells and the bottle of magic drops ... Right now the Leilara drops were used for good, to heal. But with Delia, they'd be used for evil, to make her hexes that much more wicked.

"I had a dream," Delia said, fussing with her dog's basket.

"A Martin Luther King Jr. kind? Or an REM, drool-on-the-pillow kind?" I asked, looking up at her.

"REM. But I don't drool."

"Noted," I said, but didn't believe it for a minute. I shifted on the floor; my rear was going numb. "What was it about? The dream?"

Delia said, "You."

"Me? Why?"

Delia closed her eyes and shook her head. After a dramatic pause, she looked at me straight on. "Don't ask me. It's not like I have any control over what I dream. Trust me. Otherwise, I'd be dreaming of David Beckham, not you."

I could understand that. "Why are you telling me this?" We weren't exactly on friendly terms.

Delia bit her thumbnail. All of her black-painted nails had been nibbled to the quick. "I don't like you. I've never liked you, and I daresay the feeling is mutual."

I didn't feel the need to agree aloud. I had *some* manners, after all. "But?" I knew there was one coming.

"I felt I had to warn you. Because even though I don't like you, I don't particularly want to see anything bad happen to you, us being family and all."

Now I was really worried. "Warn me about what?"

Caution filled Delia's ice-blue eyes. "You're in danger."

Danger of losing my sanity, maybe. This whole day had been more than a little surreal, and it wasn't even nine a.m. I laughed. "You know this from a dream?"

"It's not funny, Carly. At all. I . . . see things in dreams. Things that come true. You're in very real danger."

She said it so calmly, so easily, that I immediately believed her. I'd learned from a very early age not to dismiss things that weren't easily understood or explainable. Maybe Delia's dreams were akin to my witchy senses—which should always be taken seriously.

"What kind of danger?" I asked. I'd finally caught my breath and needed a glass of water. I hauled myself off the floor and headed for the small break room in the back of the shop. I wasn't the least bit surprised when Delia followed.

"I don't know," she admitted.

I flipped on a light. And froze. Delia bumped into my back.

We stood staring at the sight before us.

Delia said breathlessly, "It might have something to do with him."

Him being the dead man lying facedown on the floor, blood dried under his head, his stiff hands clutching a potion bottle.

❧ Chapter Two ❧

There hadn't been a murder in Hitching Post in nearly five years, not since Mrs. Wallerman "accidentally" ran over Mr. Wallerman after finding out he'd taken up with a young clerk from the local market. When the jury took a look at the multipierced, bodacious young mistress and heard the story of the salacious affair, they found Mrs. Wallerman innocent on all counts. The people of Hitching Post had their own sense of justice and weren't afraid to exercise it.

Perhaps that's why there is a dead man in my shop, I reasoned.

I was clearly grasping at straws.

"Maybe it's not murder," I whispered to Delia as we sat on stools behind the counter in the front of the shop as sheriff's deputies cordoned off the back room. I gripped my locket firmly to help ward off other people's energy. My stress level had already shot through the roof. "Maybe he had a heart attack or something."

He being Nelson Winston, a local lawyer. How he'd

wound up dead in my shop was beyond me. As far as I knew, he'd never even been a customer.

"Right," Delia said, rubbing her dog's ears. She'd been unusually quiet since we'd found the body, and there was a dazed look in her eyes. "Because heart attacks cause people to bleed profusely from their heads."

I didn't appreciate my cousin's sarcasm, though I was actually grateful for her company. I bit my fingernail and focused on the crowd gathered outside, which had tripled in size, thanks to the sirens. Half the crowd was waiting for their potions; the other half consisted of curiosity seekers. Word hadn't leaked yet that there was a dead body inside the shop. However, it was only a matter of time before the county coroner's van arrived and the whole town, locals and tourists alike, camped on my doorstep.

"This is a nightmare," I mumbled, sinking my head into my hands.

Delia dragged her fingertips across the wooden tabletop. "What's in the potions that make them so deadly, anyway?"

"Good try." I wasn't taking that bait.

Currently, the secret ingredient, the Leilara tears, was known only to my father and me. Eventually the knowledge would be passed down to my oldest child. If I had kids. I could practically hear my biological clock ticking—and forced it to be quiet. Now wasn't the time to be thinking about how if I *didn't* have kids, the Leilara secret would have to be shared with Delia.

She narrowed her eyes. The dazed look was still there. "At least I've never killed someone with my magic."

"*I* didn't kill him!"

"He had one of your potion bottles in his hand," she

pointed out. "And your aunt Marjie tried to shoot him last week. Obviously, you have motive."

I winced. Marjie *had* scared Nelson out of her yard the week before. "It was a warning shot," I said weakly. "And her motive isn't *my* motive."

"But family is family." She shrugged. "Just sayin'."

"Well, stop sayin'."

"Touchy."

If only there were a potion that would make Delia keep her opinions to herself, like sudden muteness. But I knew there wasn't. I didn't even have to check the grimoire to see if there was anything close. I supposed I could conjure a hex to use on her—I did have the ability. But I'd always chosen to reject my voodoo heritage and never use harmful spells.

It might be time to rethink that particular principle.

A uniformed deputy came down the back hallway and eyed me warily. I cringed as he headed for my wall of potion bottles. Floor to ceiling, narrow black shelving held a variety of faceted glass bottles of every jewel tone—it was a stunning, eye-popping, colorful sight that made customers' jaws drop in awe.

My bottles were custom ordered from a glass blower who had a studio on the outskirts of town. Each was a piece of art. There was no doubt that the violet-hued bottle Nelson held was one of my own.

But how had he gotten hold of it? I couldn't remember ever selling a potion to him—and a quick look at the wall of bottles revealed none were missing. I needed to check with my two part-time employees—my father and my best friend, Ainsley—to see whether they'd ever sold him a potion.

Plus, it was strange the bottle was violet. I divided potion bottle colors by gender. Men received blues, greens, and yellows, and women purples, pinks, and oranges. Red was used solely for love potions and it was the only color reserved for both genders.

Because the bottle was violet, the potion within couldn't have possibly been made for him. But as I'd made hundreds of potions with that color bottle, there was no way I could pinpoint who it had once belonged to.

Biting my nail, I turned my back on the deputy removing the bottles from the shelves. I understood why it had to be done, but I hated strangers touching my things.

I jumped when Delia's dog licked my elbow. Cautiously, I patted his head.

"What's his name?" I asked, desperate for any topic that would help me forget about the deputies traipsing through my shop.

I expected an answer like Lucifer or El Diablo, and was quite surprised when Delia said, "Boo."

"As in Boo Radley?"

We were in Alabama, after all, home of *To Kill a Mockingbird*.

"No, Carly, not Boo *Radley*," she said as if I'd insulted her. "Boo *Berry*."

"Like the cereal?"

"Yes. Boo for short," she said, patting his head. He swiped her hand with his little pink tongue.

I couldn't help from asking. "Why?"

"Were you expecting something like Satan?" she asked, her right eyebrow arched severely.

"Not at all," I lied, trying to look innocent. "Just curious."

"The first day I brought him home he climbed on the kitchen table and crawled into my Boo Berry box. He managed to eat most of the little marshmallows before I found him."

"You eat Boo Berry?"

I had pictured Delia having pints of blood for breakfast, raw steaks, small children—that sort of thing. The whole Boo Berry image was going to take a while to get used to.

Her other eyebrow rose sharply. "You don't?"

"I'm more of a Count Chocula girl."

Suddenly, I felt a subtle shift in the air, an intangible awareness. Senses heightened, my skin tingled—my witchy senses at work. Danger was near—a danger I knew all too well. I didn't need to turn around to know who was standing behind me.

"I knew these potions of yours would get you in trouble one day," he said.

I could hear the smile in his voice and knew one would be on his face when I turned around. It was.

Oh, Sergeant Dylan Jackson, investigator for the Darling County sheriff's office, didn't look dangerous. Not on the surface, leastways. Not with his big moss green bedroom eyes, long dark lashes. Not with that boyish grin of his. Not with the way his hair curled out from under a well-loved ball cap.

But I knew better.

After all, I'd almost married the man.

Twice.

No one was more dangerous—to my heart.

"Dylan," I said, my throat bone-dry. "I heard you moved back to town."

I'd heard it from about a hundred people who felt the need to tell me in grocery aisles, the post office, walking around the Ring. . . .

He'd been gone for almost a year, having taken a job with a police force farther south after our second failed attempt at getting married. It had been two months since he returned, and it had taken a lot of hard work and a small miracle to not face him before now.

"You might have been able to keep avoiding me if there wasn't a dead man in your shop."

Because there was no denying that I *had* been avoiding him, I said, "I didn't kill Nelson."

"Thou dost protest too much?" Delia said, her slivers of eyebrows still nearly touching her hairline.

Yes. A mute potion would be handy. I was determined to create one straight off.

Dylan wasn't wearing his uniform, thank goodness—it always made me a little hot under the collar. And he knew it. He still had that half smirk as he said, "Any idea why Nelson is dead in your shop?"

I was grateful Dylan didn't dwell on my avoidance of him and mention the time last month when I had seen him jogging on the river walk and dove behind a bush so I didn't have to talk to him. He'd simply shouted, "Watch out for the fire ants!" and kept on running. And damned if I hadn't been stung by those little buggers. And by how he'd been able to pass by so easily. "No, and I can't figure out how he got in, either."

There was no sign of forced entry. I didn't have an alarm system—no one in the county did—but now I regretted that decision.

"Who has keys?" Dylan asked.

"Me, my parents, Ainsley. That's it." I didn't feel the need to explain that none of them could possibly be involved with this mess. Dylan knew them well enough to make that leap himself.

He folded muscled arms. "Did I hear that your aunt Marjie tried to shoot Nelson last week?"

Indignant, I jumped off my stool. "It was a warning shot! You know how she feels about big-city lawyers sniffing around her inn, ignoring all her No Trespassing signs."

Every year Marjie received numerous offers to buy her inn, the Old Buzzard, but she wasn't selling. Lawyers for big hotel chains, however, didn't like taking her no for an answer.

"But Nelson Winston isn't a big-city lawyer," Dylan said, his intelligent eyes watching me carefully. "He's a local."

"Even worse," I mumbled. "He should have known better than to be snooping around Marjie's yard."

Someone banged on the door, yelling, "Carly! I need me a potion, chile! Hurry up already."

Dylan looked to the door, then back at me. "Mr. Dunwoody give a forecast this morning?"

"Sunny with a chance of divorce," Delia supplied.

With a low whistle, Dylan said, "That explains the crowd."

"How soon will I be able to open?" I asked, hanging on to my locket for dear life.

"A day or two," he said.

I let out a cry. "You're kidding."

He gave me a shrug. "Sorry, Care Bear."

Delia snickered.

Seeing red, I warned softly, "Do not call me that."

He lost that right a long time ago. When he left me at the altar. Twice. Though if I was being completely honest, I was the one to run away the second time. But it had been entirely his fault.

"Sure thing." He winked.

Winked. The nerve!

Someone else pounded on the door, and he added, "I'll send some deputies out to break up the crowd and cordon off the front of the shop."

Dylan had shifted so he stood just a bit in front of me, and I tried to keep my gaze from admiring his backside. Wearing a paper-thin Atlanta Braves T-shirt and a pair of old jeans, he was long, lean, and muscled. It was hard to look away.

"Good luck," Delia scoffed. "You'll have a riot on your hands. Mr. Dunwoody forecast a divorce, remember?"

I gazed at the crowd. "Can I take any supplies from the shop?"

"No. Everything has to be processed first."

Dang. I bit my lip. There were supplies enough at home, but in their raw state. The real problem was that the Leilara was hidden away in the room behind me. Without it, my potions were simply good homeopathic remedies. But those remedies would have to do. There was no way I would risk sneaking the Leilara bottle from its secret spot—especially not with Delia sitting out here. "Tell your deputies to announce that potions can be picked up at my house at four this afternoon and to line up by number." I stood up. "I should get going. I have a lot to do."

"I could help you with those potions," Delia said.

"Good try again," I said to her.

Delia pretended to examine her jagged nails.

Dylan said to me, "I'll come by your place later and take your statement."

"To my house?" I asked.

"You have a problem with that?" he asked.

"Yes."

He smiled. "I promise not to snoop through your underwear drawer while I'm there. Well, maybe a little snooping."

I frowned at him.

"I'm kidding, Care Bear. I'll be there on official business. I'll *officially* search your drawers. You might have evidence hidden away."

"You're not funny," I said.

"I think he is." Delia smirked.

I couldn't imagine this day getting much worse.

Until someone pounded on the front door. "Carly! Carlina Bell Hartwell, open this door right now!"

I knew that voice well.

My mother had arrived.

❧ Chapter Three ❧

By herself, my mother, Veronica "Rona" Fowl, was a force to reckon with.

With reinforcements, she was plain ol' impossible to ignore. Although I couldn't see my mother (only hear her), I spotted Eulalie, Hazel, and Marjie Fowl with their noses pressed against the display window—they must have pushed their way to the front of the crowd. Their breath created little fog clouds on the glass. The three were fraternal triplets, sixty-five years old, and never married. A hundred years ago, they might have been called spinsters or old maids, but these days, the townsfolk called the three the Odd Ducks.

I sometimes used that term, too, but mostly I called them my aunties. They were my mother's older sisters.

"Carly, open up right now!" my mama hollered from somewhere in the crowd.

"That's my cue to go." Delia stood up and scurried toward the back door.

My cue, too. I didn't want to face my mother right now.

She was going to have a thousand and one questions. Maybe I could sneak out the back as well. . . .

"I see you in there, Carly!" my mama shouted. "Don't even think about sneaking out of that shop!"

She could see me; however, I still couldn't see her—she was "vertically challenged," as she liked to say—but her tone meant business. I heard that loud and clear.

I sighed and looked at Dylan. "Do I have to?"

"She can't come in here," Dylan said. "This is a crime scene."

The phrase turned my stomach.

I yelled toward the window. "Dylan says you can't!"

"Dylan Jackson!" my mother yelled. "Don't make me call your mama."

Dylan's lip twitched. "Go around back, Miz Fowl. Carly will meet you in the alley."

I looked at him. "I will?"

"I don't want her calling my mama."

"No," I said darkly. "Anything but that."

He rolled his eyes. "Let it be, Care Bear."

I stomped on his foot as I headed for the back door.

"Hey, now! No need for violence."

Somehow he always managed to bring out my temper.

I kept my eyes averted from the break room as I passed. The coroner hadn't yet arrived, so the body was probably still lying there. On the floor. Dead.

There was no time right now to think about who had killed Nelson—or why—as I stepped out into the back alley. I had to deal with my mother first.

Crime-scene tape had already been strung tight from my shop to the stand of trees opposite the back door. Dylan followed me out as I ducked under the tape. My mama had just turned the corner at the end of the alley and sashayed toward me.

The sight of her took me by surprise.

"What on earth is your mama wearing?" Dylan asked.

I let out a deep breath. There had to be a good explanation. . . . There always was with her.

All five feet, two hundred pounds of my mama had been poured into a skintight, sparkling white minidress; her normally short, bleached blond hair was hidden beneath a lion's mane of a curly platinum blond wig; and she wobbled on four-inch golden stiletto heels. Her ample cleavage was in full view, her bustline enhanced with quivering fringe.

I braced myself for impact as my mother reached out and grabbed me in a bear hug. "Carly! What happened? Tell me *everything*!"

"Can't breathe," I gasped.

Mama let go. Her big brown eyes sparkled with excitement. "Rumor has it someone got themself killed inside your shop." She leaned in and whispered in a loud voice, "You didn't go killin' someone, did you, sugar? I know how hot your temper can get sometimes."

Dylan chuckled behind her.

"Nelson Winston is dead, and, no," I said, holding on to my temper with all my might, "I didn't kill him."

Mama's hand flew to her mouth. "Nelson? Didn't Marjie try to shoot him last week?"

"Warning shot!" I cried. My silver locket grew hot in my palm as I squeezed it tight. Bits of my mama's and Dylan's energies were starting to creep in on mine. Mama's enthusiasm; Dylan's uneasiness. I drew in some deep breaths to try to keep their feelings at bay. If they kept encroaching on mine, I was going to have to step aside—far aside. At least ten feet. Distance usually helped in situations like this.

"Where are the Odd Ducks?" Dylan asked. "They were with you a minute ago, weren't they?"

"They aren't real fond of the police," my mama said, batting her long fake eyelashes.

An understatement, for varying reasons.

Dylan was going to have to interview Marjie, and I couldn't help but wonder if he'd be shot at, too.

Marjie had a bit of a trigger finger.

"Mama?"

"Yes, honey?"

"Why are you dressed like that?"

"Oh! Nothing to worry your pretty little self about." She patted my cheek.

Which made me worry. A lot. I had a feeling this little getup probably had something to do with her wedding chapel, Without a Hitch, and Mama's crazy schemes to increase business.

Right now, I didn't want to know.

In fact, I was pretty sure I never wanted to know. That fringe scared me.

The coroner's van pulled into the alleyway and made my heart drop clear into my stomach.

"You two should go," Dylan said.

"Before they bring out Nelson's dead body?" Mama asked.

"Yes, Mama. Before then."

Mama pursed her lips. "Can't we stay for just a few seconds more? I just want one little peek."

Mama had a morbid streak a mile wide, plus she liked to gossip. A story like this would have all the town biddies gathered round her for weeks.

"No," I said, and steered her toward the end of the alley.

"Was there a lot of blood?" Mama asked.

"Where's Daddy?" I asked, hoping for an ally.

"Still at his fancy conference. He'll be home tomorrow morning."

My father, Augustus Hartwell, was the director of the Hitching Post Public Library, and had been away at a national library conference for a few days. I thought he'd be back by now. "Does he know about this outfit?"

She smiled a Cheshire cat grin. "He will soon enough, but just wait till you see what he'll be wearing."

"Daddy has an outfit, too?"

"Of course!"

Now I was getting *really* worried. Especially if his had fringe, too.

I motioned over my shoulder toward the police tape. "Could you do me a favor and not tell him about what happened here until he gets back? He'll just worry, and there's nothing he can do about it now."

Mama patted my cheek. "As long as you don't tell him about this costume if he calls."

"Deal," I said without hesitation.

Dylan called after us, "I'll be over later, Carly. Don't forget."

I planned to turn off all the lights and hide in my bedroom with a box of cookies.

"I still have a key, remember," he added.

Dang! Why hadn't I gotten around to changing those locks?

Best I clean out my underwear drawer.

Just in case.

*   *   *

I borrowed my mama's wig (she told me to keep it because she had a spare), and made my way around the Ring, along the sidewalk, past the bakery, the candle shop, a book and gift shop, a jewelry store, Emmylou's Café, and into the storefront next to mine with no townsfolk recognizing me.

I didn't think the disguise was all that good, so it must have been the arrival of the coroner that had captured their attention.

Whatever the reason, I was grateful for the distraction as I pulled open the door to Caleb Montgomery's law office.

The picture of spiffy Southern gentlemanly perfection, Caleb himself sat at the desk in the reception area and busted out laughing when he saw me.

"Wait, wait," he said. "Let me get my camera."

I pulled off the wig and threw it at him. "Do and die."

"Homicidal suddenly, aren't you? I heard you offed Nelson Winston."

I sank into a neutral-colored armchair across from him. "I didn't off anyone!"

"What about your aunt Marjie? Did she off him?"

"It was a warning shot!"

Caleb Montgomery had been one of my closest friends since grade school. These days he was the best quickie divorce lawyer in town. His office was decked out in high style with expensive furnishings and decor. However, he'd yet to find himself a good receptionist—it was hard to live up to Caleb's high standards.

Which also might explain his short-lived relationships.

"Fair enough," he said. "Marjie could hit a moving target at a hundred feet with her shotgun. If she wanted to shoot someone, that person would be full of shot by now."

He spoke from painful experience. Once when he was a teenager, Marjie caught him sneaking into her shed, where (rumor had it) she stored her homemade liquor. She'd gone after him with a BB gun. He still had a pellet or two stuck in his rump.

I still felt bad about the incident—after all, I'd been the one to start the rumor. "Well, as far as I could tell, Nelson wasn't full of holes, but he did have a big crack in his head."

Caleb leaned forward. "What was he doing in your shop?"

"No idea. I was hoping you might know something."

"Me?" His gray-blue eyes widened. "Why me?"

"You're both lawyers."

"So?"

"Maybe he told you something lately?"

"I can't speak to the dead, Carly."

I sighed. "It would be nice if you could."

He ran a hand over his hair to check for flyaways, despite the fact that there hadn't been a dark hair out of place since grade school. Caleb was the persnickety sort and wasn't afraid of hair products. Or starch. His white button-down shirt was pressed to within an inch of its life. "Can't say he had any enemies."

Nelson had no enemies I knew of, either. He was about ten years older than I was—just over forty—wasn't married, had no kids, and lived in a big house overlooking the Darling River. He was popular around town, taking on cases for little to no fee. He gave back to the community and was personable and outgoing.

"Well," I said. "Someone killed him. In my shop. Why?"

"Did you ever sell him any potions?"

"I don't think he ever came into the shop at all. At

least not while I was there. I need to check with my daddy and Ainsley."

He tapped a pen on the desk. "Are you sure Aunt Marjie is innocent?"

"Caleb."

"Fine, fine." He drummed his fingers on the desktop. "Seems to me that whoever had a grudge against him likely had one against you, too."

It was an angle I hadn't thought of. "Me? Why?"

"Why else would his dead body be in *your* shop? How many enemies do you have?"

I bit my lip. "None that I know of."

"Liar, liar."

"Okay. A few." People who'd come to me for advice and hadn't liked what I said. Plus, as my mama mentioned, I had a bit of a temper and wasn't afraid to speak my mind. "I have a hard time believing this is about me, though. What kind of cases was Nelson working right now?"

Caleb leaned back in his seat. "The only case I know of is Coach Butts's. Nelson took it over recently from a Birmingham firm."

That's right. I should have remembered that. The case was the talk of the town.

Coach Floyd Butts. A perfect surname for such a jack-ass of a man.

Even though Coach and his wife insisted the last name was pronounced *Boots*, everyone around here still said *Butts* behind their backs. We were a childish lot.

Until four months ago, forty-year-old Coach Butts was the high school gym teacher and the local youth baseball coach. That was until an audit concluded he'd pilfered league funds to the tune of twenty thousand dollars. At first he'd hired a fancy firm to defend him, but he fired them abruptly and then, at his older sister, Bernice's, urging, hired Nelson. Bernice Morris worked as Nelson's secretary, and had talked Nelson into taking the case pro bono as a favor to her.

It was quite the favor.

Especially since following Coach's arrest his personality had taken a bit of a dark turn. He'd picked more fights around town in the past few months than I could count. Coach had become a very angry man, raging against . . . life in general.

The town was split fifty-fifty on Coach's guilt. I'd had Coach Butts for ninth-grade PE, when he was fresh out of college. I knew darn well he used to try to peek up the girls' shorts when they climbed the ropes. I had serious doubts about his innocence.

Nelson had quite the challenge defending him, but as far as I knew he'd thrown himself into the case and supposedly was doing a stellar job.

"Do you know why Coach fired that Birmingham firm?" I asked.

"Nope."

"Can you find out?"

Caleb narrowed his eyes. "Why?"

"Do I need to remind you that there's a dead man in my shop?"

It didn't escape me that Coach Butts was one of my known enemies—ever since I reported him for looking up those shorts.

I didn't have much to do with him these days, except through interactions with his wife, Angelea, who I'd gone to school with. I didn't agree with their relationship— they had started secretly dating while she was still a student in high school, and even though she'd been eighteen it still made my stomach turn a bit, with him being a teacher and all. They'd been married twelve volatile years now and had been separated more times than I could count, venturing off to date other people. Their latest breakup was a ten-month-long stretch last year that I thought would seal the fate of their marriage once and for all.

But they always seemed to come back together, despite probably being better off without each other. Currently, they had been back together for almost six months now.

It might be a record for them, one that probably had more to do with keeping up appearances in light of Coach's recent run-in with the law than anything. Especially if the rumors that she was stepping out on him (again) were true.

Angelea was one of those frustrating women who sought her worth in a man. Any man, it seemed, married or not.

She was what my Grammy Adelaide would have called a vixen, and Grammy Fowl would have called a tramp.

I just called it sad.

Angelea was a loyal customer. In fact, I'd just seen her on Wednesday morning when she came in for a sleeping potion to fight her insomnia. We talked about a lot of things but never her husband—she knew how I felt about him and how he felt about me. He despised me so much that she had to keep her potion habit secret from him, hiding her bottles in her car, her yard, and at her friends' houses.

The more I thought about Coach, the more my witchy senses tingled. Something was off with him. Way off—I could feel it in my witchy bones. And if my witchy senses were involved, that meant he was either in danger . . . or he *was* the danger. Could he have had something to do with what happened to Nelson? It wasn't a possibility I could rule out at this point.

Standing, I grabbed the wig from the desk and put it back on.

"What's with the wig?" Caleb asked.

"It's my mama's."

"Enough said."

"I've got to go. I have potions to make."

"I heard about the forecast." He eagerly rubbed his hands together. "Can't you skip the potions this once? Or give them fakes or something?"

Technically that's what I was going to have to do, since I couldn't use the Leilara. I hoped the potions would have a placebo effect and no one would be the wiser about the concoctions missing the secret ingredient.

Rolling my eyes, I said, "You get enough business on your own." Divorces were more common here than one would think.

"You're no fun."

I strode to the door and turned back to look at him. "When are you going to let me set you up with someone?"

"Let me think." He tapped his chin. "Never? Save your matchmaking for someone else, Carly Hartwell."

He was a confirmed bachelor—a hazard of his job. Not because of the long hours he worked, but because of all the marriages he'd dissolved.

But . . . I knew he craved love like I craved peanut butter. He just wasn't as open to it as he could be. That's where I could help—if he'd let me.

"One of these days," I said, "I might make a special love potion just for you. You'll never know what hit you.

Head over heels in love. Married, babies, picket fence, even a dog."

He turned a bit green, shifted uncomfortably, then snapped, "Don't people have to be receptive for the potion to work?"

He had me there. There were a couple of glitches with my magic potions. First, a rule called the Backbone Effect. The recipient of a potion had to *want* the change it would bring about, consciously or unconsciously. It was named that way because the force of a person's willpower, their backbone, trumped magic every time. The rule was the only protection against using potions to trick unsuspecting intendeds, which wouldn't be fair to anyone involved, and was especially important when love potions were concerned. Whoever drank the potion had to *want* to fall in love, something I made very clear when creating an elixir so no one would expect miracles.

The second rule was the Curatio Principle. My potions couldn't fully heal chronic or terminal illnesses. They, however, could lessen the side effects and slow the progression of certain diseases. Again, warnings were given so no one would expect miracles.

"I think you're more receptive to love than you think, Caleb."

He laughed. And kept laughing.

Crossing my arms, I narrowed my gaze on him. "You know, I have been thinking about brushing up on my hexes. If getting married is such a curse to you, a hex might be just the thing to find you a wife. . . ." I raised an eyebrow. "Since hexing has no rules at all."

His eyes narrowed, and I saw a hint of the shark he was in the courtroom. "You wouldn't dare."

Fortunately, I wasn't all that scared of him. I wiggled my eyebrows and adjusted my wig. "You never know...."

I smiled as I walked out into the spring sunshine. But as I turned toward home, I wasn't thinking about Caleb and his nonexistent love life.

All that was on my mind was Nelson Winston.

And who killed him.

And if his murder *had* somehow been a message for me.

◈ Chapter Four ◈

Nelson Winston.

I'd known him for just about forever—mostly in passing, a casual acquaintance. Although he was a good ten years older, he was as active in the community as I and we often bumped into each other around town.

Because he'd always been friendly but reserved, I suspected he subscribed to a version of Patricia Davis Jackson's views of my potion making and me. In Dylan's mother's eyes, I might as well have devil horns sticking out of the top of my head. And, okay, it probably hadn't helped any that I had worn a sexy devil's costume to Dylan's and my engagement party and prodded Patricia with my pitchfork, but dang if the woman hadn't deserved it. She'd never been shy about her dislike of me.

Maybe Nelson's opinion of me wasn't as *devilish* as Patricia's, but he'd never gone out of his way to chat with me, and I once saw him pick up one of my potion bottles at a charity event and roll his eyes before setting the bottle back down.

Certainly there were a few townsfolk who didn't believe in my magic. Usually there was a telltale look in the eye that gave those people away. A distance, a wariness.

On the whole, most everyone around here accepted me with open arms. And those who didn't? I didn't pay them much mind. "To each his own" was one of my personal mottoes. I certainly didn't have to be best friends with everyone in town. As long as they let me be, I let them be.

And when they poked, I took out the pitchfork.

Nelson had never poked—he'd never so much as nudged. He'd just kept his friendly distance.

Which was why it made no sense whatsoever that he was laid out in my shop with his skull cracked open.

"Good mornin', Miss Carly," Mr. Dunwoody called out as I passed by his house. "New hairdo?"

"A diversionary tactic." Almost home, I dragged the wig off my head, figuring it was safe enough; no one had followed me from the shop. "And it was hardly a good morning for me," I added, leaning against his wrought-iron fence.

Like most on the street, Mr. Dunwoody's house was mid-nineteenth century, large, and rambling with additions and add-ons. Grand live oaks, ginkgos, and hickory trees crowded the big yard. The house had been recently painted a nice bright white. Its shutters were blue, the front door red, and it looked every bit as patriotic as the flag hanging limply from the pole attached to the porch column.

My gaze shifted to the right, to the house next door. Mine. It had been my mama's childhood home, and when she and the Odd Ducks had inherited it from Grammy Fowl almost three years ago they turned around and sold it to me for pennies on the dollar to keep it in the family, since Mama was happy living behind her chapel and the Odd Ducks already had places of their own.

My house didn't look near as nice as Mr. Dunwoody's. Sure, it was just as big and rambling with all its additions, but it was a good thing the wind wasn't blowing, as a stiff breeze might knock it right on over. I'd been slowly renovating, but I was a mediocre do-it-yourselfer at best, and the kind of expertise I needed cost much more than I could afford. At this point, I was so deep over my head that I was either going to have to seriously brush up on my home-improvement skills or move back to the guest quarters above my mama's wedding chapel—where I'd lived for the ten years after my high school graduation.

"Tee-hee!" Mr. Dunwoody giggled, his dark face alight with amusement. "I saw you sprintin' down the street this morning. You're gettin' faster. Mighty surprised to see you home so early. Did you give them all the slip?"

He sat in his usual daytime spot on his front porch in his fiery red rocker, drinking sweet tea at ten in the morning. Everyone knew the "tea" was really bourbon on the rocks with a twist of lemon, but he liked to keep up appearances. He'd nurse that drink until noon, at which time he'd switch to real tea, then finish up his day with some plain hot tea, specially ordered from a shop in town.

Seemed to me that his days were a bit upside down, and I often wondered (and was surprised I didn't already know) if he had steak, potatoes, and gravy for breakfast, and eggs, ham, and grits for dinner.

I frowned at him. "They'll be around soon enough, after the coroner leaves my shop."

"Heard about that bad bit of bad business," he said, leaning so far forward in his rocker he nearly tipped right off the porch and into his prized rosebushes. "What's the full scoop, Miss Carly?"

I wasn't the least bit surprised he already knew what happened. It was very difficult to keep news like a murder from spreading in a town the size of Hitching Post.

"You think ol' Marjie got the last laugh on that boy?" Apparently amused, he rocked backward and let out a high-pitched *tee-hee-hee.*

I didn't even bother with saying it was a warning shot. "What do you know about Nelson, Mr. Dunwoody? Did he have any enemies?"

He raised his glass to me. "Just your aunt Marjie."

Now that I stopped and thought about it, I had to wonder *why* Nelson had been sniffing around Marjie's inn. Having been born and raised in Hitching Post, he knew what to expect if he did. . . .

"Do you know why he was at Marjie's the day she shot at him?"

"Can't rightly say." This morning Mr. Dunwoody also looked the picture of gentlemanly perfection in his Sunday best, complete with suspenders and polka-dot bow tie. He'd been an eccentric math professor at a local college until he retired ten years ago, and at seventy he still dressed as though he were going to work every day. His wife had passed away almost thirty years ago, and as long as I'd known him he'd been a bachelor with a busy social calendar, never lacking a female companion. Though he was a bit of an odd duck himself, his quirky charm and natural good looks never failed to land him a date. He always insisted his forecasts were based on sta-

tistical calculations, but I suspected something else....
There was an air of magic about him.

"Most everyone else who goes snooping wants to buy
her inn," he added. "Maybe he did, too?"

I supposed it was a possibility—Nelson was a successful lawyer who might have wanted to spread his wings as
an entrepreneur. Which wasn't all that easy in Hitching
Post. Town bylaws prohibited new construction without
jumping through a million hoops (in an attempt to pre-
serve the small-town charm), so buying a preexisting
building was the only real option. Aunt Marjie had a
prime location and an already established inn.

Kind of.

I glanced down the street. Each of my aunts owned
her own bed-and-breakfast inn on this road, and each
place reflected the personality of each aunt. Next door
to the left, I spotted Eulalie hanging her clothes on the
line behind her inn, the Silly Goose, which was light and
airy; across the street, the Crazy Loon, Hazel's place, was
brightly colored, with all kinds of whirligigs and lawn
decorations in the front yard; across and farther down
the road, the Old Buzzard was Marjie's place, aptly
named indeed, as it was painted a dull, dark brown and
had little ornament, not so much as a flag or a flower box.
No surprise that she'd never ever, not once, had a guest
in her inn. Which was just the way she liked it, reflected
by the No Vacancy sign posted on her rickety fence.

Once when I was little, I'd asked her why she'd opened
the Old Buzzard in the first place if she never intended on
filling it with guests, but she'd only grunted. Later I'd
learned that the triplets had a pact: What one did, they all
did. When Eulalie and Hazel had opened inns, Marjie had

no choice but to open one as well. Majority ruled with the Odd Ducks—but it didn't mean they had to like the verdict.

Marjie obviously objected.

One would think that at sixty-five one of them would break the pact at some point, but so far I hadn't seen it happen and wondered if it ever would. The Odd Ducks were pretty set in their ways.

I noticed a note taped to the door of the Old Buzzard. Probably another No Trespassing sign aimed at keeping solicitors, possible guests, and just about anyone who was breathing away.

Marjie took eccentric to extremes.

Auntie Eulalie (also known to some as the "normal" sister) spotted me, smiled, and paused in her hanging of a washcloth to wave at me like she was fixing to take flight, her bejeweled pastel turban nearly slipping off. She was theatrical, to say the least, mostly because when she was younger someone had mentioned she had an uncanny likeness to Meryl Streep. It was true— she did, even now. Eulalie, however, had taken the compliment to heart and spent her life being as dramatic as possible.

Meryl had nothing to fear—there was no competition, except in my aunt Eulalie's head.

Blue jays cried overhead as I looked across the street at the Crazy Loon. Auntie Hazel with her frizzy, flaming red hair was engaging in the same task as Eulalie, except on her line amid the towels were pinned brightly hued undergarments for all the town (and her guests) to see. Flashy bras and tiny G-strings.

Lord help me.

"Now that I think on it, there was a bit of gossip going

on about Nelson the other day at the library," Mr. Dunwoody said, leaning forward. Sunbeams caught the silver streaks in his dark hair, making them sparkle.

The library automatically made me think of my daddy, who'd been working there since he was a little boy running errands. Now he was the director—and openly admitted there were times he wished he could simply shelve books all day. Although he technically should be the one running the Little Shop of Potions, he knew early on that he wanted to stay with the library and abdicated the potion making to me, at Grammy Adelaide's okay.

"Oh? What's that?"

"Nelson had been talking about taking a highfalutin job in Birmingham."

"A lawyerly job?"

"I heard tell."

"From whom?"

He scratched his chin. "Can't recall. If I do, I'll let you know."

As I pondered why Nelson was thinking about a new job, I heard a shrill voice echo down the street.

"Carleeeee! Caaarleee! Yoo-hoo! Yooooo-hoooo!"

Dang, I should have kept the wig on.

I glanced at Mr. Dunwoody, who was wincing at the noise—much as I was. "Do you think I can pretend I don't hear her?" I asked.

"Miss Carly, I do believe my half-deaf brother in Mobile can hear Emmylou Pritcherd."

Mr. Dunwoody made a good point, despite Mobile being a good six hours to the south.

"Carleee! Yoo-hoo!"

Daring a peek, I saw a flash of bright purple bearing down on me. As I braced for impact, I looked back at Mr.

Dunwoody, who had scurried into his house so fast his chair was still rocking violently in his wake. Chicken.

"Whoo-eee," Emmylou exclaimed as she bustled up. "Didn't think you heard me!"

Her restaurant, Emmylou's Café, was three doors down from my shop, and she'd been a frequent customer since moving to town two years before from California, on a quest to immerse herself in Southern culture because she'd loved the movie *Steel Magnolias*.

I often wondered why Emmylou hadn't moved to Louisiana, where the film had been set, but had never dared asked. Once Emmylou got to talking, one rarely snuck in a word edgewise, and rare was the conversation with her that didn't include a Southern expression she'd memorized . . . or twenty. Only her sincerity made Emmylou the least bit tolerable.

"Good morning, Emmylou. You feeling well?"

She looked a bit red in the cheeks, and there was a controlled wildness in her bright blue eyes. In her early forties, she was tall and trim, with bottle strawberry-blond hair, a button nose, and naturally plump red lips. She wasn't beautiful, but she was pretty, and had immediately caught the eye of Dudley Pritcherd, the accountant who kept the books for her café and catering business. One of my love potions later . . . and they'd been happily married for more than a year now.

She fanned her face. "Oh, I'm fine. It's Dudley I'm worried about." Her eyebrows drew downward, and her voice dropped as she added, "I finally had a chance to give him the potion you made, but so far I can't hardly see any effects, despite my pulling out all the stops. All. The. Stops. I don't hardly know what else to do. You have to help me!"

Two days ago, Emmylou had stopped into the Little Shop of Potions, looking for a potion for Dudley, who'd suddenly gone from Dudley Do-Right in the bedroom to Dudley Do-Wrong. Very wrong. Very, well, dud-ly.

I had concocted a virility potion, one of my lowest doses. I'd found it was better—much better—to start off on the mild side, or risk side effects that rivaled those of the popular little blue pills men of a certain age took to combat bedroom . . . dudliness.

Although some potions (and liquid hexes, too) could be splashed on another person or worn like perfume, Dudley's potion had to be ingested. And, trust me—a little went a long way.

"You don't think that . . ." Color rose high on her cheeks.

"What?"

Her nose wrinkled. "You don't think he's fallen out of love with me, do you? Could that be the cause?" Waving a hand, she shook her head. "No, that's crazy. The potion you gave us guarantees love, right?"

"Well," I began, "people can fall out of love, but I don't think that's the case here. Dudley loves you."

She nodded. "Of course he does! I was just being a little neurotic because it's been so long since—"

I held up my hand to cut her off. I did not need to know. Even at a low dose, the potion should have worked—my potions were, after all, magical.

Unless . . . Was this a case of the Backbone Effect at work?

If so, since force of will was more powerful than the Leilara drops, the potion wouldn't have worked because Dudley *wanted* to stay dud-ly.

But that didn't make much sense, so I searched for

another reason why the potion might have failed. "Did you give him the whole bottle?"

"Oh yes. Poured it straight into his after-dinner beer."

Aha! "That particular potion wasn't supposed to be diluted." Some potions could be mixed with other liquids, but not that one. "It lessens the effect. Remember?" No wonder he'd been such a dud. Emmylou and I talked about the necessary steps to take before she left the shop yesterday. Plus, the instructions had been printed on a nice, neat little tag.

She rocked on her heels and smoothed her lavender miniskirt, then fluffed the ruffles on her bright purple blouse. "I remember. But it didn't just *lessen* the effect. It did *nothing*. Not so much as a—" Her gaze lingered on the limp flag.

I held up my hand, palm out. "I don't need the details." Why did people always think I needed the details? "The potion needs to be in its pure form for maximum"—I stressed the word—"*potency*."

"But, Carly, I can't just give him the potion straight from the bottle."

"Why not?" Dudley hadn't ever had trouble taking one of my concoctions before. When she didn't say anything, realization hit. "You didn't tell him you came to me for a potion?"

This happened more than I liked, someone slipping another person a potion. If not for the Backbone Effect it would make me a nervous wreck. But because of that rule, I knew that the potions would have little effect on unsuspecting targets—unless they were unconsciously amenable to the potion's treatment.

She fidgeted with her big-hooped earring. "I didn't want to hurt his feelings. He's already feeling so poorly about not being able to ... I hoped the potion would give him back a little confidence. You can help with another potion, right? Please tell me you can help." Her voice dropped. "A girl has needs, you know?"

I knew that, too. If Emmylou had a clue about my near-celibate life, she'd probably melt on the sidewalk in a puddle of disbelief. Or maybe *relief* that she didn't share my fate. Well, up till now.

"I can help, but you're probably going to have to tell him about the potion." I couldn't imagine how she'd get him to drink it otherwise—plus, he'd probably welcome the help. "The shop's closed today, but stop by tomorrow. Hopefully by then I'll reopen."

Emmylou heaved an exasperated sigh. "Tomorrow? I've got to wait till tomorrow? Really?"

"Nothing I can do about it. Sheriff's orders."

Her hands fluttered over her chest. "I heard about poor Nelson Winston. Bless his heart."

Inhaling deeply, I decided this wasn't the time to explain to Emmylou that in this town "Bless your heart" was a thinly veiled put-down and not at all the endearment Emmylou thought it was.

Or maybe she did know. "Were you friends with Nelson?"

She waved a hand. "Of course. Isn't everyone? He and Dudley were close, and he's been my lawyer since moving to town. I thought him to be a perfectly lovely man. A true gentleman. I was sorry to hear about his passing, especially the way it happened. Tragic. Dudley's beside himself."

Well, that wasn't going to help his *dudliness* at all.

I couldn't help thinking about what Emmylou said. Nelson did seem to be friendly with everyone in town—

but obviously someone had had an issue with him. "Did you hear Nelson was thinking about taking a job in the city?"

Her eyes widened. "I hadn't, but I'm not surprised. He's a mighty good lawyer, and the case with Coach Butts has garnered him a lot of attention."

Heat bugs buzzed as I once again wondered if there was a connection between Coach Butts and Nelson's death. And how I could find out.

Emmylou tucked a strand of hair behind her ear. "Well, I best be going. I'm meeting Dudley for a picnic later to hopefully take his mind off Nelson, catering two wedding parties tonight, and tomorrow I'll be taking the food truck to the church's white-elephant sale and Johnny Braxton's extravaganza. Lots to do! Busy, busy, busy! But I'll be sure to make time to stop in and pick up that potion."

Johnny's extravaganza. I'd forgotten all about it—but now Mama's costume made some sense. Johnny Braxton was my mother's biggest competitor, always trying to woo couples to his chapel, The Little Wedding Chapel of Love, with themed events. There was nothing my mama liked better than showing him up, even if it meant playing unfairly.

She surely had something planned to sabotage his event.

As I watched Emmylou strut away, her ruffles flouncing, she suddenly whirled around. "I just had a notion. You know who might have more information about Nelson?"

"Who?"

"Nelson's girlfriend."

"He has a girlfriend?" This was the first I had heard of it. "Who is she? Someone local?"

"Oh, I don't know *who* it is. Just that he has one. A woman can tell these things, and there was definitely a new girl in his life. Someone serious, too, if his behavior was any indication. Find her, Carly Hartwell, and you'll find the answers to some of your questions."

❧ Chapter Five ❧

The phone was ringing as I came in the back door, the one that led straight into the kitchen. I snatched the cordless from the wall and breathlessly said, "Hello!"

"Heavens above, child. Do you know what your mama is up to?"

"I'm sorry, I think you have the wrong number."

"Not funny, Carlina Hartwell."

"Daddy, I'm busy," I said, trying to head off my father's vocal, impassioned disapproval of my mother's behavior. "You knew what Mama was like when you asked her to marry you."

"Thirty years ago, Carly, and yet do I have a ring on my finger? I am a man long-suffering. A man aggrieved. A man who—"

Roly and Poly ran into the kitchen and proceeded to flop at my feet and roll back and forth.

They were aptly named.

I sat on the plywood floor and gave the two cats belly rubs—something most cats didn't care for but mine loved. Usually they came to work with me every day, but

I couldn't very well take them this morning, when I was on the run from a mob.

"Daddy," I interrupted before he launched into a full-blown soliloquy. Augustus Hartwell had been waiting four decades for my mama to marry him and there was still no wedding date in sight. My mama didn't believe in marriage, but my daddy, a hopeless romantic, still hadn't given up hope of getting a wedding band on her finger.

"She's going to send me to an early grave."

Despite knowing better, I asked, "What does she have planned?"

"I'm not sure, but she's plotting something to compete with Johnny Braxton's country-music, weekend-wedding extravaganza. All I know is that Johnny's making himself up to look like Johnny Cash," my father said, "and is having a karaoke-party weekend, so I can only imagine what your mama will do."

Pain was beginning to pulse behind my left eye, and I wished I had some white-willow bark, which was great for getting rid of headaches, at home instead of only at my shop.

Fluffy Roly, who was mostly white with a light gray head and tail, nudged her face into my hand and looked at me with bright green eyes. Chubby Poly, who had medium-length dark gray fur with patches of muted orange on his face, hopped up on the counter. He glanced at me with his big amber-colored eyes, then stared longingly at the treat canister.

I didn't need to tap into his energy to know what he was thinking. Poly was always hungry.

"We don't have a lot of time," Daddy said, "and with me being out of town, I need your help talking your mama out of any potential plans."

I nearly laughed. "No one has the ability to talk Mama out of anything."

My father breathed out a long sigh, the kind only a man who'd lived with my mother for thirty years could produce. "Kidnap her or something. We don't need to borrow any more trouble from Johnny."

It was true—we didn't. The Hartwell/Braxton feud rivaled the Hatfields and McCoys. The thing was, Daddy wasn't kidding about the kidnapping.

"Daddy, I don't think—"

A knock sounded on the front door and my head snapped up. The townsfolk couldn't possibly be here already. I'd told them four o'clock.... Usually they respected my wishes on the rare times I had to work from home.

Another knock, this time louder.

"Think what?" he asked.

"I have to go, Daddy. Someone's at the door."

"But your mama . . . We have to stop her."

"I'll have to call you back," I said, and hung up.

I dislodged Roly from my lap, and before Poly knocked the whole canister off the counter I gave both a treat.

A slight breeze billowed the white sheers in the living room. Thankfully, the big windows were shaded by the trees, or else the place would have been truly stifling. Ceiling fans lazily stirred the hot air; the air-conditioning hadn't worked since I'd bought the place.

Construction debris was scattered across the room. Moving boxes, furniture covered in old sheets, boxes of nails, screws, and tubs of wall putty. Rolls of insulation, stacks of drywall, and reclaimed pine floorboards took up one side of the large space. It was a dusty mess—and the sad fact was that the whole house looked the same. Every single room was undergoing a transformation.

A shadowy figure lurked behind the leaded glass in the old oak door. Creaky hinges squealed as I pulled open the door. My eyes widened when I saw my visitor. "You again?"

"Don't look so shocked," he said.

"What are you doing here?" I asked, holding on to my locket.

Dylan Jackson said, "I heard there's an underwear drawer in need of searching. Aren't you going to invite me in?"

"No."

His green eyes flashed and his voice dropped to a sensuous level. "It's not like I haven't seen your panties before."

A *whoosh* of betraying desire suddenly swept over me. I tried my best to ignore it. Casually, I said, "I burned those when our relationship went up in flames."

Literally went up in flames. Though the fire had been accidental, I swear.

Still wearing his dark jeans and faded tee, he looked damn good standing there. I hated that I noticed.

"You have a thing for setting things aflame, don't you?"

Once. It had only been once.

Okay, twice. But the first time was when I was a teenager and didn't count. Much. Deciding to ignore his barb, I said, "What're you doing here?"

He shifted his weight and the playfulness in his eyes disappeared, replaced with a sharp intelligence. "I told you earlier I'd have a few questions for you. So either you let me in or you can come down to the jail and do this formally."

Since he put it that way, I stepped back so he could pass. I wasn't all that fond of jails, even the teeny-tiny one owned by Darling County. "By all means, come on in."

He stepped inside and took a look around. "I love what you've done with the place."

It had been more than a year since he'd last been in my living room. It had been a work in progress back then, too, but now it was just a plain ol' war zone.

"Home sweet home," I said, nudging aside a hammer with my foot.

Roly, the little trollop, came running in from the kitchen. Dylan bent down and rubbed her tummy as she flopped on her back and rolled about in ecstasy. "I think she remembers me," he said.

"Some men are hard to forget."

"That doesn't sound much like a compliment."

I sat on the arm of the sofa. "Because it wasn't."

Dylan said nothing. Just kept rubbing Roly's tummy. I could hear the cat's loud purrs from several feet away.

I looked over my shoulder, toward the kitchen, wondering where Poly had gone off to, since he usually never left Roly's side unless food was involved. No doubt he was probably still trying to figure out how to get the lid off the treat jar. I couldn't blame him. I could use a cookie about now, too.

Dylan glanced around the living room, peered into the dining room, and beyond that into the kitchen. "Is the whole house like this?"

"Every nook and cranny."

He leveled his gaze on me.

"What?" I asked in response to the question in his eyes. "Just say it."

Slowly, he stood up. Roly still lay on the floor, her little gray nose twitching with happiness.

When he remained silent, I said, "You're either wondering why I don't just hire someone to finish the place or you're wondering why I don't just pack up and move back to the apartment above my mama's chapel until this place is livable. Either way, you already know the answers, so you can keep your opinions to yourself."

The corner of his mouth twitched with the hint of a smile. "I didn't say a word."

Oh, that smile. It did things to me. Warm, delicious things. "What did you need to ask me?"

The sooner he left, the better.

He pushed aside a do-it-yourself renovation guide and sat on the edge of my coffee table. He was all business now. "How well did you know Nelson Winston?"

"Not very. Just in passing."

"When was the last time you saw him?"

"You mean alive?"

The humor was back in his eyes as he drawled, "Yes, alive."

I tapped my chin. "Technically, I saw his backside as it ran down the street the day Marjie shot at him. Before that, I can't rightly recall."

He let my words settle for a moment before he said, "What day was that, when Marjie shot him?"

"Shot *at* him."

"At," he conceded with a roll of his eyes.

I squinted, trying to think back. "Last Friday. No, it was Saturday, because I remember I'd just come from helping at my mama's buy-one-get-one-free wedding-day special."

"Buy one, get one free? Weddings?"

Nodding, I said, "A twofer. Two for the price of one." I bit my thumbnail. "There weren't many takers. Only two couples, in fact. Sisters marrying brothers. It was nice. The whole chapel was packed."

Unlike my almost-wedding days.

He drew in a deep breath and when something in his eyes flickered, I suspected he was thinking of those doomed weddings as well.

I couldn't help myself from asking, "How is your mama these days?"

"Just fine," he said tightly. "Do you know if Marjie talked to Winston before she shot *at* him?"

"Don't know." I swung my foot and made a mental note to rub some antibiotic lotion on my bramble scratches. They were starting to look red and angry. I flicked a speck of lint off my white shorts and reached down and ran my hand over Roly's body. She purred contentedly, her tail swishing.

Because I was feeling slightly guilty I'd brought up his mama, I said, "I heard Nelson had a girlfriend. Not sure if it's true."

"Who?"

"Don't know who."

"Who'd you hear it from?"

"Emmylou Pritcherd."

He grunted and jotted down her name. "She know Nelson well?"

"Apparently he and Dudley are close friends, and Nelson was her lawyer for business stuff. But other than that, I don't know."

"You're not knowing much, Care Bear, are you?"

I glared.

He glared back.

Maybe it was a good thing we hadn't gotten hitched. Either time.

Though sometimes it didn't feel good at all. Most times, in fact. Especially when that wide gaping hole in my heart was aching.

Like now.

I tried my best to ignore it. "Did you know Nelson was working on Coach Butts's case?"

"It's all the talk around town."

I bit my thumbnail. "Something is definitely going on with Coach right now. Something . . . not good. I can't help but wonder if it's connected to Nelson being splayed out in my shop."

"And how'd you make that leap, Care Bear?"

I clenched my fists. The nickname was getting to me. "Just a feeling."

"A witchy feeling?" he asked with a hint of cynicism.

My temper was inching up. "My feelings are rarely wrong."

He scoffed.

"What? They're not."

"Maybe. But they can be *misinterpreted*."

Not this again. I wasn't ready to rehash failed wedding attempt number two. I'd like to just forget all about it.

To forget how Dylan and I had run away to Georgia to elope after our first attempt at a wedding had gone horribly wrong, thanks to his mama.

To forget how, as I stood alongside him in a sweet little chapel, wearing a flirty white chiffon dress and holding a small bouquet of lilies, I'd opened myself up to feel his energy.

To forget that instead of feeling the same love and joy

I was, I'd been overwhelmed by his doubts, fears, and hesitation.

It had gone downhill from there, culminating with me knocking over a candelabrum as I ran out of the chapel.

I never told anyone why I'd run out. Only Dylan and I knew the truth: His reservations about defying his mother . . . about *me* . . . had doomed our relationship.

There was no *misinterpretation* about that.

I attempted to keep the topic on point. Stubbornly, I said, "I think there's a connection with Coach."

"I doubt Coach has anything to do with what happened with Nelson. Why would he? Word is that Nelson was about to get him off scot-free. This isn't about your grudge with Coach, is it?"

I ignored his implication. I no longer held a grudge against the man; I simply didn't like him. "You should dig a little deeper. Maybe get Coach's alibi."

"Let it go, Care Bear."

Oooh, that name. Before I took a swing at him, I jumped off the couch and said, "Are we done?" I'd said my piece. He could go. Immediately.

He snapped his notebook closed. "For now."

I stormed to the door and held it open, my Nikes kicking up dust in my wake. Dylan languidly rose to his feet and strolled to the doorway.

He wore a half smile as he passed by me, brushing so close that I could smell his aftershave. "Don't be leaving town."

I smiled so wide, my cheeks hurt as much as my heart. "I wouldn't dream of it. Look what happened the last time I did that."

"Carly . . ."

Suddenly, shouting cut through the tension-filled air.

Dylan looked at me. "Sounds like Hazel."

I stepped onto the rotting front porch and peered down the street. My aunts Hazel and Eulalie were standing nose to nose in the middle of the road, hollering at each other.

"It's not a full moon, is it?" I asked. Sometimes Hazel went a little wild when the moon was full.

"Next week," he said.

Something to look forward to.

When I heard the mention of "brassiere" in the argument, I decided to referee. Dylan followed, never one to miss out on a good show.

My aunts were standing, showdown style, in the middle of the street.

"Give it back, Eulalie!" Hazel shouted.

"It's mine!" Eulalie yelled back.

The pair was playing tug-of-war with a rather large-cupped, bright pink bra trimmed with black lace.

"You wish," Hazel said, eyeing Eulalie's small chest.

Eulalie's eyes went wide. "I'll have you know I've been using those chicken-cutlet doohickeys to enhance my décolletage."

I looked over at Mr. Dunwoody's house to make sure he wasn't hearing this argument. He was nowhere to be seen, but Dylan was looking more than a little amused.

"It's mine," Hazel said. "Give it back!"

"No!"

Sad to say this wasn't the first time they'd faced off over undergarments. Eulalie was a bit of an instigator. She often snitched Hazel's lacy bits off the clothesline because Eulalie felt confrontations helped hone her acting skills—and the street was as good a stage as any.

Hazel, however, never quite realized she was a pawn

in Eulalie's theatrical games, and was quite possessive about her underwear. She wasn't backing down without a good ol' catfight.

I was about to step between them when, at the end of the block, I saw a dark pickup turn onto the street. It swerved left and right, a wild zigzag. We needed to get out of the way. "Let's move to the sidewalk," I suggested loudly.

They ignored me.

Reaching into the fray, I grabbed the bra and pulled. I figured where the bra went the aunts would follow. Instead, they turned on me.

"Carlina Hartwell, how dare you?" Hazel chastised. "This isn't going to fit you, either."

I swore I heard Dylan chuckle, but I didn't have time to look over my shoulder and glare at him. I was too busy watching the truck as it zigged and zagged down the street. It bumped over a curb and sideswiped an oak tree. The loud noise succeeded in capturing my aunts' attention.

They immediately recognized the danger, released the bra, let out loud quacks, and scattered. With the sudden slack on the bra, I pitched backward onto the street. I squeaked out my own little quack as the truck bore down on me, its grille seeming to smile menacingly as it grew closer and closer.

Before I knew what was happening, I was scooped up and whirled around, and landed with a thump on the narrow strip of grass between the sidewalk and street in front of Mr. Dunwoody's house. In a blur, the truck zipped past, jumped the curb, rolled over my front hedge, and hit my front porch with a deafening crash.

The end pillar wobbled, gave out, and fell onto the yard. There was a moment of silence before a loud cracking noise filled the smoky air. As if in slow motion, the porch roof pulled loose from the rest of the house and came crashing down. The whole rotted structure seemed to collapse into itself—most of it landing on the hood of the dark truck. All that remained standing of the porch was a set of brick steps and a plume of dust and chaos.

Hazel cried hysterically, and Eulalie shouted, "I'll call for help!"

"You okay?" Dylan asked me, his warm hands cupping my face.

In a bit of a stupor, I nodded.

Slowly, I sat up. Dylan gave my chin a nudge, then took off running toward the hissing truck, a beat-up old black Chevy. A truck I suddenly recognized as Coach Butts's. My legs wobbled as I stood and stumbled toward the wreck. Dust fell from the sky like brown snow.

Smoke rose from the hood of the truck as I caught sight of Dylan's grim face. "Is he okay?" I asked, fearing the answer.

Coach Butts was slumped over the steering wheel, his face a grayish white color, except for bright red slashes of fresh cuts. He was definitely not all right.

"He's unconscious," Dylan said, pulling him out and placing him on the ground. "But alive."

I narrowed my gaze on Dylan. "Do you still think Coach had nothing to do with what happened to Nelson?"

"Not now, Carly," Dylan said darkly.

I was about to argue that now seemed like a fine time for him to tell me I may have been right when a flash of color in Coach Butts's beefy hand caught my attention. It was a potion bottle.

Dropping to the ground, I took the lavender bottle from his palm, turned it over, and found the hallmark the glass-blower used for my wares. It had definitely come from my shop, and looked a lot like the sleeping-potion bottle that I'd given his wife, Angelea, a couple of days ago.

If he had drunk it, it might explain the crash.

It was missing its stopper, and when I took a whiff of the empty bottle, I scrunched my nose at the lingering smell. It definitely wasn't my sleeping cure that had been in this bottle; I didn't recognize the smell. At all. It wasn't a scent from *any* of my cures. It made me very curious what had actually been in this bottle—and if that was why Coach was now passed out.

Dylan leaned over the prone man and shouted, "Coach! Coach! Wake up!" He shook him gently. A gash on Coach's head oozed a thin line of blood.

Neighbors started gathering round as Coach moaned and slowly blinked his eyes. They were unfocused, searching. He opened his mouth, mumbled something.

"What was that?" Dylan asked.

Coach focused his eyes, saw me, and shakily pointed in my direction. Even though his words were slurred, they were perfectly understandable as he uttered, "She poisoned me."

❧ Chapter Six ❧

Poisoned.

Coach Butts had accused me of poisoning him, the low-down, no-good louse.

Hours after the ambulance had driven away with Coach Butts, I sat alone on my brick front steps—which stood free-form in the midst of all the debris—and surveyed the damage the crash had caused, not only to my yard and house but to my reputation. Word had gotten out about Coach's accusation. I had already fielded a few calls from people wanting refunds on recent potion purchases.

Dylan hadn't said much about Coach's claim, but had put the potion bottle into a plastic evidence bag and taken it away. I had the uneasy feeling I'd be seeing him again soon.

Half the town, including my mama and aunties and the insurance man had already been here and gone. A Dumpster was on order, and a clean-up crew scheduled to show up first thing Monday morning.

My yard was quite the sight. My front porch was

DOA. Thankfully, insurance would cover most of its repair, which was great because my budget might have been able to cover some nails and screws but little else.

With the way my potions sold, one might think I was rolling in the dough, but that couldn't be further from the truth. Beyond the overhead of keeping the shop open, supplies, paying Ainsley, and repaying my parents for the first Wedding That Never Happened . . . there wasn't all that much left. What remained was sunk into the money pit behind me.

Hearing harried footsteps coming down the sidewalk, I glanced up. My best friend, Ainsley Debbs, was barreling toward me with a take-no-prisoners stride and a sweet smile. She was a mass of contradictions, that Ainsley.

"What kind of hot mess did you get yourself into?" she cried as she stepped onto the walkway leading up to the house, an enormous pocketbook hooked over one shoulder.

I let go of my locket and wiggled my hand. "It's more like a lukewarm mess."

Wiggling her way next to me on the step, she laughed. "That's right. Your mess-o-meter is higher than mine on account that you burnt down that little chapel in Georgia that one time."

"Accidentally."

"So you say." She looked at me out of the corner of her eye. "You know, you never did tell me exactly what happened that day."

"Mostly because I'm trying my hardest to forget. The fire was an accident," I said softly, emotion clogging my throat. I tugged on the hem of my shorts and wished that I really could forget. It would make things so much easier.

She studied me for a long second before nudging me

with her shoulder. Gesturing to the piles of debris, she said, "Has your mama seen this mess?"

Grateful for the change of subject, I glanced around. "She just left." My mama, thank the heavens above, had been dressed in her usual garb of shorts, flowy top, and platform wedges. I wasn't sure I could have dealt with the fringe after all that happened. Frowning at the mess, I said, "She took pictures to put on the Internet."

Ainsley laughed. "Your mama is two cups of crazy."

"More like six cups." I poked her with my elbow. "Thanks for coming over." I needed her help with the love potions if I was going to get a batch done before tonight.

"Not a problem. I got Francie to keep the Clingons for me."

The Clingons were the collective nickname of Ainsley's three kids—four-year-old twin boys and a three-year-old girl who was in a perpetual bad mood.

"I just had to promise to bring her a box of wine and one of your hangover potions, since she's fixin' to drink the whole box once I pick up the kids."

"Understandable."

"Perfectly."

Francie Debbs, Ainsley's mother-in-law, was a saint in my eyes. Never mind the rambunctious boys, but three-year-old Olive's tantrums were enough to make me want to stay celibate just to make sure I never had a child like her.

And that was saying something.

"They take after their father, you know," Ainsley said, brushing off some pebbles from the steps.

"I know," I said, playing along. Truth was, Ainsley had been a hellion from the time she learned how to toddle right up until her wedding to Carter Debbs. It was amazing what marrying a pastor could do for a troublemaker.

Now a part-time RN and a part-time employee of mine, she had mostly tamed her inner wild child.

Mostly.

Even though she was generally generous, loving, caring, and patient, there were still a few times her bossy, devilish, you-only-live-once side came out.

Karma had bitten her on the butt big time with those kids.

"You do have stuff here to make the hangover potion, right?" she asked, a bit of a wild look in her amethyst eyes. But that wildness might have been because in her haste to get out of the house, she'd put makeup on only one eye. It looked very *Victor/Victoria*.

Her light brown hair was pulled back in a loose ponytail, and her deep cleavage was spectacular in a form-fitting sundress. I'd always been envious of her hourglass figure, which only became more enviable after she had the babies.

"Actually . . . I had to leave the magic drops at the shop."

It was no secret that I used magic in my potions. The only secret was what that magic was. I thought about the lab analysis the potion bottles Dylan had collected today would be undergoing and wasn't too worried if any traces of the original potion that was in that bottle showed up. The Leilara drops would appear only as a *Liliaceae* (the fancy name for lily family) derivative. Its true origin would remain safe. Not that anyone (except for my cousin Delia) really cared what the magic was, only that it worked.

What I wondered about most was what had been in that bottle *after* my potion. That smell . . . I shuddered. Pushing it out of my thoughts for now, I said, "I have some wild carrot, ginger, and thyme for a homeopathic hangover cure.... It'll probably work well enough."

Ainsley clutched my arm. "Well enough isn't good enough. Unless I pay a small fortune, Francie is the only one who will keep my kids for me. You know my mama won't do it."

Oh, I knew. Ainsley's mother claimed she drew the line at caring for one mischief maker. She also claimed that I had been a bad influence on Ainsley during our growing-up years.

As if.

Plus, Ainsley's mother was best friends with Dylan's evil mother, Patricia.

Enough said.

"Francie doesn't ask much," Ainsley said. "Only a box of wine and a hangover potion. We have to get those magic drops."

"How?" I asked. "The sheriff's office has the shop closed off."

She wiggled her eyebrows. "Where there's a will, Carly Hartwell, there's a way."

"Break in, you mean?"

"Well, of course we have to break in to the shop. Didn't you hear how Francie's the only one who will look after the Clingons? I *need* that hangover potion before I go home. Besides I don't think it's breaking in if you own the place."

She had a point. "Well, I suppose one quick run into the shop won't hurt anything." Nelson's dead body had already been hauled away—I wouldn't be disturbing him none. "Plus, I still have all those love potions to make ... Having the drops would set my mind at ease about that."

"Well, you don't need to worry about those love potions now," Ainsley said.

"What do you mean? Why not?"

"Haven't you noticed that no one's here?"

I glanced up and down the street. There were still a few neighbors rubbernecking from the accident, but Ainsley was right. No one was lining up to get my love potions.

"Where are they?" I asked, my nose wrinkling in confusion.

"Not coming."

"Why not?" I asked for the second time in a few seconds.

"It might be because they think your potions done poisoned Nelson and Coach Butts and don't want to be the next one carried away by the coroner."

I gaped at her.

She shrugged. "I told you it was a hot mess."

"Coach Butts is perfectly alive, thank you very much."

"Barely, so I hear told."

"More than barely." I might have been pushing it with that one. He'd looked downright awful on that stretcher. "People really think I'm guilty?"

"I don't know about guilty, necessarily. But they think your potions are tainted."

My potions were magical, not poisonous.

Something darker was at work here. Something stronger than my magic.

Something evil.

"Don't tell me you're going to let a little crime-scene tape stop you from getting into your own shop," Ainsley prodded.

Some leopards just couldn't change their spots.

And her mama thought I was the bad influence? Ha!

We stood at the mouth of the alleyway that ran behind the shop. The emergency vehicles had gone and all that remained was limp yellow tape strung across the back door of the Little Shop of Potions. The roads around the Ring were busy as the tourists came in for the weekend.

"You know I'm not above bending the law from time to time," I said. "B—"

She jabbed a finger at me. "You better stuff that 'but' I hear coming right back down your throat, Carlina Hartwell."

She stood a good four inches shorter than me, but I was pretty sure she could take me in a street fight, no problem.

In all honestly, I had no qualms about breaking into the shop.

My jitters came from the memory of Nelson's body on the break room floor. I wasn't sure I was prepared to see what was left behind.

I shuddered at the memory of all that blood, but then pulled myself together. If I could poke prissy Patricia Jackson in her dimpled derriere with a pitchfork, I could reclaim my shop. Whether I could regain my shattered peace of mind was a question I didn't want to face right now.

Someone had broken into my shop and killed a man. I had to figure out who had done it and why, if only because I didn't want to be fearful every time I walked into my shop. The shop my grandmother had built.

"Let's go," I said, linking arms with her like we were Dorothy and the Scarecrow off to see the Wizard. Her being Dorothy, of course, and me being without a brain for even thinking about crossing the police line.

"Woo!" Ainsley cried victoriously, smiling wide. "That's my little coconspirator!"

As we crept suspiciously down the alley, delicious smells floated out from the back door of Emmylou Pritcherd's café, making my stomach rumble. The rear doors of her food truck that doubled as a catering van were open, and I stopped short when I saw her on all fours.

"Emmylou?"

"Don't mind me none," she said, sweeping a hand over the metal floor. All around her, trays of food were piled high, ready to be hauled to wedding receptions. "I lost one of my contact lenses. Brand-new one, too. It's a monthly one, and I knew I should have switched to the daily kind after my last exam." She glanced up, one eye closed. "Or maybe have that laser surgery. Do y'all know anyone who had it?"

"One person," Ainsley said. "He went blind from complications."

Emmylou's jaw dropped.

I frowned at Ainsley. She'd been joking, but Emmylou hadn't caught the humorous tone in Ainsley's voice.

"Maybe I'll keep with the contacts," Emmylou said softly, continuing to run her hand along the floor.

At least the truck was clean. Spotless—Emmylou was a bit of a neat freak. "Do you want some help?" I asked.

"No, no," she said. "Not enough room for all of us in here. Aha!" she cried, lifting a finger. "Got the little sucker. I'll just go clean it off, and it'll be good as new." She came down the truck's ramp. "Y'all hungry? Do you want to come inside for a bite?"

Ainsley gave me a tug.

"We can't," I said. "We have to break into my shop."

Emmylou smiled. "I'm sure there's a story there. You'll tell me later? I've got to get moving."

I agreed, and as soon as she walked through the back door of her restaurant, I looked at Ainsley and said, "Blind?"

She laughed. "What? It was funny."

I smiled. "You're touched in the head."

"I know. Come on." As we headed toward my shop, she said, "We can't really get arrested for going in, can we?"

"I'm not sure. It is a crime scene."

"Carter will surely bail me out of jail if we get arrested. He can't handle the Clingons on his own for more than a minute."

Not many could.

"You're probably on your own, though. Sorry," she said matter-of-factly.

Pastor Carter Debbs wasn't all that fond of me and my magic and tended to keep his distance. I liked him only because of how much he loved Ainsley—and the fact that he loved her enough to let her choose her own friends.

"Your mama would probably bail you out," she said.

An image of my mama snapping my picture as I clung to jail bars flashed in my head. "I'd probably call Caleb."

"Caleb does have prior experience springing you out of jail."

"I was cleared of all charges," I said emphatically.

She smiled so devilishly I thought she might have a pitchfork of her own hanging in the broom closet at her house. "I was just sayin'."

A crow cawed in the distance as I rolled my eyes and wiped my brow. The afternoon had turned steamy, and I wouldn't have been the least bit surprised if storms rolled through later on.

As we approached the back door of the shop, a strange tingling stopped me in my tracks.

"What?" Ainsley said, looking up at me.

"Something's not right."

"Are your witchy senses acting up?"

She'd started calling them witchy senses almost a decade ago after we saw the Spider-Man movie and she compared my ability to Spidey's senses. It had stuck. As had her fascination with Tobey Maguire; she had even gone so far as to name one of her twins Toby (with the spelling changed so Carter wouldn't catch on).

I nodded. My witchy senses were indeed acting up, and I couldn't help but remember Delia's strange warning this morning. After finding Nelson's body, I thought it had been about him. But maybe I'd been wrong. Maybe her warning was about something else entirely. . . .

Ainsley and I tiptoed closer to the shop, and I soon saw what had triggered the feeling. The back door was ajar.

Ainsley stuck out her flip-flopped foot and pushed the door open wider. "Yoo-hoo!" she called out.

My heart hammered as if I expected someone to actually reply. Thankfully, there wasn't so much as a "boo" from Nelson's ghost.

After a moment of silence, she looked at me. "No one's home. Come on." She grabbed my arm and made to duck under the crime-scene tape.

I grabbed her arm and pulled her back.

"What?" she said, clearly exasperated, if her pout was any indication.

"We should call Dylan."

A loud voice rumbled from behind us. "Good decision, Care Bear."

⁓ Chapter Seven ⁓

If Dylan Jackson called me Care Bear one more time, I might have to throw something at his head.

He stepped out from behind a small Dumpster.

"Were you following us?" I asked.

"Don't flatter yourself. I saw you two hooligans standing at the end of the alley and suspected something might be up."

"So you did follow us," Ainsley accused.

He glanced at me, then at her, and apparently decided I was the lesser of two evils. Underneath all that boyish handsomeness, he was a smart man.

"I watched to see what you were up to. And what exactly are y'all up to?" he said, narrowing his eyes on me.

"How's Coach Butts doing?" I asked. "Did you just come from there? Had he drunk whatever was in that bottle?" If it tasted as bad as it smelled, he was probably lucky to be alive.

Certainly Dylan recognized my diversionary tactic, but he had to also know how much I wanted an update.

"Coach is fine." Dylan adjusted his ball cap, sliding it

up, then back down on his head. "He didn't drink anything. Claims the bottle was empty when he found it."

"Then what was wrong with him?" Ainsley asked.

"It turns he hadn't been poisoned at all. He has diabetes and hadn't been watching his insulin level closely enough."

Ainsley frowned. "He could have died from diabetic shock."

"Could have," Dylan said. "But he's fine now. He'll be released from the medical center later today."

All that was well and good, but . . . "Why was one of my potion bottles in his hand? Why did he claim he'd been poisoned by me? Why'd he ram his truck into my house?"

Dylan said, "Apparently Coach had been hearing the rumors all morning about Nelson dying in your shop, so when he found one of Angelea's potion bottles in her car while he was cleaning it out, he rightly associated the bottle with you, and when he started feeling poorly, he began believing you'd somehow poisoned him. You know how he feels about you and your potions, so it was easy for him to make that leap, especially with his being a bit delusional because his sugar levels were off."

I sincerely doubted Coach had been cleaning his wife's car; there wasn't an altruistic bone in his body. More than likely, he'd been snooping to see if she was cheating on him again, and found the bottle during his search. Angelea often hid her potion bottles in her car.

"Plus," Ainsley added, "he's never liked you, especially after you almost got him fired that one time."

I huffed. "He should have been fired. Fact is, Coach wasn't poisoned from one of my potions, and neither was

Nelson. We have to stop these rumors before they put me out of business."

"Actually," Dylan said, "we don't know how Nelson died yet."

Dark clouds gathered on the horizon. "What do you mean, you don't know? His head was cracked open like a ripe watermelon."

"Oh, great," Ainsley said, sighing heavily. "I'm never going to be able to eat watermelon again."

"It wasn't *that* cracked," Dylan said. "The autopsy and toxicology will tell us more."

"How long's that going to take?" Would I have a shred of a reputation left?

"Not sure. Days. Weeks. Depends."

I bit my thumbnail. This wasn't the news I wanted to hear. "I forgot to tell you earlier, but I don't think that bottle belonged to Nelson, the one he had in his hand when he was found."

"How do you know?" he asked. "I thought you said you weren't sure if he was a customer."

I explained about the color discrepancy with the bottle being violet and all, and, to his credit, he said he'd look into it. Probably to make up for doubting my witchy senses earlier.

"Now that we've got that cleared up," Dylan said, "are you two ready to tell me what y'all are doing here?"

"Well . . . ," Ainsley finally said, brushing a lock of hair off her forehead. "It's like this. Carly's witchy senses were acting up, so we came over to the shop to see why. And luckily we did, because this here door's wide open. Look for yourself."

Dylan leaned around me and looked. He straightened, all business. "And you didn't open it?"

"It was like this when we got here," Ainsley said. "Well, except for I might have pushed it open a little more with my toe." She wiggled her piggies.

Dylan shot me a look. "You didn't open it?"

"No, I don't even have my keys. They're in my purse, which is still in the shop." A fact that I hadn't thought too much about until right that moment.

His eyes shifted to Ainsley, scrutinizing her.

Hands on hips, she said, "Don't be looking at me that way, Dylan Jackson. I don't have my keys, either. I lost them a couple of days ago."

Now it was my turn to stare at her.

She said, "What? I told you about that."

She had. I'd forgotten all about it.

"When was this exactly?" Dylan asked.

"Wednesday," she said. "Why?"

Then she looked at me, then at the door, then back at me and said, "Uh-uhn. No way."

"There was no forced entry," Dylan said. "Where'd you lose your keys?"

"That's the crazy thing," she said. "I don't know. I'd walked to a couple places that afternoon. The pharmacy, the library, the bakery to order the boys' birthday cake, over to Johnny Braxton's place to drop off the payment for renting the party room at the Silo for the boys' birthday, over to Emmylou's Café to check the catering menu, and then to Carly's house to pick up my paycheck so my check to Johnny wouldn't bounce, and then I stayed and had a cup of tea with Carly, Mr. Dunwoody, and the Odd Ducks. Then I went home. The next morning, I went to drive to the grocery and my keys were gone from my purse. I backtracked to all those places I went to, but no one had seen them. I had to change my locks." She glanced at me. "Not that we ever lock the doors at the house, but it made Carter feel better."

She and Carter lived in the hundred-year-old rectory on the church property. I'd never told her, but the old place gave me the heebies.

Dylan's eyes had glazed over during part of that rundown, but he snapped to when she finished up. "But you had the keys at some point that day for sure?"

"My library card is on my keychain, and I checked out two books and three videos. You can't be thinking someone stole my keys. That's crazy. I'm always keeping an eye on my pocketbook."

"Where is it now?" Dylan asked.

Ainsley had the grace to blush. "Sitting on Carly's front steps."

I held back a smile, afraid she might give me a good shove if I started laughing.

Dylan simply closed his eyes and mumbled something under his breath.

"The door doesn't look like someone busted in this time, either," I finally said, examining the doorframe. "Someone definitely has a key, unless they're a master lockpick." There were two industrial dead bolts on the back door, my lame attempt at security.

Dylan ducked under the crime-scene tape and said to us, "Stay here."

"Do we have to?" Ainsley asked me as he disappeared through the doorway. "I want to go in."

"You can go, but I won't look good in prison stripes."

She frowned. "No, you wouldn't."

I cracked a smile, Ainsley stayed put (she wouldn't look good in prison stripes, either), and it wasn't long before Dylan was back.

"Nothing seems disturbed," he said, pushing my pocketbook into my hands. He started to close the door behind him when Ainsley grabbed hold of it.

"Wait!" she cried.

"What?" he said.

"I need a hangover potion."

He looked my way.

I said, "On account that Francie Debbs is going to be drinking a whole box of wine tonight."

Tipping his head, he still looked confused.

"On account," I continued, "that she's been keeping the Clingons all day for Ainsley and will be in need of some liquor to recover after they go home. Which means she'll probably have a big headache tomorrow."

"Ah," he said. He held open the door for me. "Be quick and don't touch anything but the potion stuff."

"I need a few minutes to make it up," I said.

He made a shooing motion with his hands. "Hurry with you, then, and take a look around to see if anything's missing or out of place I didn't notice."

I swallowed hard as I ducked under the tape and quickly made my way down the back hallway. Immediately, I was overcome with the comforting, familiar scents of the herbs I used in my potions. It felt like a hug from my grandmother, and all my muscles relaxed in response.

Pulling in a deep breath, I forged ahead. I could do this. No problem.

I kept my gaze averted from the break room and bustled toward the shop. I nabbed an empty magenta bottle from the shelf and gathered ingredients from bins and baskets. All around me I noticed that my inventory had been rummaged through, and a few potion bottles even lay broken on the floor, but nothing seemed to be missing.

I carried all my supplies with me into my workroom and closed the door behind me.

The space was small, filled mostly with a built-in cabinet my granddaddy had made just about fifty years ago, a short counter, and a small sink. There was a pass-through cut into the wall between here and the front of the shop so I could chat with customers and keep an eye on them while I made their potions.

The opening was purposefully high, so people could see only my head and shoulders and not my hands. I quickly propped up the drop-leg table work surface. Behind it, a series of cubbies and drawers filled the wall to the ceiling.

I could tell the sheriff's office had been in here, as all the *visible* drawers had been searched. For a moment, I worried that one of them might have found my secret compartment, but I drew in a deep breath and tried to keep calm. My granddaddy had been a master carpenter, and I doubted many of the sheriff's deputies—other than Dylan—were smart enough to even suspect there were secret spaces in this cabinet, let alone ten of them, most of them empty.

Rushing, I removed two decorative spindles and pulled three drawers out of place. Behind those, I removed a hidden box—a decoy filled with two hundred dollars—and set it aside. I pushed a corner on the bottom of the cube and a foot-long panel lifted. I pulled that out and reached my hand inside. From the right side, I pulled on a box and lifted it out of the hole.

As with every other time I've done this, I held my

breath as I lifted the top off the carved wooden box. Inside, nestled in a bed of cushioned velvet, lay the grimoire, a small leather-bound journal filled with homeopathic recipes.

Picking up the worn leather book, I held it between my hands and could practically feel folk magic pulsing between my palms. I reached into the hidey-hole and nudged the box from the left side and carefully lifted it out.

Two entwined lilies had been carved into its top—an image identical to the one on Delia's and my lockets. I lifted the lid off the box and gazed at the stunning engraved sterling silver bottle swaddled in luxurious velvet.

Slightly tarnished, the bottle stood about six inches tall and had the diameter of a half-dollar. More a flask than a potion bottle, this container held exactly a year's worth of Leilara drops. Tears, really.

Leila's and Abraham's tears.

As I grated wild carrot, I thought about my great-great-grandparents. Of how Leila had fallen in love with Abraham and followed him from New Orleans up to northern Alabama, and, in the hope that her love was strong enough to change his sinister ways, turned her back on her family, who warned against marrying the voodoo practitioner.

Of how every day was a struggle for her to keep her energy pure, because she could feel his darkness. She had no charmed locket like Delia and I had; she simply had a heart full of love and good intentions.

I thought of how they'd married and had a daughter who'd inherited her mama's way of feeling other people's emotions and her talent for folk-magic remedies.

And of how one June day, while picnicking along the

Darling River, when Abraham was bitten by a poisonous water snake, Leila felt his pain, his anguish. She tried to save him by sucking the venom from his wound.

Of how they both died, wrapped in each other's arms.

And of how every year on that day—and only that day—an extraordinary double lily blooms in the spot where they died and cried magical tears.

Engraved vines and lily leaves decorated the outside of the bottle. I pulled the stopper from the Leilara and carefully inserted a dropper and extracted two teardrops, depositing them into the hangover potion. Steamlike white tendrils rose from the liquid and swirled into a spiral before dissipating. Tomorrow, Francie Debbs wouldn't have so much as a twinge of a headache.

A few minutes later, after I'd cleaned up a bit, a knock came on the door just as I had finished putting the Leilara back into its hiding space. Since I didn't need it for the love potions, because my customers had abandoned me, I'd leave it here. I liked knowing it was safe and sound.

"Carly? You going to be all day?"

I grabbed the potion bottle and opened the door.

Dylan's face peered inside the workroom, and he looked around suspiciously.

"I'm done," I said, holding up the bottle.

He gave a sharp nod and walked ahead of me toward the back door. I couldn't help myself from admiring his backside. I wasn't proud of that fact, but, hey, some things were impossible to ignore.

Ainsley, standing at the back door, strained to see any goings-on. I held up the bottle, and she grinned ear to ear. "Lordy be!"

The bottle slipped from my grasp, and using moves I

didn't know I had, I made a grab for the falling bottle and was able to get my hand under the glass just in time. I wasn't able to catch it—only break its fall. It hit my palm and rolled off—into the break room.

Ainsley let out a cry and came rushing toward me. "It's not busted, is it?"

Dylan threw his hands in the air at her intrusion into his crime scene.

I simply stared in horror as the bottle rolled over the spot on the floor where Nelson Winston had been lying dead as a doornail a few hours earlier.

A large smear of blood had colored my off-white tiles a rusty brown. I immediately felt queasy, but Ainsley had no qualms as she rushed past me, stepped over the blood-stain, and snatched up the potion bottle.

"Out!" Dylan ordered her, pointing down the hallway. Without a fight, she slunk away, the potion bottle clutched to her chest. "I'll wait for you outside, Carly."

I felt glued to the ground. Stuck there, staring at all that blood. I felt a hand on my elbow.

Dylan said, "Come on, Carly. Let's go." He tugged, and I slowly rose to my feet, a bit wobbly.

"I'll have to scrub for days. That stain's never going to come out of the grout." I grew queasier just thinking about it.

"No you won't, Cinderella. Someone's coming in later today to clean up. A professional crew. Stain magicians."

"Really?" I asked.

"Really."

I was beyond grateful, because I couldn't imagine taking a scrub brush to that floor.

Looking around, I said, "Why did someone break in but not take anything? Nothing is missing."

He leaned against the wall. "I don't know. Yet. But I'll figure it out."

As I walked into the alley, leaving my shop behind, I really, really wanted to believe him.

But I had the uneasy feeling that Nelson's murderer was going to great lengths to keep that from happening.

❧ Chapter Eight ❧

Ainsley and I sat in Déjà Brew, the only coffee shop located in the Ring, sipping iced coffee.

"What now?" Ainsley asked, dragging her straw through the mocha liquid, swirling the ice into a mini tornado.

Condensation dripped from my cup onto my shorts, leaving a dark shadow on the white fabric. "We have to find out who Nelson was dating. You never heard anything about him dating, did you?"

"Not a peep, and I'm surprised. I tend to hear all the gossip either through church events or at Dr. O'Leary's office. That place is nothing but a hen house—you should hear all the squawking."

Colley O'Leary was the only ob-gyn within Hitching Post's town limits, and Ainsley worked for her a few days a week.

I set my cup on a paper napkin to absorb the drips sliding down the side of the glass tumbler. "But no squawking about Nelson?"

She shook her head. "Nothing about a girl. Only some buzz about Coach Butts's case."

"What kind of buzz?"

"That that Nelson was going to get Coach off, free and clear."

Dylan had said the same earlier. Tearing an edge off the soggy napkin, I rolled the paper between two fingers. "Win because Coach isn't guilty? Or because Nelson is such a good lawyer he'd get him off?"

"Not guilty. Coach has been claiming all along that someone forged his name on those checks, and talk is that Nelson could prove it true by getting some fancy handwriting analysis done. He's been waiting on the report that was due any day now." She shrugged. "It may have already come in."

A handwriting analysis . . . that would answer a lot of questions. I wondered if Dylan had found one in the search of Nelson's office.

Ainsley took a sip of her coffee, then said, "Everyone's speculating that Coach is so dang angry and picking fights all the time now because he's innocent and feels like he's getting railroaded. I have to admit, if I were falsely accused, I might be picking fights, too."

"He has been getting into a fair share of trouble lately, hasn't he?"

"Fighting with everyone under the sun, including Angelea, Bernice, and Nelson, so I hear told."

Angelea and Bernice I could understand—it was easy to snap at family. "Why Nelson?"

"Word is Coach wasn't happy with how slowly Nelson was working to clear his name. He was getting mighty impatient."

"How'd Nelson handle Coach's outburst?" This could take the case in a whole new direction. . . .

"Cool as could be. Calmed Coach right down. Like I

said, Nelson believed he'd clear Coach's name for good when that handwriting analysis came in."

The scent of blueberry scones wafted through the shop as I tapped my fingers on the tabletop. "Okay, for conversation's sake, let's say Coach is innocent." It was hard for me to even say those words. "If Coach didn't take the money, then where is it? Twenty thousand dollars doesn't just vanish." Maybe Angelea Butts had it; that might be why she wasn't sleeping so well these days.

I suddenly had a ridiculous image of her sleeping on a mound of hundred-dollar bills. I smiled. That would explain some things.

Ainsley shrugged. "I don't know."

"But if he *wasn't* innocent, and Nelson found out he wasn't, maybe Coach got scared and killed him to keep him quiet? What?" I said at Ainsley's dubious look. "It could have happened."

"Not likely, darlin'," Jessamine Yadkin said in her raspy voice as she set a plate of cookies on the table. She'd obviously been eavesdropping—a regular Darling County extracurricular activity.

I could have kissed her for the cookies. I grabbed one up and took a big bite.

"No reason for Coach to kill him," Jessa added. Her brassy-colored hair was piled atop her head and held in place with two pencils. Heavy wrinkles pulled at the corners of her bright blue eyes and bracketed her mouth. All those years of smoking hadn't been kind to her but didn't dull the sparkle in her eyes.

I mumbled heartfelt thanks for the cookie over a mouthful of oatmeal chocolate chip, then said, "What do you mean, no reason?"

Jessa cocked a plump hip and tightened her bright

pink apron strings. She was sixty, if a day, and happily married to her second husband, Odell. She'd owned this place for as long as I could remember and made the best coffee in all of Darling County. "Nelson couldn't rightly say anything even if Coach had given him a full confession on a silver platter. He's bound by attorney-client privilege." She winked. "I learned all about that when my first husband was incarcerated. It's basically a gag order for Nelson."

The cowbell on the front door jangled as a young couple walked in, holding hands. The man wore a T-shirt that said I JUST GOT HITCHED IN HITCHING POST, ALABAMA.

Jessa said to them, "Y'all have a seat, now. I'll be right with you."

The newlyweds sat at a table in the corner and gazed dreamily at each other. Tourists, probably only in town for a weekend elopement. They were adorable, and I sure hoped theirs wasn't the divorce Mr. Dunwoody had predicted.

"So, there wasn't no motive on Coach's part to kill Nelson, leastways if the killin' was because Coach stole that money," Jessa added before sashaying away to the newlyweds' table.

"Jessa is right." Ainsley broke her cookie in half and watched warm chocolate stretch from one side to the other.

"Well, someone killed him." Admittedly, I wouldn't have been devastated to see Coach behind bars. I had never liked him, and especially not now that he'd accused me of poisoning him. "We have to find that girlfriend."

Ainsley nodded.

Jessa ambled by, and I snagged her apron string.

"Have you heard about Nelson having himself a girl-friend?"

Jessa's eyes widened. "You don't say. He did?"

"So we heard." I dropped what was left of my cookie on my plate, my appetite suddenly gone.

"Not one I know of, darlin'," Jessa said. "The only person I've seen him with lately is Johnny Braxton, and whoo-ee, were they going at it right outside this here door. They were shoutin' at each other something fierce before Johnny stomped off."

"You sure it was Nelson and not Coach?" Ainsley asked.

Jessa smiled. "Coach sure is making a name for himself lately, isn't he? But no, it wasn't him. It was Nelson — I saw the whole thing clear as day."

"When was this?" I asked.

Jessa looked upward, as if searching the recesses of her brain. "Two, three days ago."

"What were they fighting about?" Ainsley asked.

"I didn't hear that much, only Nelson saying he didn't care anymore. By the time I made it outside to eavesdrop properly, Johnny was already storming away."

Didn't care anymore? About what? "Did you tell this to Dylan?"

"Didn't think of it till just now." She tightened her apron. "I'll give him a call straight off." She hurried into the kitchen.

"You know," Ainsley said, wetting her thumb to dab up cookie crumbs from her plate, "I've been thinking on what you said to Dylan earlier, about the potion bottles and how there are colors for men and women...."

Ainsley already knew my color-coding system since she worked for me. I picked up my cookie again. I couldn't bear to leave it uneaten—plus, I didn't like the way Ainsley was eyeing it. "What about them?"

Shifting left and right, she wouldn't look me in the eye. "It's just that at the white-elephant sale, there's a new booth that—"

She was interrupted by Jessa, who had barreled up to the table. "I've just realized y'all should talk to Bernice Morris about Nelson's personal life. If anyone knows about a secret girl, it'd be her. She'd probably also know why Nelson was gettin' on with Johnny something fierce."

Brilliant! Bernice was Nelson Winston's secretary and had been for years. Of course she'd know all his secrets. "We've got to talk to her."

Ainsley looked at her watch and stood up. "*You've* got to talk to her. I've got to be getting to the market to buy a box of wine. But you'll call me to let me know how it goes?"

It was getting late, almost supper time, and for a moment, it felt like finding Nelson's body had happened days ago, not this morning.

We settled up with Jessa and walked outside, where the scent of rain hung heavy in the thick air.

"Storm's coming," Ainsley said unnecessarily. She pecked my cheek and hurried off, headed for the market. Calling over her shoulder, she added, "You be careful, Carly. Y'hear?"

It was the second time today I'd heard that sentiment, and as I set off toward Bernice's place I decided to take it to heart.

Bernice lived on the other side of town, near the Darling Playhouse Cinema, which was, appropriately, half playhouse and half movie theater. I'd seen many a movie sitting in the worn red velvet seats, on the screen draped with golden fabric.

As I started across the Ring and headed toward Bernice's house, I suddenly realized that I couldn't go knocking on Bernice's door—unless I wanted it slammed in my face.

Bernice Morris was Coach Butts's sister.

There was no way she was going to talk to me about Nelson's murder, especially if she'd heard the rumors that I'd tried to poison Coach.

Gnawing my thumbnail, I was debating what to do when I spotted Emmylou and Dudley Pritcherd on their hands and knees crawling around a blanket near the big gazebo in the picnic park.

Had she lost her contact again?

"Yoo-hoo! Carly!"

Emmylou's high-pitched voice sliced through my soul. I hid a cringe and walked over. Dudley sat back on his haunches in the grass, a pinched look to his handsome face.

"Good afternoon," I said. "You two doing well?"

Emmylou gave a brief shake of her head, as if warning me to not talk about Dudley's bedroom dudliness.

As if I would.

"We've been better," she said.

Dudley added, "Much better. Afternoon, Carly." He bent back over, bringing his nose down close to the grass and sweeping his hands over the blades.

"You lose your contact again?" I asked Emmylou.

"I wish," she said, tears pooling in her eyes. "It's my wedding ring this time. It flew off my finger while we were sitting here," she said, clearly exasperated. "Went thataway." She pointed vaguely behind Dudley.

Still on the hunt, he peered into the depths of the thick lawn.

"I can't believe it," she said. "I knew it had come loose, but not that loose. It's this weight I lost. Sympathy weight."

"Sympathy weight?" I asked.

Dudley's big blue eyes looked pained as he glanced up. "Emmylou . . ."

Ignoring him, she said, "Dudley's lost so much lately that I've lost some, too, just worrying about him. Look at him. Just look. Shrinking away. Isn't he shrinking, Carly?"

Dudley gave me a pleading, "please don't look at me" gaze, but the truth was, he had lost a lot of weight, and he hadn't been a big man to begin with.

Before I could say anything about his appearance one way or another, Emmylou added, "Do you have a potion for that? Weight gain?"

Dudley dragged a hand through his curly brown hair, rolled his eyes, and went back to crawling around.

"Depends on what's causing the weight to come off," I said. "A tried-and-true doctor would be needed for something serious."

There was a good chance Dudley's health was why he was having bedroom issues in the first place. Emmylou hadn't said anything at all about him losing weight when she came in for the potency potion a couple of days ago.

"I'll tell you what's causing that weight to come off," she said, fluffing the ruffles on her blouse.

"Emmylou, sweetheart," Dudley murmured, sitting back on his haunches. "Carly doesn't need to know."

Actually in this case I was kind of curious.

"Pish-posh," she said. "It's just Carly. Maybe she can help. It's this trial."

"Coach Butts's trial?" I asked.

Emmylou nodded. "Dudley was due to take the stand next week."

Was. Now with Nelson dead, that timeline was likely to change.

"Emmylou." Dudley sighed, a scarlet stain spreading across his cheeks. "Really."

She paid him no mind. "You know Dudley's the one who found the accounting discrepancy in the first place, right? He keeps the baseball league's books."

Dudley had discovered the mistake after a check to buy new uniforms for the team had bounced.

"He was to testify against Coach, and was worried the town wasn't going to like what he had to say." She *tsk*ed loudly. "Plus that old biddy Bernice Morris can't stop spouting off, trying to ruin Dudley's reputation."

"Emmy," Dudley pleaded quietly.

Bernice? Coach's sister? Nelson's secretary? The one who probably wouldn't talk with me even if I came bearing an oversized check with her name on it? "What is Bernice saying?"

Emmylou threw her hands in the air. "I can't believe you haven't heard! Seems to me she's been telling everyone who will listen that Dudley made a *mistake*. That Dudley wasn't *qualified* to run the audit. That maybe even Dudley was the one who *stole* that money and is framing Coach. She even talked Nelson into getting another accountant to perform a second audit on the books, as if that was going to help the cause. It's *outrageous*."

I glanced at Dudley, who looked like he wanted to dig a hole and throw himself in. By Emmylou's theatrics, I suspected this wasn't her first retelling of this story, and wondered who was the bigger spouter—her or Bernice.

With one look at the gleam in Emmylou's eyes, I figured I already knew the answer to that.

Tucking a strand of hair behind her ear, Emmylou said, "She's a bitter old pill, that Bernice, one who has it out for Dudley. It's tearing him up, and I'm sure she's pleased as punch about that."

My brain whirred with information. The first thing that jumped out at me was that Bernice wasn't old. She was maybe fifty at most. The second thing was that Dudley did have easy access to those funds. The third was wondering about the outcome of the second audit. The fourth was that Bernice had never seemed the vindictive type to me. "Why would Bernice have it out for Dudley?"

"Well, it all goes back to—"

"Oh, dear God," Dudley muttered, apparently going straight to the Big Guy for help with the ground opening up and swallowing him whole. "Emmy, stop."

She brushed him off with a grand wave of her hand. "It's all because of Angelea Butts."

"Angelea?" I wished I had a folding chair and some popcorn for this show. It was getting interesting.

"On account of Dudley once dated Angelea, while she was on a split with Coach." She tittered. "Before he met *me*, of course. Bernice seems to think Dudley's still holding a candle for Angelea, and that framing Coach is his diabolical way of getting her husband out of the way. Have you ever heard anything so plumb crazy in all your days?"

A chair, popcorn, and a big Diet Coke with a bendy straw.

"Angelea and I are just friends," Dudley said to me in a desperate whisper.

I suddenly recalled the rumors that Angelea had been cheating on Coach recently. Was she stepping out with Dudley? He did have a guilty flush about him—but that coloring could also have come from Emmylou's over-sharing.

Emmylou rolled her eyes and possessively latched onto Dudley's elbow. "If anything, Angelea is still *pining* for Dudley. For Bernice to think differently is just plain crazy."

Dudley looked like he wanted to shove a spoonful of macaroni salad down Emmylou's throat to keep her quiet. Clearly he was a proud man who didn't like airing his dirty laundry to outsiders. He'd probably keel right over if he knew Emmylou had come to see me about his *dudliness*.

Thunder rumbled in the distance, and a fat rain drop plopped smack-dab on Emmylou's forehead.

Looking upward, she squealed, "Our picnic!" and started gathering up their supplies.

Dudley muttered something that sounded like, "Divine intervention."

"Do you want help looking for the ring?" I asked.

Dudley said graciously, "Go on home before you get soaked to the bone, Carly. I'll come back later with a metal detector. It'll turn up."

Emmylou was making quick work of packing her picnic basket. "Let me wrap some of this up for you, Carly."

"You don't have to. . . ."

"No, no. I insist." She shoved a tin of corn bread into my hands. "I'll come by the shop tomorrow to see you," she said with a saucy wink.

For the virility potion.

"What for?" Dudley asked.

"For you, darlin'," Emmylou cooed his way. "I'm sure Carly has something for stress."

Before I could say I did in fact have a stress potion, Dudley spoke first.

"Thank you kindly, but I'm fine. I don't need any potion," he protested, his cheeks bright pink. "Especially not from . . ."

He trailed off, his blush turning red.

"Not from Carly," he was going to say. I just knew it.

It was like I'd been hit by a two-by-four. Even my regular customers believed the rumors. Dudley never had trouble taking one of my potions before.

He glanced at me apologetically before Emmylou patted my arm. "There, there, Carly. This will all blow over soon enough. How is Coach, by the way?"

"He's fine," I said. "Turned out he had a diabetic reaction. He'll be back home before nightfall."

"Diabetes, really?" Emmylou said. "That's interesting. That poor man, bless his heart. Bless *your* heart." She smiled sympathetically.

I glanced between the two of them, and it was clear as day that neither believed what I'd said about the diabetes.

"I need to get going. Thanks for the corn bread," I said.

Emmylou gave me a little wave and wrinkled her nose. "See you tomorrow, Carly."

Nodding, I walked off. As soon as I rounded the corner, I dumped the corn bread in a trash can.

❦ Chapter Nine ❧

I was at a loss about what to do. Bernice Morris surely had some answers to my burning questions, but getting her to divulge them to me was going to take a small miracle.

A raindrop splashed my cheek, and I swiped it away as I headed down the tree-lined sidewalk toward the river walk at the bottom of the hill. It continued to sprinkle, but the storm held off for now.

Despite the weather the river walk was crowded, but I managed to find an empty bench. Most of Darling River was calm and flat, but every half mile or so it would suddenly form into rough water with rapids and small drop-offs—nothing too dangerous, but exciting enough for an afternoon of fun. From where I sat, I could see several kayakers bouncing over and dipping under the churning white water, and I hoped the storm would hold off until they were safely on land.

I needed to figure out a plan to get Bernice to talk with me. I was sitting there staring at the water, mesmerized, really, when I suddenly felt a presence studying me.

I glanced up and found Johnny Braxton leaning against the iron safety fence not four feet away.

The look in his eyes matched the storm clouds above.

Johnny had always been cordial to me, less so to my mama and daddy. He was a shrewd businessman who was all about money, and it showed in the way he dressed. From his silver-tipped boots to his fussy bolo tie.

He jutted his chin and stroked his white grizzled beard. "What's your mama up to?"

I shrugged as a raindrop glanced off my shoulder. "Beats me."

"She's not planning to sabotage my weekend extravaganza, is she?"

Yes. Yes, she is. "You know my mama."

I recalled how my daddy told me that Johnny was going to dress as Johnny Cash for his extravaganza, and I couldn't quite picture how he planned to pull that off, as there was no resemblance whatsoever.

Around seventy, Johnny was not a young man by any means, but he was big and muscular with a wide barrel chest and beefy arms. When I was younger, there was something about his physique and the way he walked that always reminded me of Popeye's nemesis, Bluto. Nowadays I thought he still looked like Bluto, though his hair had long since turned white and his muscles had atrophied some.

Once upon a time, Johnny had been considered a catch, especially since he had a fat bank account and a big ol' house, but money couldn't make up for his rotten personality, and he'd remained a bachelor most of his life.

It was a little ironic that he ran one of the most popular wedding chapels in town, though I supposed I could

say the same of my mama, with her matrimonial cynicism.

I wondered again what he had been arguing about
with Nelson but couldn't quite screw up enough courage
to ask. I wasn't frightened of much, but this man scared
me some.

"It would serve her best to mind her own business and
stop trying to steal mine," he warned, keeping his voice
low. "And best you remind her of that."

Apparently after all these years he also hadn't learned
that no one told my mama what to do. I stood up, ready
to go toe-to-toe with this man three times my size. I
might be scared, but I was never one to back down from
a challenge. I latched onto my locket and said, "Is that a
threat, Mr. Braxton?"

"Just fair warning," he answered lightly. "No one
messes with my bottom line and gets away with it."

"How much money do you rightly need?" I snapped.
"You already own half the town." He owned his chapel,
several reception venues and party halls, and a couple of
restaurants, too.

"More, if I have a say in it."

"What does that mean?"

"It means I always get what I want."

"I know what you *need*," I said sassily.

His tone was sharp as he said, "And what is it I need,
young lady?"

A poke from my pitchfork would work nicely. "You
need yourself a woman to soften up your hard edges, Mr.
Braxton. You should come see me about my matchmaking services. You're never too old to find love."

Though, truth be told, finding someone to love him
would be quite the task.

Thunder rumbled, and Johnny looked to the skies before glancing back at me. "Why would I do that? I heard tell you've been poisoning people with those potions of yours. Isn't it cruel how vicious some rumors can be?"

I narrowed my eyes. Had he been fanning the flames of those rumors? "Seems to me I heard my own rumors about you fighting with Nelson in front of the coffee shop a couple of days ago. Now, what was that fight about, Mr. Braxton?"

His jowls tightened in anger. In a low warning tone, he said, "You should mind your business, too, Miss Carly." He tipped an imaginary hat. "Have yourself a good night, now."

A good night. Ha! It was turning out to be anything but.

The skies had opened on my way home, and I'd come in the back door to a dark kitchen. The power in my house had gone off, yet everyone else's on the street was just fine.

Roly and Poly were nowhere to be found, and I suspected the big chickens were hiding out under my bed — their usual spot when it was storming.

I'd left my damp shoes on the back door landing and now stood in the kitchen in my sopping socks, watching the ceiling drip.

Letting loose a string of curse words that would make my daddy blush, I grabbed a Crock-Pot from the cabinet and set it under the leak.

Rain pounded the roof, and I found two more leaks in the living room. I set a saucepan under one and an empty kitty-litter container under the other before heading upstairs to my room to change.

As I was running home in the rain, I'd tried to come

up with a good plan to get Bernice Morris to spill what she knew of Nelson's private life to me.

I needed a lie. A whopper that would convince her to give me some information—despite the fact that she probably hated my guts.

The storm had darkened my bedroom, and it took me a second to remember why the light switch didn't work when I flipped it on.

No electricity.

I moved about in the murky light, first to check to see if the cats were under the bed (they were) and then to my closet to change out of my wet clothes. I slipped into a pair of drawstring shorts and a T-shirt before thumping down the hall to the bathroom (dang light switch!) to dry my hair with a towel. I set a wastebasket under the drip near the tub.

I glanced in the mirror at my freckled face and groaned at the sight of my hair. Without a hair dryer it was going to frizz like a used Brillo pad.

As I stared at my reflection, I wondered what on earth I'd done to bring today's mess upon myself.

Nelson dead in my shop.

Johnny Braxton threatening me.

Rumors that my potions were poisoned.

I squeezed my eyes shut and braced my weight on the pedestal sink. In a town this size, a rumor like that could put me out of business fast. Despite the truth of the matter, people would believe what they heard. Even tourists would hear snippets and stay away.

It didn't matter that mine was one of the more successful shops in town.

Or that my potions worked wonders on people.

Only that people heard that one man had died and another had wrecked his car after drinking my potions.

Why?

The word kept echoing in my head, bouncing off reasons why Nelson had been found in *my* shop.

Why? Why? Why?

There were no answers.

I might not know why now, but I'd find out. I wasn't going down without a fight.

With a new determination, I headed downstairs to gather up more buckets for the inevitable leaks, and candles in preparation for nightfall. Lightning flashed and thunder cracked.

I checked the breaker in the kitchen, but it didn't show that I'd blown any fuses. I opened my front door to check on the neighbors' houses and almost fell into my pile of porch debris.

I'd almost forgotten about the porch. My anger simmered as I stomped toward the kitchen, to the phone book in a drawer. I'd call and see if the cleanup company could come tomorrow instead of Monday to haul the debris away. I found the number of the county company, but as soon as I picked up the phone, I found it dead.

Lots of that going around today.

I slammed down the receiver, walked over to the pantry, and pulled out a jar of peanut butter. After grabbing a spoon from the drawer, I twisted off the peanut butter cap and dug in.

Within minutes, Poly was downstairs, twining around my legs, meowing for his fair share. He could smell peanut butter from a mile away, I swear.

I grabbed another teaspoon from the drawer, dipped

the tip into the jar, the smallest of dabs, and set it on the floor.

Poly looked at the spoon, then back up at me.

"It's enough," I said.

He flicked his long gray tail in displeasure.

"Take it or leave it."

The cat wouldn't touch a mouse with a ten-foot pole, but offer him some peanut butter and he was in kitty heaven. It was no surprise when he started lapping at the spoon.

It would take Roly another few hours after the storm stopped to come out from under the bed. I had no doubt that as soon as Poly finished his peanut butter, he'd go back upstairs and lord it over her that he'd had a treat and she hadn't.

He was a braggart like that.

Roly was patient, however, and would exact her revenge on him later.

I tapped my spoon on the edge of the plastic container and thought about Bernice and Nelson. There had to be a way to get information from her.

Maybe I could send Ainsley. She had a way about her that made people tell her things. Of course, if Bernice knew Ainsley was only after the info to help me out, then Ainsley would be sent packing with a firm, sweet smile and a zucchini loaf.

Southerners were polite like that.

Poly stared up at me with baleful eyes.

"No more," I said, and finally had to turn around so I wouldn't be persuaded.

I shoved another spoonful of peanut butter in my mouth and let it melt. What was going to happen with the trial now that Nelson was dead? Coach would need another lawyer, and surely the case would be delayed.

I continued to tap the spoon and noticed that the skies outside were lightening, but it was still raining. Drips plopped from my ceiling into the Crock-Pot.

Wait a sec. . . . The perfect plan was forming in my head. It just might work.

If I went to Bernice and explained that I needed the information on Nelson because I was convinced that whoever killed him must have been the *real* embezzler, trying to stop the case from going to trial by killing Nelson because he was going to expose the true culprit, then maybe she'd open up. Especially after I added that by finding that person, I'd be proving Coach's innocence once and for all, and oh yeah, clearing my own name and saving my reputation.

The fact that my argument was all made-up gobbledygook (except for the clearing-my-name part) was beside the point.

Ha! It was genius, if I did say so myself. The perfect lie concocted to weasel some much-needed information.

Poly wandered off, and I was feeling right proud of my plan as I set my spoon in the sink and put the peanut butter away.

So much so that my motive for my faux argument barely registered until I set the peanut butter jar back in the pantry.

And realized it might not be so phony after all.

In fact, it was the only thing that had made sense all day long.

What if Coach really *was* innocent? And what if the real embezzler heard the buzz about Nelson getting Coach off scot-free? Would he or she have killed to stop Nelson from taking the case to trial, to stop new evidence from being revealed?

New evidence like a second audit and a handwriting analysis?

Hmm.

I walked over to the dining room window and stared out at the falling rain. From this spot, I could see Mr. Dunwoody on his front porch, sipping his evening tea, rocking away while watching the storm march eastward. Leaves fluttered in the wind, and broken twigs littered our yards.

If Coach's new lawyer didn't know what he was doing . . . Coach would be found guilty of embezzlement. Locked up. And the embezzler would get off clean as could be with twenty thousand dollars.

It sounded like the perfect motive to me.

I just had to figure out who that person could be.

If he or she even existed.

I was still clinging to the belief that Coach was guilty, but since this was the only lead I had, I'd work with it until proven otherwise. And in order to do that, I needed Bernice Morris's help.

As I stared outside, I spotted movement near Auntie Marjie's fence.

I squinted, but didn't see anything out of place.

But there . . . a bush shook. As I watched, a head popped up above the fence, looked left, then right, and then ducked back down again.

Someone was sneaking through Aunt Marjie's front yard.

Someone with a death wish, apparently.

And just as I had the thought, a shotgun blast split the air.

∾ Chapter Ten ∾

The gun blasted the trespasser out of his hiding spot in the bushes and sent him scurrying for better cover.

I jumped into action before there was another murder in Hitching Post today. Hightailing it out my back door, I dashed toward my aunt's house.

Mr. Dunwoody's loud *tee-hee-hee* reverberated as I sprinted down the street, my bare feet slapping on the wet brick road. Aunt Marjie stood on her front porch, a shotgun balanced against her shoulder, one eye squinted.

"Don't shoot, Aunt Marjie!" I shouted.

One of these days she was going to hit someone, and I didn't think she would look good in prison stripes, either.

Marjie yelled, "Come out of those brambles, you son of bitch, or I won't miss next time!"

I hurdled Marjie's front fence (I was getting good at it) but nearly fell because of slippery landing area. Standing firm, I put myself between her gun and the culprit. I didn't think she'd shoot me.

At least I hoped she wouldn't.

"Could you put that gun down, Aunt Marjie?" I huffed, trying to catch my breath.

"This ain't your business, Carly. Get on with you, now," she barked. "I've got a city slicker to pop holes in. He's gonna look like Swiss cheese when I'm done with him."

Another round of Mr. Dunwoody's *tee-hee-hee*s echoed. I was glad he was having a jolly good time.

What sounded like pitiful mewls emerged from the bushes behind me. I wasn't sure what had set the trespasser to crying—the Swiss cheese threat or the brambles. Those thorns hurt something fierce.

"The gun, Aunt Marjie," I said firmly. Pleading never carried much weight with her—she saw it as a sign of weakness.

Heaving a sigh, she slowly lowered the weapon, though I noticed she still kept a finger on the trigger. She was itching to bag herself a city slicker.

"Thank you," I said.

"He has exactly ten seconds to get himself out of my yard. Do I make myself clear?"

"Perfectly," I said.

"Eight," she intoned.

I spun around, crouched, and stared into the face of a terrified man.

"Six."

"Get up!" I yelled.

Like a deer caught in headlights, he just stared at me, making those pitiful sounds.

"Four!" Marjie yelled.

"Tee-hee-hee," Mr. Dunwoody laughed.

"Three!"

I grabbed the guy's arm and pulled. Brambles tore at his fancy—yet soggy—suit as he found his feet.

"Two!"

I threw a glance at Marjie, who'd once again braced the gun on her shoulder.

More mewling came from the city slicker.

I glanced into his terrified eyes, said, "Sorry," and gave him the biggest shove I had in me.

He tumbled backward, right over Marjie's fence and onto the sidewalk.

The public sidewalk.

I winced at the sound of him hitting the cement. A long, drawn-out moan filled the air.

"He didn't break my fence, now, did he?" Marjie asked with an accusatory tone.

Marjie's fence had been falling apart for years. It was only the brambles that kept it from crumbling.

"No, ma'am," I said.

She grunted and went back inside, slamming the door.

Giving the brambles a wide berth, I walked around the fence. The rain had stopped but moisture hung thickly in the air, and I was sweating like crazy.

The trespasser lay in a fetal position on the sidewalk. Blood oozed from small scrapes and punctures from the thorns. I didn't see any bullet holes.

I crouched down. "Jeez, do you have a death wish?"

Wide, terrified eyes blinked at me. His perfect white teeth chattered as he said, "I thought they were kidding about the gun."

"Didn't you see the No Trespassing signs?" There were enough of them. I saw five with just a quick glance around the yard.

"I thought they were kidding about the gun," he mumbled again.

Taking pity on the poor thing, I grabbed his hand helped him to his feet.

Wobbly, he reached out for Marjie's fence post, and I said, "I wouldn't do that if I were you."

He immediately snatched his hand back, as if it had been electrocuted.

"Who are you?" I asked as I picked leaves off his once-fancy suit.

"John Richard Baldwin, ma'am."

At least his teeth had stopped chattering, but his eyes were still wide. Shock, I reasoned. "What are you doing here, John Richard Baldwin?"

He blinked as though I'd asked him to name all the presidents in alphabetical order. Bits of shrubbery clung to tufts of light brown hair that stuck out in every direction. His face had been scratched to hell and back.

"Working, ma'am," he finally said.

"Working where?" I prompted, leading him down the sidewalk toward my about-to-be-condemned house.

Aunt Eulalie came out onto her porch and said, "Did she get him?"

"Nope," I said.

"Dang!" She spun and went back inside.

John Richard looked at me. "Is everyone in this town bloodthirsty?"

I led him across the street to my freestanding set of steps. "Pretty much. Who do you work for?"

His eyes brightened a bit, and it was good to see some color in his cheeks that wasn't from the bloody scratches. "Doughtree, Sullivan, and Gobble." With a flourish, he handed me a damp business card.

"I see." I'd heard the name before. It was the Birmingham law firm that had been trying to get Aunt Marjie to

sell her inn. It was also the firm that had once repre-
sented Coach Butts, until Coach fired them to hire Nelson. "Sit."

He glanced around. "Where?"

I dusted pebbles off the damp brick steps. "Here."

"You're kidding."

He wasn't much younger than I was, maybe three or
four years, but with his baby face and naive air, he
seemed more like a high school boy than a big-city lawyer. I pegged him to be fresh out of law school. "If you're
worried you'll ruin your suit, I'm afraid it's too late for
that."

He glanced down and let out a small cry, as if just noticing all the rips.

I left him whimpering and ran inside for some rubbing
alcohol and cotton balls. When I came back out, he had
his head in his hands. "I'm going to get fired for sure."

"Hush," I said, dabbing his hand with the alcohol.
"They're not going to fire you. You weren't successful in
your quest, but no one in the firm has been. They can't
fire the lot of you. There won't be anyone left to make
fun of Gobble's last name."

He yowled at the sting, then gave me a halfhearted
smile. "We do have ourselves a good time around
Thanksgiving."

I could imagine.

"Who's your client?" I asked. "The one who wants the
inn so bad?"

"Can't say, ma'am."

"Can't or won't?" I dabbed at his cheek and he let out
a hiss.

"Can't." He grabbed the bottle from me. "I'll do that.
I don't know who the client is. Just that it's someone

who's willing to pay a bunch of money for what looks like a fire trap."

It was true—the Old Buzzard did look like it could burst into flames at any moment. But appearances weren't everything. Its location near the town square made it prime real estate.

He glanced around at the rubble. "What happened here, anyway?"

"Someone drove his Chevy into my porch."

John Richard's eyes lit. "Are you lookin' to sue him?"

Although suing Coach Butts held a certain appeal, I shook my head. "I think he did me a favor, actually. The porch needed to come down. Saved me demolition costs."

Plus, now insurance would pay for the debris removal and new construction.

His face fell. "If you change your mind, you have my card. I should go." Standing, he looked down the street, toward the Old Buzzard. "I can't believe she shot at me," he said in wonder. "Thank goodness she's got bad aim."

"Nothing wrong with her aim, John Richard. Let that be fair warning to you."

For a second he said nothing, only looked at me as if seeing me for the first time. "Who're you exactly?"

"I'm Broom-Hilda."

"Like the witch from the funnies?"

I nodded. "Exactly."

Rolling his eyes, he said, "Is everyone in this place crazy?"

"Plumb."

"Good to know for when I come back."

"Back?" I asked, capping the alcohol bottle.

"I've got to get that old lady to sell. My career depends on it. Time is of the essence. There's a big fat bonus involved if the old lady sells by the end of the month. I don't intend to fail like the last guy." He winced. "Not that he could help it and all, dying the way he did this morning. It wouldn't surprise me none if that crazy lady shot him dead." John Richard headed for the sidewalk.

I scurried to catch up to him and said, "The last guy? What was his name?"

"Supposedly he lived in this nutty place." His eyes rolled up as if he were searching the corners of his brain for the correct name.

"Nelson Winston?" I supplied.

Snapping his fingers, he said, "That's it! You knew him?"

"Not very well." I didn't think finding his dead body changed the status of our casual relationship. "He was working for *your* law firm?"

"Freelancing, hoping to get a full-time gig. It was suggested to the senior partners that getting a local involved might help the cause. Fat lot of good it did them." John Richard shrugged.

"Suggested by whom?"

"Don't know. But now this is my chance to prove myself to the firm."

Birds chirped as what he'd said about Nelson's moonlighting sat heavy in my mind. Mr. Dunwoody had heard talk about Nelson looking for a new job in Birmingham, but to work for *that* firm in particular? The one Coach had fired? It was an odd coincidence, to be sure, and I had to wonder if Coach had known. With his hair-trigger temper these days it might have been enough to set the man off but good. Maybe that was why Nelson was found with a cracked skull in my shop.

Or maybe I was grasping at straws simply because I wanted Coach to be guilty of *something*.

The latter was definitely more likely.

John Richard said, "Anyway, thanks for saving my hide."

I didn't like the determined gleam in his eyes. "If you want to keep that hide safe, I recommend you stay away from the Old Buzzard. Far, far away." If his career depended on Aunt Marjie selling, he ought to start spiffing up his résumé.

"Thanks for the advice."

I watched him walk away, knowing I'd see the young fool again.

Hopefully without bullet holes.

✎ Chapter Eleven ✎

Early the next morning, I dragged my hot, sticky self out of bed and headed to Déjà Brew. No electricity meant no morning coffee. Which meant a cranky me.

On my way out the back door, I gave the frame a swift kick, which resulted only in me stubbing my toe. I thought I actually heard the old house laugh at me as I hopped on my bike, Bessie Blue, and headed down the street, trying my best to ignore the sting in my toe and the pile of debris in my front yard.

Mr. Dunwoody sat on his porch and held his glass up high in a salute. "Morning, Miss Carly."

With a halfhearted wave, I growled out, "Mornin'," and kept on pedaling. I was a witch on a mission for some much-needed caffeine.

Last night, I'd dropped all my refrigerated and frozen goods off at Aunt Eulalie's so they wouldn't spoil, and I used her phone to call Jasper Cates, the electrician who'd been working on my house off and on since I'd bought it. Unfortunately, he was in Mobile for the weekend. That left me two options: I could rough it at my house with cold showers and no coffee, or I could pack up the cats and move back to the apartment above Without a Hitch, where my mama would have twenty-four-hour access to me.

Neither option held much appeal, but roughing it won out by a slim margin.

As I passed the Old Buzzard, I noticed that Aunt Marjie had added yet another No Trespassing sign to her front yard. I had a feeling it wouldn't keep John Richard Baldwin away.

Most of Hitching Post was still asleep at this time of the morning, a little past six thirty, but it was only a matter of time before it bustled with business. Both Eulalie's and Hazel's inns were at capacity, and Johnny Braxton's weekend extravaganza was bound to draw tourists and locals alike.

My plans for the day were in limbo, depending on whether I could open up my shop. No matter what, I needed to track down Bernice Morris. Someone had made this murder my business by killing Nelson in my shop. I had to figure out who and why before my livelihood went down in flames.

Flames reminded me of my ill-fated second wedding, which reminded me of Dylan. I didn't want to think about him, so I pedaled harder. Faster.

Right now I had one suspect in Nelson's murder: the real embezzler.

If there was an embezzler other than Coach.

Obviously, my suspect list was sadly lacking.

I had to find out who else had access to those funds—and I knew just who to ask. Dudley Pritcherd. I could probably guilt him into just about anything after the way he'd treated me yesterday. Southern guilt was just as good as Catholic guilt. Maybe a touch better when used on Southern men who'd rather swallow their tongues than unwittingly insult someone. Dudley owed me.

Then I thought about Bernice spouting that Dudley himself might be the embezzler. . . . He didn't seem the dishonest type, but I couldn't deny he could have taken those funds easily. I had an easy way to find out whether he felt guilty or not. . . . I could simply tap into his energy when asking him about the money. I would be able to feel his guilt.

If he *was* guilty . . . well, I'd cross that bridge later.

Morning sunbeams set the town aglow, sparkling on dewy grass and giving a sunshiny "anything's possible" feeling to the day.

I wanted to enjoy that mood, but I felt more like flipping it the bird.

Grumpily, I parked my bike and pulled open the door to Déjà Brew. For a second, I stopped and breathed in all the aromas. Coffee and blueberry muffins and cinnamon scones.

Better. Much better. My mood immediately improved.

My mouth watered as Jessa looked up from refilling a customer's cup and then down at the oversized watch on her wrist.

As she tucked a pencil into her rat's-nest hairdo, her bright eyes sized me up. "You're up and at 'em early this morning, Carly. Busy day at the shop?" She scooted around the horseshoe-shaped counter, picked up the cof- feepot, dropped her voice, and added, "I saw the cleaning crew working there last night."

I sidled up to the display cases as Jessa filled a to-go cup with a dark brew and tried to wrestle on a lid. I didn't even want to think about the cleaning crew—and what it was cleaning. "I'm not even sure if I can open today." I glanced around. The coffee shop wasn't too crowded this early, but I dropped my voice anyway. "Have the tourists heard the news?"

"About the murder?" She continued to fight with the coffee lid. "Oh yes. It's all the talk."

I slumped. "Then it probably doesn't matter if I open today or not. No one will come in, anyway."

"Hush, now, with that kind of talk, darlin'. Not *everyone* thinks you poisoned Nelson and Coach."

I rolled my eyes. "Just some of them?"

She shrugged. "Small-minded folks."

Odell Yadkin, Jessa's husband, came out from the kitchen, covered in flour. A smile spread across his plump face when he spotted me. "Miss Carly, you're out and about early this morning!"

I eased myself onto a stool. "I was up early reading about electric panels."

"Stimulating," Odell quipped, cracking himself up.

"Necessary, unfortunately. My power's out. The old wiring up and died."

"Lots of dying happening lately," Odell said, still cracking jokes.

Jessa elbowed him, giving him a stern look.

"It's okay," I said. After all, I made the same joke last night.

Jessa said, her eyes sparkling with humor, "No power explains what's wrong with your hair. Bless your heart."

Unfortunately, I wasn't in a joking mood. The humidity in the air added to the insult of not being able to use a hair dryer, so I'd twisted my thick blond hair into a sloppy knot at the base of my neck. I patted my head, checking for loose strands. "Is my hair really looking that bad?"

"Not if you're Mrs. Neumeyer," Odell said, setting a tray of cookies into the display case.

Mrs. Neumeyer was Hitching Post's oldest resident. At 103, she still worked at the county clerk's office three days a week filing wedding licenses. She looked every bit a stereotypical elderly librarian, from coiled bun to orthopedic black shoes.

The old lady was spunky, though, so I didn't mind the comparison all that much. Besides, there wasn't much I could do with my hair without electricity. I should've been grateful for running water at this point, even if it was ice-cold. However, after the electricity was fixed, I was going to have to look into replacing the air-conditioning, which hadn't worked since the Clinton administration, if I didn't want to melt to death in my sleep come summertime.

I might need to rob a bank in the meantime.

I glanced at Odell. "You don't happen to know anything about electricity, do you?"

Jessa threw her head back and laughed. Odell shook his head at me, then frowned at her before heading back into the kitchen.

Jessa lifted her eyebrows and said, "You should ask Dylan for some help. He's handy."

I knew exactly how handy the man was. My cheeks surely aflame, I said, "That's okay. I'll muddle through."

As she continued to fight with the lid, she said, "Suit yourself" in a way that told me she thought I was making a big mistake. She'd always had a soft spot for Dylan Jackson.

I knew the feeling. And I also knew Jessa. She wasn't one to give up so easily, and I could only imagine what kind of plan she was concocting.

"You can leave off the top, Jessa," I said, desperate for some caffeine.

With a grateful sigh, she slid the cup and its lid across the counter and leaned down on her elbows. "Have you heard anything else about what happened with Nelson, darlin'?"

The murder.

I added a bit of sugar and a little half-and-half to my cup before taking that amazing first sip. "Not much. Have you? What's the latest gossip?"

Next to Mr. Dunwoody and my mama, no one knew gossip like Jessa.

"Besides you poisoning everyone?"

"Yeah. Besides that." I snapped the lid on my cup without a bit of trouble.

"I must've loosened it up," Jessa said, referring to the lid.

"Must have."

"Anyways, I've been keeping an ear out for any talk about Nelson having a girlfriend, but no one knows anything. Maybe you heard wrong?"

It was possible Emmylou Pritcherd had been mistaken, but I was a big believer in women's intuition, so I wasn't ready to let the notion go. It did make me wonder who the woman could possibly be and why—if she truly existed—the relationship was so hush-hush.

What were they hiding?

Nelson's secretary would surely know if he had someone special in his life. It was too early to pay her a call right now, so I'd have to bide my time.

Hopping off the stool, I took a five-dollar bill out of the pocket of my shorts and slid it across the counter.

"You want a muffin to go, darlin'?"

Shaking my head, I said, "Thanks, but I'm not very hungry."

Jessa rang up my order and reached over into the display case and pulled out several of Odell's chocolate fudge cookies. She stuck them in a bag and handed it to me. "On the house."

"Thanks, Jessa."

"If I hear anything, I'll call your place," she yelled as I headed out the front door. I knew she'd be eavesdropping on every conversation at the shop that day, and I hoped someone would let something slip.

It was only after I left that I remembered my home phone was as dead as Nelson.

Outside it was still quiet, the humid air barely stirring. I placed my bag of cookies in my wicker basket and set out on my way. Steering with one hand and holding on to my coffee with the other, I decided to take the long way home—the route that passed my shop. I wanted to check on it and make sure nothing else dreadful had happened there overnight.

As soon as I circled around the Ring, I spotted Emmylou and Dudley almost exactly where I'd seen them the day before. Only this time Dudley had a metal detector with him, and Emmylou was bossing him about.

"Try there," she said, pointing toward a flower bed.

I slowed Bessie Blue as my witchy senses kicked up, a forewarning. Waves of energy suddenly washed over me. My nerves began to dance with anger and anxiety and a deep bellyache nearly doubled me over.

This happened to me sometimes, either when I was distracted or when someone else's emotion was so powerful that it could break through my highly refined defenses. In this case, I was distracted *and* picking up strong emotions from both Dudley and Emmylou. My psyche had been tag-teamed.

I took a few deep breaths, trying to rebuild the wall between their energy and mine. I put my coffee cup in my basket and set my kickstand. My palms grew sweaty and my heart pounded as I walked up to them. My stomach hurt something fierce, a painful gnawing sensation, and I wondered which one of them had the ulcer.

Most likely it was Dudley, if his pale face was any indication. No wonder he'd lost all that weight. One of my potions would do him wonders. I could make him one as soon as my shop opened. . . .

But no. He didn't want any of *my* potions.

"Oh, Carly!" Emmylou cried. "We can't find it anywhere!" She nibbled her lip and wrung her hands.

The anxiety I was feeling was clearly coming from her. I took a step back, hoping the distance would help me block their emotions, but between them, I was overwhelmed.

My hand curled around my locket. Warmth flowed into my palm, and I took a few deep breaths as I slowly detached myself from their collective maladies.

Feeling better, I said, "It?"

"My ring!" Emmylou said, her gaze glued to the ground.

"Right." Her wedding ring—the one that had flown off her hand yesterday afternoon.

"It'll turn up, Emmylou," Dudley said, wiping his brow with a handkerchief. "Patience."

"I refuse to believe it's gone," she said, continuing to wring her hands. "It's custom made by a jeweler in Huntsville, you know." She sighed. "We have special en-gravings on the inside of our bands. Show Carly the en-gravings, Dudley."

He stared at her a second before just doing as she bid. He slid the ring easily off his finger and handed it over.

"See?" she said.

4-ever & 4-always

Sunlight glinted off the teardrops in her eyes, making them sparkle. "We used the number four instead of spell-ing out f-o-r on account of Dudley being an accountant." She tittered. "On account . . . that's funny."

I glanced at Dudley—he seemed embarrassed by the way his wife carried on.

I didn't blame him.

Now probably wasn't the best time to ask him about keeping the books for the baseball league. I made a men-tal note to track him down later to ask him some ques-tions about who all had access to the league's checkbook.

"Cute," I said.

"Absolutely darling," she added wistfully, handing his ring back to him. "But now my ring is gone!" Her gaze settled on me. "Will you help us look for it? We'd be most thankful."

"Now, honey. I'm sure Carly has things to do," Dudley said softly, his cheeks a bright, guilty pink. He still wouldn't look at me in the eye. "She doesn't need to spend her morning helping us."

Because his tone clearly conveyed that he'd rather I just go so he wouldn't have to face me, I said, "Oh, I have a few minutes I can spare."

Emmylou smiled gratefully, but Dudley merely stared at the ground. How he was functioning with that kind of stomach pain bewildered me. He had a high pain toler-ance, that's for sure. The desire to heal him with a potion was impossible to ignore. I was, after all, a healer by nature. But I refused to try to talk Dudley into trying one of my cures—he would have to come to me.

Dudley had manners enough not to argue. I said, "Where have you looked?"

"Everywhere," Emmylou said, gesturing wide. "Maybe someone found it last night? We should put up Lost flyers. Perhaps offer a cash reward?"

"It couldn't hurt," I said. The picnic park was popular with townsfolk and tourists alike. It was a nice place to hang out, have lunch, fly a kite. . . . It was very possible someone could have found the ring already.

As I helped search, Emmylou fell in step with me. She dropped her voice and said, "Do you think you'll be able to reopen your shop today? I can stop by any time. Any time at all."

The wildness I'd seen in her eyes yesterday was back. Apparently she was still in the market for a virility potion. "I'm not sure. I haven't heard from the sheriff's department yet." I glanced over my shoulder and saw that Dudley kept glancing at us. "Do you think stopping by is a good idea? I'm not sure Dudley's too keen on using any of my potions."

She winced. "I was hoping you wouldn't pick up on that. You have to ignore him. He's just nervous, with what happened to Nelson and Coach."

I was done explaining that Coach had had himself a diabetic reaction. It was a waste of my breath. What exactly had happened to Nelson was still up in the air. I shook the image of him on my break room's floor out of my mind.

"You know the potion won't work unless the person taking the potion is amenable to it—it's part of the magic."

"That's not just a rule for love potions?"

One of the first potions she ever bought from me was a love potion for Dudley. They'd been dating a couple of months at that point, and I warned her then about the Backbone Effect—that his heart had to be ready to accept it in order for the potion to work.

They were married not long after.

"The rule goes for all potions," I said.

With her foot she swept the grass around us, separating blades, looking for that platinum band. Frown lines pulled at the corners of her eyes. "Well, I don't think that will be an issue. No one wants to fix this problem more than Dudley."

"But?" I asked.

"I don't rightly know how I'm going to get him to drink a potion. But," she drew in a deep, determined breath, "where there's a will there's a way."

I looked over my shoulder at Dudley and suddenly had the feeling he didn't get much say in their relationship. Maybe his *dudliness* was his way of having some control. . . .

"Well, I'm not sure if the shop will be open or not, but you can stop by later and see. Or call."

"I'll pop in after I'm done at the white-elephant sale."

That's right—she'd mentioned yesterday that she'd be taking her food truck over there today. She made the most heavenly cakes, and suddenly I was starving. I was grateful for those cookies Jessa had sent home with me.

I helped search the area for ten minutes more before I decided it was time to leave. I glanced at my watch, ready to make an excuse, when my eye caught something glittering in the grass.

"Oh!" I said, pointing. "Look!"

Dudley came running as Emmylou dropped to the ground and snatched up the silvery band.

Her sudden happiness vanished in an instant as she held up the bauble. "False alarm. It's just a tin party favor."

Tin rings were as common around Hitching Post as brides and grooms.

Dudley patted Emmylou's shoulder. "Don't worry. We'll keep looking."

She sniffled and nodded.

"I'm sorry, but I have to get going," I said.

"Thanks for your help, Carly," Emmylou said.

"Yes, thanks," Dudley echoed, actually sounding grateful.

I said, "I hope it turns up."

Emmylou said, "You don't happen to know any spells or such that could find it, do you?"

"Emmy," Dudley warned.

She ignored him. "A spell would be right useful about now."

"Sorry," I said. "I'm a healing witch only. Mind, body, heart, and soul."

"What about your cousin?" Emmylou asked. "Would she have a spell?"

"Delia?"

She nodded.

If Dudley thought my potions were bad, he deserved a dose of Delia's hexes. But I couldn't do that to them. "No, I don't think so."

"That's what I figured," Emmylou said, wringing her hands.

"I need to get going. Good luck—I hope you find the ring," I said to them, and turned to walk away. After a few steps I slowly twisted myself around. I just couldn't keep myself from bringing out a verbal pitchfork. "Dudley?"

Dark eyebrows raised, he said, "Yes?"

"If you want some help with your stomach pains, come see me, okay? I've got a potion that will work wonders."

His hand went directly to the spot on his stomach that had been hurting me as well, and his eyes widened as if wondering how I'd known.

I gave him a wink, hopped on my bike, and pedaled away.

Behind me, Emmylou's voice carried easily in the quiet morning. "Your stomach? What's wrong with your stomach? Is it hurting? Why didn't you tell me? Do you need to see a doctor?"

I smiled the whole way home, suddenly at peace with the sunshininess of the day.

Chapter Twelve

It was a little after eight when someone knocked on the back door. I abandoned my do-it-yourself book, stepped over Roly and Poly, who were splayed out on the cool wooden floor, and trotted into the kitchen.

I swished aside the thin white curtains covering the back door's window and peeked out. My heart near to stopped.

Dylan Jackson was peeking in.

A deep ache settled in my chest, and I wasn't altogether sure if the throbbing was his or mine. I had to get my stress levels under control—or lock myself in the house before I was completely overwhelmed with everyone else's energy.

Clutching my locket tightly, I tried not to think too hard about him hurting—or else I would *definitely* start picking up on his feelings.

I wasn't sure I could deal with that. I'd only opened myself up to his energy once—that time at our second, and final, failed attempt to get married. I'd barely recovered from that experience, and it wasn't something I wanted to open myself to again. I took a few deep breaths, building up my walls against his energy.

Pulling open the door, I silently cursed that meddlesome Jessa, and turned on my most saccharine Southern belle voice. "My, my. Dylan Jackson, what a surprise."

The engine of his truck parked in my driveway ticked as it cooled off. His lips quirked into a sassy grin. "You do something new with your hair?"

"Jessa has a big mouth."

He laughed, a deep, muffled sound I liked more than I should. "But a kind heart."

I agreed, though I questioned her motives for sending Dylan over here. I doubted she cared about my electrical woes; she had matchmaking on her mind.

Poor woman was going to be terribly disappointed.

"She shouldn't have bothered you with my hair troubles," I said.

"No bother at all." He waited for me to invite him in.

I wasn't sure I wanted him in. Having him close only served to remind me of all I'd lost.

He adjusted his ball cap, held up a toolbox, and said, "I heard you needed a handyman. I tried to call to let you know I was coming over. . . ."

"Along with my electricity, my phone's out, too."

"Well, it's good Jessa sent me over. I can probably get both up and running."

It was a nice offer, but I didn't really want him hanging around all morning. "Surely you have other things to do. What with the murder and all."

"I always have a few minutes for you, Care Bear."

I ignored the sting of the endearment and eyed him warily. "Can you really fix it?"

"I can surely try."

My head warred with my heart, but common sense won out. "By all means, then. Come on in."

He clucked as he passed by. "You'd invite the devil himself in if he could fix your electricity, wouldn't you?"

I think I just did. I plastered myself against the door so we wouldn't brush against each other. "Have you seen my hair?"

"Unfortunately."

I pinched his arm.

"Yow!"

"Sorry. My hand slipped."

He scowled and headed for the electrical panel, stopping to examine the Crock-Pot full of water on the floor that I'd yet to dump.

Looking up, he assessed the ceiling, then looked back at me. I shrugged. He shook his head and popped open the electrical panel's door and started flipping breaker switches.

As if I hadn't already done that.

The fact that he knew where the panel box was didn't escape me. Once upon a time, he'd spent a lot of hours in this house.

Leaning against the counter, I said, "What's new with Nelson's case?"

He went about unscrewing the front of the panel from the box, revealing a maze of wires. "A few things."

"Like?" I prodded. It was my shop Nelson had been found in, after all. I had a right to know some of these things.

"First things first: You can open your shop today. Business as usual."

It was good news, but I hardly felt like celebrating. Business would hardly be usual, what with Nelson's murder yesterday and the town thinking I was making tainted potions. However, I scared up some gratitude, because I knew Dylan had to have pulled some strings to get me back in the shop today. "That's great. Thanks."

Setting the metal frame on the ground, he said, "Second, did you happen to notice the lack of blood in your break room yesterday?"

"Lack of blood? Are you kidding me? It was pooled under Nelson's head, spreading out like some sort of red halo." Nausea suddenly rolled through my stomach, which was weird, because I wasn't the type who was normally affected by such things.

Systematically, he tugged on wires. "But not on the walls or the cabinets."

"Thank the Lord for small favors."

"Nelson wasn't killed in your shop, Carly." He glanced at me. "Someone planted him there."

Planted. Like a petunia or a daisy. "If he wasn't killed there, where was he killed? At his house?"

"His place had been ransacked, and there were signs he'd been ill recently, but there was no blood to be found."

"Ransacked?" I swallowed hard. "Had there been a struggle?"

"I don't think there was a struggle. It just looks like someone was searching for something."

"Like a secondary audit report?" I asked.

He glanced at me. "How did you know about that?"

"I ran into Emmylou and Dudley." I adopted Emmylou's high-pitched voice and said, "Apparently Bernice Morris thinks that Dudley stole the money from the baseball league and framed Coach so Dudley can get back together with Angelea Butts—they dated a while

back. She's outraged at the accusations, by the way. Emmylou, not Angelea. Simply *outraged*."

Dark eyebrows lifted, and he cracked a smile. "You do
a good impression of her. But she can rest easy, at least
about the audit. We found that second report in Nelson's
house, and it confirmed Dudley's initial findings. He
didn't tamper with anything. Bernice is just desperate to
prove her brother's innocence."

"Is he innocent?" I asked.

"Those checks with his signature are pretty damning."

"Ainsley said she heard that Nelson had also ordered
an independent handwriting analysis to prove Coach's
name had been forged. You didn't happen to find that in
Nelson's house, too, did you?"

"No, I didn't. You're certainly hearing a lot of things."
I shrugged innocently. "It's a small town."

He went back to work on the panel. I watched him for
a few minutes before I said, "I don't suppose it matters
whether Nelson was killed in my shop or not. Someone
wanted him found there for a reason. Why?"

"Revenge is my best guess."

"Revenge on me?" It was the same theory Caleb had
brought up yesterday. Maybe he'd been right all along.

Crouching, he rooted through his toolbox and came
out with a pair of wire cutters. "Who've you done wrong
lately, Care Bear?"

I bit my thumbnail. "I did have a strange run-in with
Johnny Braxton last night." I told Dylan all about it.
"But that seemed to have more to do with my mama
than me."

"He's on my list to talk to," Dylan said.

"Because of the fight he had with Nelson?"

He lifted an eyebrow. "You're not snooping into this case, are you?"

Of course I was. "Not at all. I can't help it if I hear things."

Grunting as if he didn't believe me for a second, he said, "Who else have you ticked off lately? There have to be others."

I crossed my arms. "*Have* to be?"

Smiling, he picked another tool from his box. "Do you deny it?"

I set my jaw. I could probably argue, but the truth was, he was right. My mouth and temper had gotten me into more trouble than I cared to admit. "Mrs. Kelvin didn't like me telling her that her teenage son's weight trouble wasn't from a thyroid problem but from all the home-made cookies he taste-tested."

"Mrs. Kelvin makes a damn fine cookie."

"I know, but Lucas shouldn't be eating all of them."

"Ain't no mama wants to hear that."

"No," I said, thinking of the scene in my shop. "She wasn't too happy with me. I did notice, however, that the last time I saw Lucas, he'd lost some weight."

As he worked on pulling down the panel, he said, "Who else?"

"Other than that, I can't think of anyone." I chewed on a nail. "Other than your mama."

His eyebrows snapped into a deep V, making me clutch my locket to maintain my witchy equilibrium.

"It's *true*," I defended. Though now thinking on it, I probably should have kept that to myself. Sometimes my tongue gets the better of me. Patricia Davis Jackson might hate me, but I didn't really think she would commit a murder quite so messy. She didn't do well with stains.

"Keep thinking," Dylan said tightly. "Something might come to you. Even the littlest of tiffs."

The mention of his mama had brought a thick, choking tension to the air about us. I let him be with the electricity and set about pacing my living room as best I could—it was an obstacle course of building materials and lazy cats.

Tiffs. Well. There were a few of those. Minor things, mostly. Like when I got into it with a mama who was talking down to her kid that one time. And when a perfectly able-bodied tourist had taken a handicapped parking spot.

Hardly revenge-worthy stuff.

"When did your power go out?" Dylan asked, his voice carrying easily. There was still an edge to it, and I could have kicked myself for bringing up his mama. When was I going to learn?

"Yesterday afternoon sometime. Are you sure you know what you're doing?" Though Dylan might be handy, I wasn't convinced he could restore my power. That electrical panel looked like a big ol' box of danger to me.

"Are you questioning my capabilities, Care Bear?"

My teeth clenched at the way he said the nickname, all syrupy sweet. "Yes. Do you want to look at my wiring manual?"

"Well, now," he drawled. "Why am I not the least bit surprised that you don't trust me?"

I walked over to the kitchen and leaned against the doorway. Dylan fussed with exposed wiring that resembled a tangle of tentacles. It looked a slight bit worse than it had just five minutes ago. Folding my arms over my chest, I said, "What's that supposed to mean?"

He glanced over, his eyes intent and focused. They locked on mine, and I could have sworn sparks flew. "It means that I know what I'm doing. That even though I *might* have some concerns about being electrocuted, I trust the decisions I'm making. That I don't need someone else to butt in and make choices for me. Without even bothering to get my opinion on the matter, I might add."

Damn me and my big mouth. Keeping my hand wrapped around my locket, I narrowed my eyes, knowing we were no longer discussing my power outage. I braced myself, ready to do battle. Anger bubbled. "Dylan Jackson, did you just compare marrying me to being *electrocuted*?"

He abandoned the wiring and straightened to his full six-foot-two. Taking a step toward me, he said, "If the shock fits . . ."

"I wasn't the one who had doubts," I snapped. "That was you."

"Oh, that's right. You use your witchiness to tap into my head for one second—unfairly, I might add—and you think you know my every thought. I dare you to go to any chapel in town and read the energy of the bride and groom. I guarantee they feel the same way at some point. Just like I guarantee you had doubts that day as well."

It took all my strength to hold my ground and not lunge at him—or turn and run. "You're wrong."

He languidly leaned against the counter. "Am I?"

"Can you fix my electricity or not?" I said, digging in my heels.

"All I'm saying is that maybe you didn't fall too far from the Fowl apple tree." He turned back to the panel and used a screwdriver to tighten some screws. "Something for you to chew on."

"The electricity," I said, my jaw aching.

He threw me a long, hard look and, being a smart man and all, knew when to retreat. He drawled, "It's as good as done."

I flipped the light switch at my elbow. Nothing happened. I cocked an eyebrow.

"It's not done *yet*, Care Bear." Apparently thoroughly amused, he gave me a slow smile.

"I don't have all day. I need to get to work. Maybe you should just leave it be." I wanted him gone. As in "long gone." I heard Alaska was nice this time of year.

His smile widened, and it threw me for a loop. Just what was he so pleased about?

"I'm done leaving things be," he said softly.

I stared. He stared back. I didn't even want to imagine what *that* meant.

"How long will it take you?" I debated whether I should leave him here alone to finish up, but I didn't trust the man to be near my underwear drawer unsupervised.

"Depends," he said.

"On?"

"You. I can be done here right quick . . . on one condition."

I tapped my foot. "That reeks of blackmail, Dylan Jackson."

He winked. Winked! The nerve of him.

"It's called negotiating," he said.

Maybe I just ought to wait for my electrician to come back to town. Then I thought about moving back to my mama's chapel—and what that would entail. "What do you want?"

"I want you to go with me to Marjie's," he said casually.

Too casually.

He wiped his hands on his jeans. "I need to get some answers from her about Nelson's murder. Having you along might loosen her lips a bit."

I sized him up pretty easily. "Are you scared to go over there alone?"

He smiled that sexy grin again. "Terrified."

If the slamming of the door in our faces was any indication, Marjie wasn't too pleased to see us.

"Go away, Dylan Jackson!" she shouted.

He had the look of a man caught in the crosshairs—which was appropriate, considering Marjie was taking aim at him with her shotgun through the front window.

"Should I be taking this personally?" he asked me.

"Can't rightly say. You did do me wrong. She's family and all, so she might be a wee bit protective of me."

"What?" he gasped. "You did *me* wrong."

Not this again.

"I'm not carin' a whit who did who wrong," Marjie yelled. "Go away!"

"I need to talk to you about Nelson Winston," Dylan shouted. "It's either here or at the jail."

"You better get yourself a warrant," she countered.

Dylan said, "Fine. I'll be back." He started down the porch stairs.

"Wait!" I cried.

"Carly Hartwell, don't you be calling him back!" Marjie yelled, her voice only slightly muffled by the window.

"What about my electricity?" I asked, trailing after him.

He shrugged. "We had a deal. No answers from Marjie, no electricity. Sorry, Care Bear. I can help you pack to move to your mama's, though."

I let out a frustrated sigh and turned to face my aunt. "Now, Aunt Marjie, I need your help here. Dylan won't fix my power unless you talk with him, and without my power fixed, I'll have to move back to my mama's. I really don't want to move back to my mama's," I said, my voice low. "Maybe you can help me out a little? I've had a rough couple of days, what with finding a dead body in my shop, Coach running his truck into my house, people thinking my potions are tainted...and no power to boot. I mean, look at my hair."

Slowly, the door opened a crack. "Your hair does look somethin' awful."

Which was saying something, considering Aunt Marjie's hair resembled a light brown tumbleweed.

"Five minutes," she said to Dylan. "Make it snappy."

I slumped in relief and sat cautiously on Marjie's wooden front step, trying to avoid splinters. She lowered herself next to me, keeping her shotgun close at hand.

Dylan kept a fair distance. "Where were you between ten and midnight night before last, Miss Marjie?"

Ten and midnight? That was new information. I hadn't realized Dylan could place the time when Nelson had died.

"Right here," she said. "Like always."

He watched her carefully—whether to see if she was lying or to spot if she was reaching for her gun, I wasn't sure.

He said, "Anyone see you?"

"Not to my knowledge." She ran a finger down the length of the shiny gun barrel as gently as if she were caressing a newborn baby's face.

Dylan held his ground. "You talk to anyone on the phone?"

"I don't have a phone."

"Is it true that you took a shot at Nelson last week?" he asked, rocking on his heels.

"He shouldn't have been trespassin'," Marjie said, fidgeting. "I have a right to protect my property."

Underneath the gruff-and-rough exterior, my aunt was a beautiful woman. My dark brown eyes came from the Fowl side of the family, and Marjie's were even bigger and darker than mine. Her skin had only a few wrinkles here and there, and despite her cranky disposition, it glowed with good health.

"True fact," Dylan said, obviously trying to smooth ruffled feathers. "Why was he trespassing? Did he say?"

"He was too busy running." Marjie smiled—apparently she found the memory amusing. "But I reckon he was snooping for the same reason everyone else does. He wanted to buy my inn."

"Actually," I said, clearing my throat, "he didn't want the inn for himself. He was representing a law firm in Birmingham who has a client who wants it."

Marjie's thin eyebrows snapped downward. "Who'd that be, now?"

She asked in such a way that I suddenly wondered if she had a target-practice list she was looking to add a name to. "Don't know."

Dylan's gaze zeroed in on me. "How do you know about the law firm and the buyer?"

I flicked a loose paint chip from the porch railing. "John Richard Baldwin."

"Who?" he asked.

"The man Marjie tried to shoot yesterday afternoon."

"He had it comin'," she interjected sharply.

Dylan rolled his eyes. "Miz Marjie, you need to lock up that gun of yours. You're going to kill someone one of these days."

"If I'm lucky." Standing, she grabbed her gun and went into the house, slamming the door behind her.

Dylan's time was up.

He stared after her for a good long minute.

"We should go," I said finally, brushing debris from my shorts. "Before her good mood shifts."

"If that was a good mood," he said, "I don't want to see her bad side."

"No," I agreed. "You don't."

As we walked through the gateway, he said, "Now, about this John Richard fellow . . ."

"Now, about my electricity . . ."

He looked at me from the corner of his eye. "Care Bear, are you negotiating?"

"I'm a quick learner." On some things at least.

We crossed the street and paused at the foot of my driveway. Bessie Blue leaned against my garage door, its shiny turquoise a bright contrast to Dylan's beat-up, mud-caked truck. Two opposites—just like their owners. Maybe that was the real reason our relationship hadn't worked out.

I bit a nail. Guilt was eating at my insides, gnawing away at a year of suspicion that Dylan was right in what he'd said earlier. The part about my apple not falling far from the Fowl tree. But there was no time to think about that right now. I squashed the guilt, banishing it for the moment. But I knew it'd be back.

"Well, I'm all for a little negotiation. How about you

tell me about this John Richard fellow while I finish up the repairs?" he said.

"Maybe." I skirted past his pickup, climbed the back steps, and pulled open the screen door. "After you're done with the fixin'."

He didn't make another comment about me not trusting him, thank goodness. Instead he said, "And how about you fix me a sandwich or something while I'm at it? I'm getting mighty hungry."

"How about *no*?"

"That's not very gracious of you," he said in a teasing tone. "Especially with me restoring your power and all."

Tilting my chin, I narrowed my gaze. "Maybe if you tell me more about Nelson's murder, we can cut a deal."

His eyes crinkled as if he knew exactly what I was up to. "Sorry. No can do, Care Bear."

My jaw jutted. Obviously my negotiating skills needed honing.

Until then, there were no two ways about it. I was just going to have to keep investigating on my own.

Chapter Thirteen

A little over an hour later, Dylan had just walked out my back door, the electricity was fixed, and the phone was, too.

Apparently, all my power woes stemmed from some sort of critter living in the walls, chewing wires for fun and giggles. Dylan suspected that the thinned wiring had been jarred loose by the force of yesterday's crash that took down the front porch. He'd jury-rigged it and told me the fix would hold for a while, but my whole system needed to be replaced soon.

I glanced at my cats and shook my head. "You two need to start earning your keep."

Roly barely lifted her head to glance at me. Poly kept sleeping, but I knew the only thing he'd be attacking was the treat canister.

"Mooches."

They paid me no mind.

I needed to take a quick (blessedly hot) shower, blow-dry my hair, and head to work, where I'd attempt to never use my break room again. The phone rang as I watched Dylan hop into his truck. We'd both held our own while he replaced chewed-up wires; I hadn't weaseled any more information from him about Nelson's murder, and he hadn't sweet-talked me into making him a sandwich.

There had been no more talk about his mama or our failed relationship, but heaviness still hung in the air between us. Tension. Anticipation. I had a feeling our conversation was far from over.

I'm done leaving things be.

The phone rang again, and I grabbed it up, grateful for the distraction. "Hello?"

A high-pitched female voice cried, "Sweet baby Jesus, Carly Hartwell. You need to get yourself to the church right now. Right. Now. Do you hear me?"

"Mrs. Jackson?"

"Ha, ha. You're hilarious," Ainsley said.

"Does Carter know you talk about baby Jesus that way?"

An aggrieved sigh echoed across the line. "Seriously, Carly. You need to get down here to the white-elephant sale at the church. I don't know how much longer she'll be here."

"Where'd the term 'white elephant' come from, anyhow?"

"Hand to God, I'm fixin' to jerk a knot in your tail, Carlina Hartwell."

I knew she was serious when she pulled out the down-home threats. "Who's there?"

"Bernice Morris, that's who. Right this here minute, she's elbow deep in macramé pot holders. I don't know how long she's staying."

"I'll be right there," I cried. "Stall! Sic the twins on her."

"Do you *want* her to leave?"

I smiled. "Oh, and if I haven't told you lately, you're the best friend a girl can have."

"Hon, tell me something I don't know."

White-elephant sales were a big chunk of the church's bread and butter and were held every other weekend. Truth be told, "white elephant" was a bit of a misnomer, a euphemism used to pretty up the truth. The sale was nothing more than a big ol' 'Bama-sized yard sale. The church donated its land and good name in return for booth or tent fees. Locals loved the chance to sell their junk, and tourists loved a big dose of local flavor.

I parked my bike near Emmylou Pritcherd's food truck and saw her loading a dolly with bakery boxes. She waved and said, "Any news about the shop?"

"I'll be opening in a little bit."

"Praise be!" she cried as she wheeled the dolly toward a booth.

"Did you find your ring?" I rubbed a finger over the bare spot on the ring finger of my left hand. I hadn't actually received a wedding ring, but for a good long while I'd worn an engagement ring. I could hardly imagine how I would have felt if I'd lost that. Even now I felt a little tug of my heartstrings at the thought of it sitting in my dresser drawer, tucked into its fancy little black box.

I probably should have given the ring back to Dylan, but I couldn't bear parting with it. Fortunately, he'd never asked for its return.

She shook her head and unloaded boxes onto a table. "Not yet. Dudley's still looking. Care for a slice of Lane Cake?"

"Definitely. I just need to find Ainsley first."

"I'll save you a piece."

For not being a native, she'd taken to making traditional Southern, boozy Lane Cake, a multilayered, bourbon-laced sponge cake with pecans, coconut, and raisins, like she'd been born and raised in these parts— and, really, I could use a little liquor right now, even if it was only ten in the morning. We all had our limits, and I'd just about reached mine for the day.

As I wove through the crowd, looking for either Ainsley or Bernice, heat radiated from the ground. The storm last night had brought in a dose of the tropics. I shaded my eyes, wiped my brow, and noticed I'd garnered some attention.

There were whispers all about me, along with some not-so-discreet pointing. I set my shoulders, lifted my chin, and refused to look like I had done something wrong. My name—my potions—would be cleared soon enough. I kept a firm hand on my locket and refused to give in to the urge to tap into the energy of those around me, to feel what they were feeling. To see whether they truly thought I was guilty or if I was just a curiosity, like one at a carnival freak show. I didn't need to be borrowing trouble, so I pressed on.

I felt someone studying me intently and looked around. I found the man standing next to a booth that sold ceramic knickknacks and had to do a double take to make sure I wasn't seeing a ghost.

It appeared as though the man was Johnny Cash himself, but upon closer look, I realized it was Johnny Braxton. He'd done a remarkable job transforming himself, shaving off his beard but leaving long sideburns. His hair had been dyed a dark brown and was slicked back in a fancy pompadour. A Western-style shirt with black piping was left unbuttoned to his breastbone, and I wouldn't have been the least bit surprised to hear him launch into a rendition of "Ring of Fire" right there on the spot.

He'd done good. Damn good. It was on my lips to congratulate him on his costume until I remembered his threat from the night before. And it also made me wonder what my mama had up her sleeve for today. Johnny's weekend bash was due to start at two today, and I was afraid that if my mama was planning to sabotage it, Johnny wasn't above some sort of retribution.

Johnny dipped his head in acknowledgment of me and kept on staring. I nodded back and tried to shake off a case of the willies.

Pushing farther into the crowd, I still couldn't find Ainsley or Miz Morris, but I did spy someone who might be able to help me out.

"Mornin'," I said to Carter Debbs, stepping up beside him. He was easy to spot in a crowd, being that he was well over six feet tall and as skinny as a whittled twig. Not for the first time, he reminded me of a big ol' tree, like a shagbark hickory, tall and thin but incredibly strong.

He turned, his eyes widening when he saw me. In his early thirties, he had a thick shock of brown hair, a dimple in his square chin, and gray-blue eyes that held a hint of mischief mixed with intelligence that came from always having his nose pressed into a book. His daddy had been a preacher before him, and the church and its congregation had been handed down to him when his daddy passed a few years ago. Ainsley and I had known Carter just shy of forever, sharing a grade in school, but she hadn't hit it off with him until she'd literally hit him.

With her car.

It had been raining, and there was a crosswalk, and she swore she braked. . . . He hadn't been seriously injured, unless one counted the way he'd fallen for her after that.

And one could count that as an injury, seeing how Ainsley was Ainsley and he was the son of a preacher man. (That song had been played at their wedding, much to Ainsley's mama's dismay.)

But it seemed to have worked out. Separately, they were both misfits, but together . . . they simply fit.

"Mornin', Carly," he said, glancing around.

The stares had followed me to his side. He tugged at his shirt collar, probably feeling the heat of the day along with the pressure of everyone around us to reach a decision on my guilt or innocence in the matter of Nelson Winston. Carter was an important man in our town, and his opinion held a lot of weight to many people. His actions toward me could either turn the tide on the rumors or bury my business for good.

Considering we didn't particularly see eye to eye on a lot of things, I honestly didn't know which side he'd choose.

"I'm looking for Ainsley," I said, trying to stay calm and not lash out at those around me. For land's sakes, most of them had known me since I was knee-high. Did they really think I could kill someone? "Is she still around?"

Sucking in a deep breath, I held his gaze and tried to convince myself that it didn't really matter much what people believed because I knew the truth. But here, now, with the blazing sun feeling like a spotlight and all these people watching . . . Suddenly I cared very much what people thought. What Carter thought.

Not enough to tune into their energy, but enough to make my heart pound and my palms sweat as I waited for him to say something, do something, to issue a verdict.

Finally, the corner of his lip lifted into a smile. "I do believe she's giving Sister Morris a tour of the house." His eyes crinkled with humor. "Against her will, I might add." He hooked an arm around my shoulders and turned me to face the home he and Ainsley shared. "Go on up. If you see little Olive, hide. She's on the warpath today."

The tension in the air around me deflated suddenly, a balloon popped by his kindness. Another thing about the shagbark hickory tree—it was able to bend and not break. I was surprised by the sting of tears in my eyes as I said, "Isn't Olive always on the warpath?"

The crowd about us slowly went back to their business, and I no longer felt any stares. Any judgment. Relief swept over me, though I wished it hadn't taken someone else's opinion for people to believe in my innocence.

He rolled his eyes. "She's a three-year-old reincarnation of General Beauregard, I'm convinced."

"Luckily, she doesn't look like him," I said, laughing. "The mustache would be a mite disturbing."

"Amen." He smiled and his eyes softened. "She has the face of an angel. Her mama's face."

And that right there was the only reason Carter and I got along.

"Go on up," he said. "I do believe they're expecting you. Ainsley, leastways."

I hemmed, I hawed, I bit my thumbnail. Finally, I pulled the words from deep in my throat. "Thank you, Carter."

After a long moment, he said, "It's Ainsley you should be thanking." He gave me a nod as he headed for Emmylou's truck, probably to snag himself a piece of Emmylou's Lane Cake. Olive tended to drive people toward liquor, whether it was in the form of cake or a box of wine. She was a high-spirited child.

I watched him go, then turned toward the house. As I did, a flash of color from a nearby tent caught my eye.

I blinked, sure I was having myself a big ol' hallucination, but the image before me didn't change. Slowly, I walked over to the table covered in small bright bottles.

My potion bottles.

Picking one up, I checked the hallmark just to be certain. Sure enough, the bottles were mine. Empty, yes, but they'd come from my shop at one point or another.

I glanced around for the vendor but didn't see anyone standing nearby. The till was sitting there, plain as day, and it was odd for someone to leave it unattended.

As I debated what to do, I heard a noise near my feet. I glanced down and saw the tablecloth flutter. A small black wagging tail stuck out from under the fabric.

Crouching, I lifted the tablecloth, and two familiar yet guilty eyes stared back at me.

I set my jaw. "Mornin', Delia."

My cousin Delia scooped up Boo and scurried out from beneath the table. She'd forgone the black cape today in favor of a long, flowing black skirt and a tiny black T-shirt. Her snowy blond hair was braided along her hairline and left loose in the back. Icy blue eyes watched me closely as I started counting how many bottles she had displayed on the table.

She clutched the little dog in one arm, football style, and her other hand gripped her dangling locket. The delicately crafted silver-linked chain looked stunning yet stark against her black shirt. "What'd you do to your hair?"

"Don't try to distract me. I'm counting."

"There are more than two hundred bottles there. Now, seriously, what'd you do to your hair? Because I want to make sure I never have it done to mine."

My jaw ached from clenching it, so I forced myself to relax a bit. It helped to focus on her dog, who was cuter than any dog of Delia's had the right to be.

I ignored her gibe about my hair and pointed to the bottles. "Where'd you get them?"

"Here and there," she said casually.

"Where here? And where there?"

She lifted one slim shoulder in a half shrug. "I buy them at my shop. People have been selling me their empty bottles for years." The other shoulder lifted as she nibbled on a fingernail. "The colors are nice."

How had I not known about this?

Then realization hit me hard. This must have been what Ainsley was going to tell me yesterday at Déjà Brew. That Delia was selling my potion bottles at the white-elephant sales. Which meant that anyone had access to my bottles, and that my color-coding system, in regard to the bottle in Nelson's hands, was moot.

I narrowed my gaze on Delia. She wasn't fooling me in the least. "You've been trying to figure out what's in the Leilara, haven't you?"

Trying to look innocent, she scrunched her nose. "The bottles are empty when I buy them."

My jaw was back to aching. Suddenly, I realized how naive I'd been. Delia had probably been buying empty bottles, yes, but she'd probably also sent in people to buy potions for her.

I was about to read her the riot act about protecting family secrets when I heard my name being shouted.

Ainsley was at the edge of the crowd, waving her arms like she was flagging a jetliner toward its gate. "She's fixin' to leave!"

I glanced at Delia. "I'm not done with you."

She smiled and gave me a little good-bye finger wave. "Try not to poison anyone today, okay? You take care, now."

I stomped away, cussing a blue streak in my head. As soon as I was in striking distance, Ainsley latched onto my arm and propelled me toward the bike rack. Bernice Morris was setting a small bundle into the wire basket of her bike.

"Hurry," Ainsley said.

I took off at a run and shouted, "Miz Morris! Wait!"

She took a look at me and quickly whipped her bike helmet onto her head and yanked her front tires from the rack. Luckily, one of the pedals tangled with the bike next to it, slowing her up. I reached her just as she threw a leg over the low frame.

"Miz Morris," I said, jumping in front of her to cut her off. "I need to speak with you."

Looking like a frightened rabbit, her eyes wide and darting, she said, "I don't believe I have anything to say to you, Carly Hartwell."

The thick humidity made the simple act of catching my breath difficult. "First, my condolences on Nelson's passing. I know you were close."

Some of the fear left her eyes, and I could easily see the resemblance between her and Coach. The same narrow eyes, the same weak jaw and long craggy nose. Her saving grace was her beautiful skin tone and plump lips.

She'd been married once, but Mr. Morris had long since passed away. She'd been swallowed by widowhood for quite a while before finally shaking off her grief and finding a job—as Nelson's secretary. It'd been four or five years now that she'd worked for him.

Those thick lips pursed into a scowl. "I was greatly fond of him. Everyone was. You took away a good man when you killed him, Carly Hartwell. But you'll get yours."

Surprised by the venom in her voice, I staggered back a bit. "You don't really believe I'd hurt someone, do you? Especially someone I barely knew? Why would I do that?"

I should've been glad she had said nothing about my supposed poisoning of her brother. She had to know Coach's diabetes had been to blame, or I was sure she'd have been the one to track me down—for retribution.

As though a steel rod were sliding down her spine, she slowly straightened an inch at a time. "You want to see my brother go to jail. What better way than to kill the person who could prove his innocence?"

The sharp and condemning tone of her voice set my teeth on edge. Wrapping my hands tightly around her wire basket, I said, "If Coach is guilty, he deserves to go to jail. If he's innocent, he deserves to be set free. That's not my call to make. It's no one's call besides a judge and a jury."

Her eyes narrowed into spiteful slits. "He's *not* guilty."

She sounded so sure, so righteous, that for a second there I completely believed what she was saying. "You mentioned that Nelson could prove Coach's innocence. Why are you so certain?"

Sunbeams lit the freckles sprinkled on her arms as she

folded them across her chest. "The afternoon of the day he died, he told me he'd finally found the proof he needed to clear Floyd's name once and for all. He said the case would be wrapped up by the end of next week."

"What kind of proof?" My curiosity was killing me.

"The second audit verified Dudley Pritcherd's findings."

People passed by, openly curious about our discussion. Ainsley hung back a bit, peeking out from behind a nearby tree.

Perspiration beaded along Bernice's brow line, just below the edge of the helmet. Wagging a finger at me, she said, "I ain't saying anything more to you, seeing as how you're the one who killed Nelson."

Not this again. "Let's say you're right, Miz Morris. Not about me, of course. Let's assume I'm not out to get your brother for a decades-old grudge, okay?" Seriously, what was with people around here? "But let's say someone killed Nelson because they want Coach to be found guilty, because that person is the real embezzler who doesn't want to be found out. Did Nelson ever offer up any suspects who could have taken the money?"

Tufts of tawny hair stuck out around her ears. "I've said it all along that Dudley Pritcherd had just as much access to those baseball accounts as my brother, and could have easily had Floyd sign checks that were never deposited correctly. Floyd wasn't one to focus on details."

Dudley just didn't seem the murderous type, but I supposed if he had taken the money he'd be desperate to keep it a secret. And since he and Nelson were friends, Nelson may have unknowingly tipped him off about any evidence that would prove his guilt.

I wondered if the police had looked into Dudley's finances as I said, "Does that mean the handwriting analysis report came back?" Had it shown that Coach actually signed those checks? Was she setting up a defense?

But no. If Nelson said he had proof Coach didn't commit the crime, there would have to be hard evidence, not just a theory.

"I have to go," she said, setting her feet on the pedals.

Taking hold of the handlebars, I said, "Before you do, did you know Nelson was thinking about leaving town for good?"

Something flashed across her eyes, and it looked a lot like betrayal. Obviously she hadn't known Nelson as well as she thought.

"Let go of my handlebars, Carly Hartwell, or I'll run you over."

There was a gleam in her eye that had me believing she would love trying. Still, I was stronger, and held on. "I know this is a mite unusual, but I think we can help each other, Miz Morris."

"How's that?"

I laid it on the line. "You want to prove that Coach is innocent, and I want to prove that I had nothing to do with Nelson's death. We're probably looking for the same person. If we pool our facts, we might be able to narrow down a list of suspects."

Her beady eyes shifted. I could tell she didn't trust me a whit, but I was banking on her desire to see her brother proven innocent being enough to let down her guard.

"Who're your suspects?" she asked warily.

I couldn't admit I had none at the moment. "I heard Nelson had a girlfriend. Maybe she'd be willing to share her thoughts with us. Do you know who she is?"

The strap on her helmet looked to be digging into her chin as she fastened the clasp. "True fact. He had a new girl in his life, but I don't know who. He kept that information to himself. But his old girl might be able to tell you something. They only recently broke up a couple months ago."

My mind whirred, trying to process the new information that Nelson had himself another girl I hadn't known about.

"Who is she?" I asked.

Malice glittered in her eyes, and for that split second her true resemblance to Coach shone clearly through. "Why," she said, her voice syrupy sweet, "I do believe it was your cousin. Delia Bell Barrows."

≈ Chapter Fourteen ≈

I was spittin' mad and seeing red.

Delia and Nelson had been a couple? An odd couple to be sure, but a couple nonetheless.

And yet yesterday morning in my shop, she hadn't said a word about knowing him well.

My cousin had some explaining to do.

As I stomped toward Delia's booth, I was waylaid by Ainsley, who quickly fell in step beside me.

"What's got your gussie up?" she asked, her cheeks red from either the sun or the exertion. "What'd Miz Morris have to say?"

"Delia," I said through clenched teeth.

Ainsley put a kick in her step to keep up with me, and pressed her hand to her chest to keep her breasts from bouncing right out of her sundress. "I don't understand."

"Delia and Nelson dated a few months ago."

"Hush your mouth!"

I shared her shock. Delia and Nelson. I couldn't wrap my head around it. He was so clean-cut and boy next door, while she was . . . Delia, black cape, skulls, and all.

On a mission, we sliced through the crowd and headed straight for Delia's booth. But all our storming and steaming was for nothing. Delia had cleared out. All that remained of her visit was tamped-down grass and a bad taste in my mouth.

I let my anger cool. "Why didn't you tell me she was selling my potion bottles here?"

"I thought you knew," she said. "I realized you didn't only yesterday, when you were talking to Dylan. I tried to tell you at the coffee shop, but then I got cut off and forgot. Delia's been selling them here for about a month now." Her nose wrinkled. "I'm sorry. I should have said something sooner."

"It's not your fault," I said. It was Delia's. "Nelson had one of my potions in his hand when he died, which made it look like one of my cures killed him. Or at least had something to do with it. But anyone could have bought that bottle and put something in it. And there's no telling where the murderer got that bottle—from me, one of my clients, or Delia."

Ainsley chewed her lip. "Hadn't thought of that."

"All this is so crazy, isn't it?" I asked, not really looking for an answer. A murder, rumors of tainted potions, Dylan's sudden presence back in my life. "Anyways, I should go. Dylan said I could reopen the shop today."

"That's good news, but don't forget it's the first Saturday of the month. . . ."

I'd completely forgotten.

Ainsley's hands settled on her hips. "You can still carry me over to Rock Creek this afternoon, right?"

It wasn't really a question if her demanding tone was any indication. I knew better than to say I had too much going on to make our monthly trip to the county seat ten miles to the south. She didn't dare drive her van in case someone recognized it, so we always took my old Jeep, pulling it out from its dusty slumber in my garage. Because I biked everywhere around town, my Jeep didn't get much use except for these little monthly trips I took with Ainsley.

"Of course," I said.

Relief flooded her eyes. "Just remember that Bixby's closes at six on Saturdays, and I don't want to cut it too close."

I understood. "We'll have plenty of time. I doubt my shop will be busy today."

Across the lawn, I saw Ainsley's twin boys climbing an old oak tree. Little Olive had herself wrapped around her daddy's leg, clinging like she was a baby cub too scared to come down from the branch it had climbed. She was wailing something fierce, and it looked like Carter was doing his best to ignore her.

Ainsley watched the scene, too, a tender, loving look in her eyes. Probably out of gratitude that it wasn't her leg Olive was attached to.

Giving Ainsley a nudge, I said, "Does Carter have any idea you ran him over on purpose all those years ago?" It had been no accident the day she hit him in the crosswalk, but a well-orchestrated plan years in the making, to get his attention. All because he never looked up from his books long enough to notice her many (futile) attempts to catch his eye. Her plan had worked perfectly. There was no ignoring a car hitting you.

A wide smile bloomed on her face. "Not a clue." She winked and sashayed away.

I watched her extricate her spirited daughter from her husband's leg before I turned toward town. It was a little surreal to be on the other end of a witch hunt, but I needed to find Delia.

And she'd better have some answers for me.

One would think that in a town based on love and marriage a shop like Till Hex Do Us Part would fail miserably. But in fact it was one of the most successful stores around.

With its mystical kitsch, it drew a crowd looking for something different, something a little darker.

I parked Bessie Blue and stood on the sidewalk facing the front of the store. I'd never actually been inside—had only passed by, sparing furtive glances through the shaded window. My aunt Neige had opened the store nearly twenty years ago but signed it over to Delia just about a year ago when Neige followed her heart to New Orleans to shack up with a scary voodoo practitioner named Xavier.

She was clearly following in Leila's footsteps of choosing the wrong man to fall for, though I hoped my aunt wouldn't share the same fate. We were hardly close, but kin was kin, and I didn't want to see anything happen to her.

My thoughts led me back to the conversation I'd had with Delia yesterday morning. The one where she warned me something bad was going to happen . . . Had she known about Nelson's death all along? Was that why she hadn't been too surprised to see him on the floor?

I supposed there was no way to find out but to go in and ask Delia flat out.

Taking a deep breath, I pulled open the leaded glass door. Long arcing shadows danced in the dimly lit shop, and it took a second for my eyesight to adjust. When it did, I was surprised to see how beautifully decorated the store was. Dark purple walls, velvet draping, and gold trim should have felt cheap and tacky yet instead seemed rich and oddly soothing. Some sort of sweet incense scented the air as I looked around, soaking in the atmosphere. Twigs fashioned into arched doorways led into smaller rooms at the back of the store. The front room held a lot of novelty items, including many, many skull-emblazoned items (no surprise there), voodoo dolls, charms, talismans, jewelry, crystals, gemstones, New Age CDs, journals, and books. A cash register and small displays of key chains and beaded bracelets sat on a long counter ran along the wall to my left. There was no one else around.

"Hello?" I called out.

No one answered, and I wondered where Delia was hiding, because I knew she was around here somewhere. As I passed display tables, I stopped to lift the fabric skirts on each one, but so far Delia hadn't turned up under any of them.

The next room, a tiny nook, held incense, beautiful pairs of tapered candles, stunning crystal candle holders, lots of jarred herbs, and small leather pouches called gris-gris that were used to hold all sorts of things from hair to bone.

Dark-stained, rough-hewn floors creaked as I made my way into the last area, the hexing room. I passed under a twig arch and into a space that made my skin tingle with the magic in the air.

Although Delia and I had been cut from the same cloth, she chose to practice the dark arts of our great-great-granddaddy, while I chose the white magic of our great-great-grandmother.

And it was a choice. Although Delia didn't have access to the magical Leilara, she could easily conjure her own potions and be quite successful at running an herbal-remedy shop.

Just as easily as I could use hexes.

We'd chosen our paths.

I shied away from hexes, wanting to help people rather than cause harm. And, of course, Delia had chosen hexes instead of helping people with her abilities.

"Delia?" I said loudly. "Hello?"

Sunshine streamed into the room from a high window, highlighting stunning handmade brooms and wands. Small cauldrons, runes, and tarot decks were also beautifully displayed on tables of varying heights.

I couldn't help but smile at the hex menu board on the wall behind a high wood-planked counter. Delia sold liquid hexes of every variety. Ones that caused baldness, misfortune, impotence, career problems, cramps, warts, cankers, relationship woes, bad breath, wrinkles . . . The list went on. As far as I knew she didn't market anything truly dangerous—nothing that would cause chronic illness or death—but it wouldn't surprise me if she knew them backward and forward.

And that was exactly why she shouldn't have access to the Leilara. Just as the tears made my healing potions magically potent, they would do the same for Delia's hexes. And that would be very dangerous indeed.

Someone had to be in the shop—it certainly wouldn't have been left unstaffed. And though I was sure Delia had employees, if one of them were here they would have helped me by now.

A swinging door behind the counter probably led to a stockroom and office space. Skirting the counter, I headed toward it and was surprised to find it locked.

I was also surprised to feel a pinprick of concern for my cousin. Had something happened to her? A vision of Nelson's lifeless body on my break room floor had beads of sweat popping up along my hairline as I imagined a similar fate for Delia. Did she even have a break room back there?

Before I went into full-blown worry mode, I tried another tactic. "Boo! Here, Boo!" I gave a short, sharp whistle and smiled when I heard a muffled bark from behind the door.

I hopped up on the counter, letting my legs dangle. "You might as well come out, Delia, considering I'm not fixin' to leave until you do."

Behind me, I heard customers come into the shop, their voices easily carrying the length of the store. Glancing over my shoulder, I saw a young couple looking at a display of amulets.

"Howdy!" I called out. "Let me know if you need any help."

The couple smiled my way and went back to browsing. I hopped off the table and walked over to the door. "And now you've got customers here," I said. "Unless you want me sending them across the street to my shop, you'd best be getting out here."

I heard a bolt slide across a metal plate and the door swung open. Delia strode out, calm as could be, with Boo tucked into the crook of her arm. He wagged his tail when he spotted me, and I reached over and patted his head.

Looking me dead in the eye, she said in a low whisper, "What do you want, Carly? This isn't about the bottles again, is it? Last time I checked, it was a free country." She set Boo on the floor and he raced off to greet the guests.

"He's friendly!" she called out.

Sunbeams fell on her like a spotlight, making her look like some sort of fallen angel. There was no denying how pretty she was—at least on the outside.

"I still have questions about the bottles," I said, keeping my voice low, "but what I really want to know is if you dated Nelson Winston."

Her locket swung back and forth as she reached for a feather duster. "Where'd you hear that?"

"Bernice Morris."

Swiping the duster across the counter, Delia rolled her eyes. "That woman never did like me."

I knew the feeling.

"So, it's true?" I asked. "You and Nelson?"

She stopped dusting long enough to nibble her thumbnail. The black polish had seen better days. "I wouldn't call it dating. We went out a few times."

"How few?"

"We were together for a month or so." She shrugged. "No big deal."

I wasn't getting that feeling. I was picking up that she had cared a great deal. "Why didn't you tell me you knew him yesterday morning in my shop?"

Pain flashed in her eyes. "I was in a bit of shock."

"Then you didn't know he'd be there? That's not why you showed up?"

"Don't be ridiculous!" she said angrily. "I came because I had a dream about you. And foolishly I thought—" She cut herself off.

"What?"

"Nothing."

"Tell me."

"You're annoying."

I ran my hand down a beautifully crafted broom. "I've been called worse."

Letting out a deep sigh, Delia said, "I just thought it might be time we start acting like family and not strangers."

She'd caught me off guard, and I found myself at a loss for words.

"It was stupid," she went on. "Obviously."

The thing was, I couldn't tell if she was serious or if she was manipulating me in order to find out more about the Leilara. Because she was right: we were strangers.

"Not *stupid*," I said, wanting to believe the best of her. But I also recognized I couldn't trust her. Not yet. Maybe not ever.

"Delusional?" she threw out.

"Closer." I smiled.

She didn't smile back.

I wandered around a bit before I got back to the reason I was here. Nelson. "How'd you two get together? You and Nelson?"

"What's with all the questions, Carly?"

"He was found dead in my shop, remember?"

"Hard to forget," she said quietly. Looking away, she grabbed her locket and held it tightly.

I thought back to yesterday morning and recalled she had been a bit off. I supposed she could have been in shock. I knew I had been.

Finally, I said, "How'd you two meet?"

"We bumped into each other at the bookshop, in the magazine section. Got to chatting. It went from there."

"And then?"

"And then what?" she asked, heading with her duster for the display of miniature iron cauldrons. Boo wandered back to us and went straight to a doggy bed tucked into a dark corner.

"How come no one knew about your relationship?" A couple like them would certainly be on the lips of every gossip in town.

"It was no one's business. We went to Huntsville a lot to dinner and the movies." Her head snapped up as another couple came into the shop. Boo went off to greet them, possibly the cutest welcome wagon I'd ever seen.

"Did he ever talk about having any enemies?" I asked.

"None. Everyone liked Nelson."

Except for the person who killed him.

"And why did you two break up?" I asked.

Her body stiffened. "We just did."

"Did it have anything to do with Coach Butts?" I could hope.

Delia looked toward her customers, then back at me, her eyes sparking with anger, with hurt. "It had nothing to do with him and everything to do with Nelson falling for another woman."

I was taken aback at her show of emotions. I'd always known her as being ice-cold, but apparently this breakup had hit her hard. "I'm sorry."

"I don't need your pity," she seethed.

"It's not pity," I said. "It's someone who's had a broken heart and knows the pain."

"Well, at least Dylan's not dead."

It was hard to argue with that.

I hated to push my luck but needed more information. "Do you know who his new girlfriend is? A local?"

She shook her head. "I don't know. I don't care."

I doubted that very much. "What about—"

Her eyes blazed. "It's time for you to go, Carly."

It was time to pull back and regroup. I nodded, and left her standing in her hexing room, looking a little lost and forlorn.

I knew that feeling, too, and couldn't help feeling sorry for her.

Which shook me to my core.

We were strangers.

Worse than that, we were enemies.

Weren't we?

And as I walked back out into the sunshine, I realized that I hadn't really learned anything new from Delia. She'd only confirmed what Miz Morris had said.

I was back to square one.

❧ Chapter Fifteen ❧

Pedaling slowly, I circled the Ring, headed toward my shop. My journey to work was a far cry from yesterday morning's frenzy.

Today there was no crowd nipping at my heels, no mad rush for any of my potions. It would be a surprise if anyone came into the shop today. Anyone other than Emmylou Pritcherd, at least.

Heat haze blurred the sidewalk, the wilting trees, and the shops straight ahead. It was going to be an absolute scorcher today, and I was mourning the lack of air-conditioning in my house. Maybe it was silly that I was living there while it was under construction, but as much as I adored my parents—and I did—moving back to within arm's length seemed so . . . suffocating. I'd just plug in another fan and make plans to get a loan from the bank to get my air fixed.

I eyed Déjà Brew wistfully. It would be so easy to go inside, pull up a stool, and pass an hour or two. Or four or five.

As I was gliding along, I recognized my desire for a

diversion for what it was. An attempt to delay what needed to get done.

My shop needed to be reopened, and I couldn't keep putting it off.

Resolutely, I kept pedaling.

In the picnic park, I noticed Dudley still sweeping the grass with his metal detector, which reminded me that I hadn't stopped back at Emmylou's booth to pick up my piece of cake. Hopefully she'd bring a slice by when she came to the shop later on. I could use some cake right about now.

As I watched Dudley swing the detector back and forth across the grass, I couldn't help the twinge of pity I felt for him. Emmylou wasn't going to let him rest until that ring was back on her finger.

Even though I fully knew I should be getting to my shop, I steered my way toward Dudley. Now was the perfect time to ask him about the baseball league's accounting books—and to see if he was harboring any guilty energy. It was a good way to put Bernice's theory to rest once and for all.

I left my bike on the pathway and walked over to Dudley. An ashen face looked up as I neared.

"I'll find it," he said, continuing to swing with the metal detector.

"I have faith."

"I'm glad *you* do."

Ah, so Emmylou's nagging was getting to him. "I'll help look for a few minutes."

"You don't have to."

"It's okay. It's helping me procrastinate on opening my shop. I hate the thought of going back in there."

His pale face turned a bit green. I had the feeling mine was the same shade.

"I appreciate the help," he said.

"How's your stomach?" I asked.

"Hurts. I'm going to the doctor later today."

The sting of rejection hurt. One of my potions would have fixed him right up. "Glad to hear it."

"It's this stress. . . ."

I was grateful for the opening. "From the trial?"

He nodded.

"Do you think Coach is guilty?"

He tipped his head back and forth. "It was his name on those checks. They'd all been made out to cash and Coach signed them."

"Seems rather foolish of him, doesn't it?" I asked, testing the waters. "I mean, it's so easy to get caught."

"It's actually not all that unusual a way to embezzle. It's just that the amounts started to add up and there weren't receipts to back up the withdrawals. And then a check bounced. That sent up big red flags."

"He had to have known he'd get caught eventually," I said.

"He's not the brightest bulb," Dudley said softly.

No. No he wasn't.

"Could someone have forged his name?" *Someone like you,* I wanted to add but didn't.

I lowered my defenses and tapped into his energy. I felt no guilt coming from him—only his stomach pain and a good level of frustration. Bernice had been wrong about him. I latched onto my locket, took a few deep breaths, and rebuilt the blockade against his pain.

"It would have had to have been a very good forger,"

he said. "Nelson was waiting to get the results from a handwriting expert."

"When was the report due?"

"Two days ago," Dudley said solemnly.

The day Nelson was killed. "Bernice said Nelson had gotten some proof that day that Coach was innocent."

He turned off the metal detector. "It must have been the report."

"She didn't say. I'm not sure she knew for certain."

"Well, I'd like to know. If those checks were forged, it changes the whole outlook on the case."

I would've liked to know, too. Because as I'd been saying . . . if Coach was innocent, it meant that someone else stole that money.

Someone other than Dudley.

Someone who might have killed to cover up the crime.

A half hour later, I decided I'd stalled long enough. I left Dudley on the picnic green, still looking for Emmylou's wedding band, and I headed toward my shop.

Tossing a look both ways before I crossed the street, I couldn't help but think about Nelson and who'd done him in.

According to just about everyone I'd talked to, Nelson was a likeable guy. No enemies. Yet someone had split his skull and left him in my shop.

My shop.

I still didn't understand why. If there was some sort of message there, it was lost on me.

I drew up in front of the Little Shop of Potions' large display window. My gaze fell on an antique cast-iron mortar and pestle. It had once belonged to Leila, and had been passed down through the family to me. I'd chosen not to use it—it was heavy and unwieldy—but I could easily picture Grammy Adelaide pounding the pestle into the bowl while she regaled me with stories of my heritage. Of Leila and Abraham. Of a love doomed from the beginning. Of a legacy born from their deaths.

My gaze wandered to my reflection in the glass. My hair still looked a sight, since I hadn't had time to shower before Ainsley called. My eyes, too, had a strange look about them. A mix of confusion, trepidation, and determination that perfectly summed up my life these days.

A shadow fell over me. "You owe me big, Carly."

I jumped as Caleb Montgomery appeared at my shoulder. I hadn't heard him coming. My nerves were frayed. "How big? And for what?"

"I'm still weighing the enormity." He leaned against the window and swiped a hand through his dark hair. "You can add it to my tab."

I owed him for many things—it was true. He'd been my partner in crime for many years. And my savior, too. After I'd been arrested for setting that chapel on fire in Georgia, he'd been the one to bail me out and convince the police it had been an accident. I'd paid the deductible for the chapel's insurance and had been asked kindly never to return once it was rebuilt.

"Well, why do I owe you this time?"

"I made some calls."

"To?"

"Friends in Birmingham. I got the scoop on why Coach Butts fired Doughtree, Sullivan, and Gobble."

I rolled Bessie Blue to a nearby bike stand and twisted a lock around her frame. "That is big," I admitted. "What did they have to say?"

"The Birmingham lawyers had tried to get Coach to

take a plea deal. Coach pitched a white-trash fit, including throwing some chairs and punching holes in the office walls."

"That's quite a fit."

"By all accounts, it was a full-blown rage. Coach went on and on about how the lawyers were conspiring with the real embezzler. He fired them on the spot, though if he hadn't they would have resigned the case. Clearly Coach is not right in the head."

"Because of the violence?" It did seem out of character. He was a bit pervy, but I'd never known him to even raise his voice.

In the shade of my shop's awning, Caleb's eyes looked more gray than blue. They held a hint of amusement as he said, "Because of the conspiracy theory. If he'd been thinking straight, he would have realized twenty thousand dollars was nothing to that firm. Hell, Coach has probably racked double that in legal fees, not that he's footing the bill. . . ."

"Ooh, I do owe you big. Who's paying?"

"Bernice Morris."

That knowledge didn't surprise me much, but it did make me feel a bit sad for the woman.

"And apparently Nelson hadn't really wanted to get involved in a case that had the town split down the middle, but out of fondness for Bernice, he signed on."

His blue button-down was immaculate, not a wrinkle to be seen as he crossed his arms. "I also heard another little tidbit. About Nelson and that Birmingham law firm."

I couldn't help a smile. "That he was freelancing for them, hoping to be taken on full-time."

Caleb's eyes filled with outrage. "How'd you know?"

"John Richard Baldwin."

"Who?"

"Long story." I bit a nail.

"Well, here's the interesting part about Nelson and that firm. He called them the day before he died and said he was no longer interested in the position—said he'd had a change of heart and was going to be staying put here in Hitching Post."

"Did he say why he'd changed his mind? Was it because Aunt Marjie wouldn't talk to him?"

"He didn't say, but I've seen this kind of thing before, Carly. Where a man is willing to pack up his life and move away on what seems like a whim."

"Oh?"

"Indeed, and usually there's a woman involved. Find her, and you'll get some answers."

It was the second time I'd heard that advice in as many days.

But finding Nelson's mystery woman was turning out to be much harder than I thought. Which only reinforced one thing in my mind.

She didn't want to be found.

᪥ Chapter Sixteen ᪥

A few minutes later, after seeing Caleb off, I decided I couldn't procrastinate any longer. I needed to open the shop.

The lock on the front door of the Little Shop of Potions turned easily, reminding me that I still needed to call a locksmith. The familiar scents of the shop greeted me, erasing some of my unease. I breathed in deeply jasmine and vanilla as I looked around, took stock.

Colorful potion bottles were in disarray on the shelves, and I noted in dismay that one or two lay in shards on the floor, knocked over by a careless hand. I guessed the "stain magicians" had worked their magic only in the break room.

The back hallway was in shadow, dark and foreboding. My feet felt glued to the floor as I trudged toward the potion room . . . and the break room. As I passed a wall plate, I cut on the lights and the shop brightened immediately, further relieving my anxiety.

The door to the potion room was open, and I peeked inside. Nothing seemed amiss from the way I'd left it the day before when I made Francine Debbs's hangover potion. I pressed onward, ready to face my fears.

Bracing a hand on the wall, I peered into the break room. Part of me had fully expected to find another dead body. . . . But all was clear. The room was immaculate, scrubbed top to bottom. My gaze lingered on the tile floor, and I knew without a doubt that it was going to have to be replaced. The walls painted. The cabinets torn out. It would be the only way I'd be able to use the space again—if it felt new. Untarnished. Mine, and mine alone.

Glancing at the back door, I noted that the double locks were still bolted. There hadn't been another break-in. Good to know.

I grabbed a broom and other cleaning products from the supply closet and went to work in the shop cleaning up broken glass.

An hour later the floors were immaculate, the potions bottles were back in alignment, and I hadn't had a single customer, even though plenty of people had stopped by to gawk through the window.

When the phone rang, I snatched up the receiver, glad to have *something* to do.

"Carlina Bell Hartwell, you have to help me," my daddy said. He sounded out of breath.

"What's wrong? Are you back in town?"

"Got in this morning. And it's your mama. . . ."

I couldn't help my smile. My mama was all kinds of wrong, it was true. "Did you find out what Mama's planning exactly? Mr. Braxton is all worked up over her sabotaging his big weekend."

"Don't I know it?"

I rather hoped she changed her plans. "Is she still planning to sabotage his weekend?"

"Of course she is. You know your mama when she has a bee in her bonnet."

"There's no stopping her."

He let out a deep breath filled with frustrated vibrato. Next to my mama and my aunt Eulalie, there was no one more dramatic than Augustus Hartwell. He had learned from the masters.

He said, "She is a freight train out of control."

"And you?" I asked, playing along. I found it was best just to humor his rants.

"I am but her caboose, being dragged along behind her by the braids of my wig."

"The braids of what?" I wasn't sure I'd heard him right.

"My wig," he repeated. "It's why I called, Carly. I'm in desperate need of your help before your mama makes a fool of me this afternoon."

A braided wig. I couldn't wait to see what Mama had in mind. "Tell me what I can do."

"First, I need you to—"

My head snapped up as the shop door swung open. "I need to call you back, Daddy."

He protested. "But, Carly—"

"I'll call you right back," I said, and hung up, feeling guilty about cutting my daddy off. But I knew he'd understand if he could see who was here.

"Is it a bad time?" she asked as she scooted into the shop, throwing a look over her shoulder as if afraid someone might see her.

Which was understandable, considering most of the townsfolk suspected I had tried to kill her husband.

"What are you doing here, Angelea?"

Coach Butts's wife was a pretty little thing, with long curly red hair, fair sun-kissed skin, and pouty lips. She and Floyd Butts had met while she was still in high school, she the head cheerleader and he the school's gym teacher. It was a scandalous relationship and the only things that had kept him out of jail and from being fired were the facts that she'd been eighteen when they started dating and that their relationship hadn't come to light until after she graduated.

When she found out she was pregnant.

They eloped right off and had come back to tongues wagging about their marriage. They weathered the storm, but unfortunately Angelea had miscarried after a month or two and had never been able to conceive again despite years of trying. Even my potions hadn't helped any.

Rumor around town was that she'd faked the initial pregnancy all those years ago to trap Coach into marrying her. . . . Why, I'd never understand. Angelea could have had her pick of men. And still did, which she regularly proved whenever she and Coach were separated.

Why they kept getting back together was beyond me.

"I need a potion made up," she said. "I heard about Mr. Dunwoody's forecast yesterday."

It seemed so long ago that he'd predicted sunny with a chance of divorce.

"You want one of *my* potions?" I asked, noticing she didn't look so good and didn't seem herself. Dark circles colored the fair skin beneath her eyes, and instead of her usual skintight jeans, heels, and tank top, she wore a pair of baggy cargo pants and a thick sweatshirt. In this heat. Something was definitely off. "Even after everything's that happened?"

Chipped manicured nails gleamed as she waved a hand. "I've known you a long time, Carly. You don't have it in you to hurt someone like that."

It was nice of her not to bring up the pitchfork incident with Mrs. Jackson. She'd been at that party.

"Plus," she added, "I don't give a damn what other people say."

Now probably wasn't the right time to point out that her husband had accused me of poisoning him. If she was willing to overlook it, so was I.

"I appreciate that," I said. "Did that sleep potion I made work okay for you?"

The mix of lemon balm, valerian, chamomile, and Leilara should have worked like a . . . well, like a charm. Since it was, in fact, charmed. But she looked like she hadn't had a good night's sleep in a month of Sundays.

Rolling her eyes, she shifted her weight and tossed another look over her shoulder. For someone who didn't care what others said, she was sure nervous about being seen in my shop.

"I didn't get a chance to use it. Floyd found the bottle and asked me a million questions." Fussing with her collar, she said, "He didn't give it back. And now the police have it, as you probably know."

The bottle had been *empty* when Coach crashed. Had he dumped it out? "This is going to sound strange, but the remnants in that potion bottle weren't those of the sleeping cure I gave you. Do you know what might have been in it?"

Her face drained of color. "In it? No . . . I don't. Was it something bad?"

"The police are looking into it. It just didn't smell like anything familiar. And the bottle was empty when Coach had it, but you say you didn't drink any, so . . . what happened to the sleeping potion?"

"I-I don't know. That's surely strange," she said, shifting her weight from foot to foot.

Her strange behavior was making me suspicious that she knew more than she was letting on. I tapped into her energy for a second and felt evasiveness wash over me. She was lying. "Are you sure you don't know what happened to that potion?"

"I'm sure," she said. "Maybe Floyd knows."

"Maybe," I murmured, wondering what she was hiding. "How's he feeling?"

"Much better. My apologies about your house. Whatever the insurance doesn't cover, we will, of course."

Bass vibrated through the floor from distant yet loud music. I glanced out the window but didn't see anything. "What's that, do you think?"

"It's probably from your mama's block party," Angelea said.

"Her what?"

Angelea smiled, and it lit her whole face. "The block party? Your mama's quite the sight, I have to tell you."

A block party. My word. I was definitely going to have to rescue my daddy—but not before I took a picture of how my mama had trussed him up. "Give me a quick sec, and I'll fix you up a love potion. Then I've got to see what's going on."

"Wait," she said, grabbing my arm as I passed by her. "It's not a love potion I want, Carly."

"But you said . . . about the forecast?"

"Right. But I don't want a love potion. I want to make sure that the breakup Mr. Dunwoody predicted is my own. I want a divorce potion. I-I actually told Floyd earlier this week that I want a divorce. We've been living separate lives for so long now. . . . This divorce is a long time coming, and I want to make sure I actually go through with it this go-round."

I felt my eyes go wide. "A divorce potion?"

"Surely you can concoct one," she said, a desperate gleam in her eye.

"Actually, I can't," I said. "Divorce falls outside my abilities." One of Delia's hexes, however, would be just the thing she needed. Not that I told her so.

Water filled her eyes. "Why not?"

"My potions are to foster love, to heal, to fix." Not to cause pain. I studied her carefully and noticed the anguish in her eyes she was trying desperately to hide. "Why do you think you wouldn't go through with the divorce?"

People came from all over Alabama to Darling County for its quickie, no-muss, no-fuss divorces. We had laws here that didn't apply to the rest of the state, grandfathered in from a time when government wasn't quite so involved in people's love lives.

"It's like Floyd has a spell cast on me, making me come back to him time and again. It's time I leave. For good."

I thought it was a sensible decision. "How'd he take the news?"

She let out a weary sigh. "About as well as you'd expect with his temper these days."

"He didn't hurt you—"

"No, no. But he was angry as the devil, punching walls, throwing things, and accusing me of cheating on him. I had to promise to give him another chance just to get him to calm down." Her voice cracked. "So I'm still living there, and now he's hurt. . . . And he's already vowed to fight a divorce if I do go through with it, dragging it out to a bitter end."

Ah, there was the rub. Quickie divorces were only quickie if both parties agreed to the terms. I wanted to ask if she had been cheating, because most of the town had heard those rumors, but I couldn't bring myself to do it.

"I just want out." Her shoulders shook and she wrapped her arms around herself.

I motioned her to a stool. "Have you two tried counseling?"

A tear dripped from the corner of her eye. "I don't think it will help. We're too far gone. As you know, we've always been at odds, but this court case has just torn us apart."

"Because he's guilty?" I prodded. I couldn't help myself.

She gave me a weak smile. "His ego has been bruised and battered," she said, not answering the question. "It didn't help that right around the time he was arrested we found out that it's near impossible for him to have kids, neither. Some sort of complication of his diabetes. He's taken that hard. So hard."

Ah. That would explain why none of my fertility potions had worked on Angelea. The issue had been with Coach. "Maybe if he comes in, I can make something that will help. . . ."

Fear filled her eyes. "Oh no. That wouldn't do at all. He's not all that fond of you, and, in fact" — she winced — "he thinks your potions are to blame for my infertility. He believes that your potions made me barren so he couldn't have kids."

"That's . . ." I was at a loss for words.

"Crazy. I know. He's . . ." She searched for words. "He's not really thinking straight right now. He hasn't been really. Not for a while. He hasn't touched me in months. He's a shadow of the man I married. I need to get out."

Once I would have thought that being a shadow of his former self wasn't a bad thing. Seeing as how his former self was a big jerk. But in light of the fact that he'd been losing touch with reality, this news wasn't good.

She looked up at me through lowered lashes. "I just want . . . I want him to get better—but without me." Letting out a deep sigh, she said, "What am I going to do now?"

Even though I didn't particularly like Coach, I did like Angelea. I hated seeing her hurting so, but wasn't sure what kind of advice to give her. Finally, I said, "Maybe you should talk to Caleb Montgomery. He's the best divorce lawyer in town, and he'll know how best to handle this."

Pulling a hankie from her purse, she nodded stoically. "Maybe I should. This stress is hurting me, too. "

"I *can* help with that."

She looked like she was about to decline, then nodded.

I left her in the front of the shop and went to work on her potion. As I took out the Leilara from its hidey-hole, I glanced at her through the pass-through.

She looked over her shoulder once again and moved off to the side, out of sight of anyone happening by.

"Are you afraid Coach isn't going to like you being here if he catches wind of it?" I asked.

"It's not that. It's just—" She tossed another glance out the window.

"Just?" I prompted as I gathered ingredients.

"It's probably silly, but I can't help but feel like someone's been following me."

I stopped working and took a good look at her. There was a hint of fear in her eyes, but when she blinked it was gone.

"Silliness," she said with a wave of her hand.

Ordinarily, I'd have agreed with her. But strange things were happening in this town. "Is there any reason someone would be following you? No one has threatened you, have they?"

Uneasily, she laughed. "I shouldn't have said anything. I'm just being paranoid."

I let my guard down to feel her energy, and a wave of overwhelming anxiety crashed over me. I quickly wrapped my hand around my locket and blocked out her emotions. She might have a smile on her face, but under the surface she was a wreck. There were definitely things she wasn't telling me, but I also wasn't sure I wanted to prod her any more than I had.

Very carefully I put in two drops of Leilara into the fuchsia-hued bottle. Wisps of magic rose into the air and wafted away.

Angelea said, "Almost done?"

"Almost." I attached two small tags with directions on how to use the potion and placed the bottles in a purple packing box.

Her head lifted and cocked to one side. "You hear that?"

Muted music—singing—filtered into the shop. I recognized my mama's voice instantly.

Angelea's smile this time was genuine. "Your mama's something."

"That she is." I needed to get out there to see exactly

what she was up to. As I quickly went about mixing the stress potion, Johnny Braxton's threat echoed in my head.

Just fair warning. No one messes with my bottom line and gets away with it.

Johnny wasn't a man to bluff. I could practically smell retribution in the wind. What that would be was anyone's guess.

❧ Chapter Seventeen ❧

I closed and locked the shop and hung a sign on the door that I'd be back as soon as possible.

Finding my mama wasn't going to be a problem—I simply followed the noise. Currently, she was belting out "9 to 5," a classic Dolly Parton song, which perfectly explained yesterday's costume of a blond wig, sky-high heels, and low-cut dress that revealed bodacious cleavage.

It appeared as though she was having her own country extravaganza, and everyone around here knew Dolly trumped Johnny Cash any day of the week.

Mama had purposely one-upped Johnny Braxton.

He was going to be fit to be tied.

I quickly picked up my pace and as I exited the Ring and rounded the corner, I found sawhorses blocking off Magnolia Lane, the next street over, which housed not only Mama's chapel but Johnny Braxton's as well.

With bass pulsing through my veins, I bypassed a large sign that boasted RONA'S BLOCK PARTY, and stopped dead in my tracks.

Lordy be, as Ainsley would say.

A stage stood smack-dab in the middle of the street in front of mama's chapel. A huge crowd was gathered round it, swaying and clapping as mama finished her song. Tents had been set up on the grounds of the chapel, and it looked a lot like the white-elephant sale except under these tents there were wedding games, like wedding bingo and a *Newlywed Game*–type contest, a dance floor, a reception buffet. There were prizes of free weddings and honeymoons.

Mama had gone all out in upstaging Johnny.

All out.

Mama shook her booty salaciously as she launched into "Jolene" at the top of her capable lungs. She shimmied back and forth, as comfortable in five-inch golden stiletto heels as she was in bare feet. Her ample cleavage was in full view, her bustline enhanced with that quivering fringe.

The crowd ate it up.

Thoroughly amused, I looked around for my father, afraid that he hadn't been joking yesterday about being sent to an early grave—or, after having seen this whoop-de-doo, he might have opted to put himself in one. Rightly so.

Though he had dramatic tendencies, my daddy wasn't the attention-seeking type. Not the least bit. In fact, he reminded me a lot of Bashful from *Snow White and the Seven Dwarfs*. Except for the fact that he wasn't a dwarf, I should say. He was tall and balding with big eyes, round cheeks, and trimmed white whiskers, and was prone to blushing.

At first I had trouble finding him—I'd glanced past him three times before I realized it was my daddy holding up the side of the chapel, looking like he was trying to blend in with the whitewashed barn board. Which wasn't even remotely possible with the way he was dressed.

Mama had outdone herself decking him out.

My father, my laid-back librarian daddy, had grown out his whiskers, wore long phony braids, a bandana headband, tie-dyed peace sign T-shirt, leather vest, tight jeans, and cowboy boots.

He wasn't quite the spitting image of Willie Nelson, not with his hooded glower, but it was close. I was impressed.

As I started toward him, my witchy senses suddenly began twitching. I stopped, turned, and found Dylan Jackson hot on my heels. "Your mama sure is something," he said, coming up beside me.

"So I've heard." He'd changed out of his jeans and into a pair of dress pants and a button-down shirt with its sleeves rolled to his elbows. A badge and gun were clipped to his belt. He was working. "Are you planning to arrest her?" I was only half kidding.

"Nah. I don't want to deal with the paperwork."

He wasn't fooling me. He adored my mama and would sooner lock himself up than cuff her.

"But," Dylan looked around, "I doubt Rona has a permit for this party, so someone will probably be along shortly to break it up."

The crowd cheered as my mama finished the song and then immediately launched into another Dolly classic, "Here You Come Again."

I figured my mother had never applied for a permit in her life. "I'm guessing Johnny Braxton will see to shutting this down—if he hasn't already."

Glancing around, I saw him stewing on the side of the

road, his jowls quivering in anger. He glared at me, and I tried not to shiver. Abruptly, he looked away and started marching toward my father.

Uh-oh.

Mama must have seen him, too, because she finished her song and cooed, "Come on up here, Augustus, darlin'." Then she said, "How about a little 'Everything's Beautiful'?"

The crowd whistled and crowed at the suggestion of the Dolly and Willie duet. I watched my daddy's cheeks redden but noticed that Johnny had veered off, out of the limelight. He stood to the side, looking like a big ol' Johnny Cash–like storm cloud waiting to bust open.

Long Willie Nelson braids convulsed as my daddy shook his head in a vehement no.

"Come on, Gus, honey," my mama purred. "Don't be shy." She turned her charms on the adoring crowd. "Ain't he cute?"

They started chanting, "Gus! Gus! Gus!"

If my parents had actually been married, this little stunt might have precipitated a divorce. Perhaps Mr. Dunwoody had been wrong with his forecast—maybe he'd meant sunny with a chance of permanent separation.

"Come on, darlin'," Mama urged, shaking her fringe in encouragement.

Never one to resist Mama's allure for long, Daddy reluctantly dragged his skinny self onstage. Wild clapping erupted.

Dylan reached over and, using the tip of his index finger, lifted my jaw from where it had fallen. I snapped my mouth closed.

I couldn't help but smile as my parents launched into the duet. Especially when my daddy started loosening up and enjoying himself, looking slightly entranced by my mama's fringe.

It had probably been my mama's plan for that trimming all along.

Both had great voices and had quite the act going. If they wanted, they could probably take it on the road and give the real Dolly and Willie a run for their money. Couples in the crowd started slow dancing, and I figured my mama would have a packed chapel tonight. Unlike Johnny, who still fumed. If eyes could throw flames, my parents would be ashes on the stage. I watched him spit, then he turned and—

"Uhhn!" I grunted.

Dylan spun me around and into his arms. "Hush now," he said, shimmying to the left.

"What are you doing?" I asked, still struggling as his gun nudged into my rib cage.

"Dancing."

Tossing my head back, I laughed. "You call that dancing?"

He shimmied to the right. "You never did teach me how to do it proper."

No, I hadn't. We'd planned to do a lot of dancing on our honeymoon . . . the one that never happened. I wiggled some more.

"Quit your squirming, Care Bear. I'm not letting go."

That's what I was afraid of.

I gave in to his embrace, and he rested his chin atop my head. We continued the pattern of shimmying to the right, to the left, to the right, to the left.

If I had a lick of sense, I'd kick his shin and hightail it out of there. But his arms felt a little too good wrapped around me.

My head rested square on Dylan's chest and I could hear the steady *whump*ing of his heart, beating hard and fast. I found it as mesmerizing as my daddy did that fringe.

My eyes widened when I spotted Auntie Hazel dancing with John Richard Baldwin, whose eyes were the size of full moons as Hazel's hands roamed his backside.

Apparently he hadn't heeded my warning about staying away. Maybe he figured the way to Marjie was through one of her sisters. He was going to learn very quickly that the three stuck very closely together.

My aunt Eulalie stood nearby, singing along to the song, and Marjie was next to her, scowling so hard I thought the top of her head might pop clear off. Although a scowl was Marjie's usual expression, this one seemed especially fierce. It didn't seem to be aimed at John Richard, which made me think that she hadn't recognized the man she tried to shoot the day before.

To her, all suits looked alike—targets.

Shimmy to the left, shimmy to the right.

Above the *whump*s of Dylan's heartbeats and my parents' rousing duet rose the thin, plaintive wail of a siren. It grew louder as the sheriff's cruiser pulled up to the sawhorses.

Auntie Eulalie made herself scarce. She was still convinced the police were after her for sneaking into Birmingham's Alabama Theatre to see the Miss Alabama Pageant as a teenager—she'd always fancied herself an unfulfilled beauty queen . . . and a fugitive.

Mama was unfazed by the arrival of the law, but Daddy's Willie impression faltered as the last notes played out—he was probably hoping the police didn't take him for the real Willie, who'd had notorious brushes with the police.

The deputies looked more amused than anything as they made their way toward the stage, the crowd parting like the Rea Sea.

I reluctantly let go of Dylan. It had been a long time since I'd been in his arms, and much to my dismay I found I'd missed it. Too much.

No sooner had I taken a step toward my parents than a hand reached out and latched onto my arm, spinning me around.

"Broom-Hilda, could I have a word?" John Richard Baldwin asked.

"Broom-Hilda?" Dylan echoed, a smile in his voice.

I didn't feel the need to explain. "I'm surprised to see you back in town so soon, John Richard."

Dylan straightened, obviously recognizing the name. I felt the shift in his air as he switched from flirting ex to interested investigator.

Multiple thin red scratches marred John Richard's determined face. The brambles had really done a number on him.

He said, "I'm not giving up until I explore all possibilities."

"So I saw. Hazel seems to have taken a liking to you."

He glanced at my aunt, who smiled and waved. "I think we're going steady now," he joked, waving back to her.

In this case, I wasn't sure who was manipulating whom. Hazel's always had a thing for younger men. I figured John Richard deserved whatever she had planned for him. That's what he got for playing with fire.

"Do you have a sec?" He tossed a look at Dylan. "Alone?"

"I don't think—," Dylan began.

"Sure," I said, smiling sweetly. "Dylan, you might want

to go help my mama deal with those deputies, or you might have a riot on your hands soon."

The crowd was starting to get rowdy, chanting, "Doll-y! Doll-y! Doll-y!"

"Don't go far, Carly," Dylan said. "There's something I need to talk to you about, too."

"Well, aren't I the popular witch today?"

Dylan strode off, and John Richard and I walked away from the crowd, down toward the river walk. Sunbeams glittered off the Darling River, the water sparkling like stars on a pitch-black night.

"What is it you wanted, John Richard?" I asked, dodging a hand-holding couple who had eyes only for each other.

Shrugging out of his suit coat, he slung it over his shoulder and ran a hand over his face, then winced at the contact with the scratches. "I could use your help. I'm looking for any hints or tips that will get me a meeting with your aunt. All I need is a few minutes of her time to explain the situation."

"And what exactly is the situation?"

"That she has a very interested, motivated buyer for her inn. A cash offer."

Chapel bells rang in the distance. "What kind of cash are we talking?"

His cheeks colored, and it looked like he waged an inner war on whether he should divulge the information. He must have finally decided that the number would help his cause. Solemnly, he said, "Millions."

I tried to keep a straight face and not gasp. "How many millions?"

"I've been authorized to offer up to four."

I whistled. "That's a lot of money for a run-down inn."

"Tell me about it. I think the client is nuts, but now the firm has upped my bonus amount if I get your aunt to sell. A bonus I'm generously willing to split with you if you help me. The money will go a long way toward fixing up your house."

"I see." Indeed, I saw very clearly that he had a death wish. If Aunt Marjie didn't get him first, I might have to drag out my pitchfork. Did he actually think I could be bought?

Instead of giving him what-for right there on the river walk, I decided to see if I could pry more information out of him before I told him exactly where he could put his *generous* offer.

I leaned on the safety railing. "About this client . . . Do you know who it is yet?"

He hedged. "It's confidential."

Hmm. "Well, do you know if the client asked for Nelson Winston specifically to talk to my aunt?"

Confusion flashed in his eyes. "Nelson Winston? Oh, right. The dead guy."

That was one way to describe him.

He pulled a fancy cell phone from his pocket, and held it high in the air as if trying to find a signal. I didn't bother telling him it was of no use. There wasn't coverage within miles. "I don't know who brought him on. All I know is that the firm offered the guy a full-time position if he convinced your aunt to sell."

I still wondered why Nelson wanted a new job in the first place. Was Caleb right? Was there a woman involved? The mystery girlfriend? At this point, I didn't know how to find out. It seemed like no one knew who she was. I would think she didn't even exist, except for what happened with Delia and how Nelson dumped her.

"So, what do you say about helping me?" he asked.

I scrunched my nose. "I don't know, John Richard."

"Come on. Is there anything I can buy for your aunt that will help sway her? Like I said, all I need is five minutes of her time. Flowers? Chocolate?"

The thought of Marjie with flowers and chocolate nearly made me laugh.

I glanced up the hill and saw my daddy walking toward us, his braids swaying. I patted John Richard on his shoulder. "I need to go. Do you really want to know the way to Marjie's heart?"

Eagerly, he nodded.

"Guns, John Richard. That'll get her attention. Oh, or bullets."

As I left him staring in wonder I went to meet my daddy.

"Bullets?" he called after me. "Are you sure?"

Smiling, I yelled back, "All the better to shoot you with."

Chapter Eighteen

"Nice braids," I said to my daddy, kissing his cheek. His facial scruff scraped my lips.

"The things I do for your mama." He took hold of my hand as though I were a wayward three-year-old and threw a look toward John Richard. "Who's that?"

"A fool with a death wish." I explained about the quest for Marjie's inn as we headed back toward the chapel. After the long tale, I squeezed my father's fingers. "I'm glad you're home."

"Carlina Bell Hartwell, you should have told me on the phone what was going on with the trouble at your shop and that buffoon running into your front porch."

"Buffoon" was about the biggest insult my father would ever utter. He used the term a lot when speaking about Johnny Braxton.

"I can't justify being angry at him, since the insurance will cover the damage."

He nudged me with his elbow. "You want your mama to set fire to the place so you can start from scratch?"

The funny thing was he wasn't joking. "Thanks, but no

thanks. I'm rather fond of the old place." As we continued up the hill, my mama's voice echoed loudly as she started singing once again.

"Did she sweet-talk those deputies?" I asked.

His eyes twinkled. "Well, yes, but she also presented them with her permit."

"Mama got a permit?"

"Not exactly. I called in a favor this morning to secure the permit when I learned what your mama had planned. I had a feeling that buffoon Johnny Braxton would call the sheriff straight off, and you know how I like to do things by the book."

"Like asking me to kidnap Mama and offering to burn down my house for the insurance money?"

His cheeks colored. "Mostly by the book."

I laughed. My parents might seem like complete opposites, but underneath it all they were a perfect match.

"Now tell me all about this business with Nelson Winston," he said. "What was he doing in the shop?"

We took our time returning to the block party, and I told my father all I knew about the case, and finished with a question for him. "You never made a potion for Nelson, did you?" He could still make potions—he just chose not to do it full-time. But he did help me out by working a few times a month on the cheap.

"No. He never came in the shop while I was there."

That's what I had figured. Nelson just wasn't a potion kind of guy. Whoever put that empty potion bottle in his hand must have done so to hurt me somehow. I purposely didn't tell my Daddy about Delia selling potion bottles. I thought his heart might have had enough excitement for one day. I changed the subject. "Daddy, Mr. Dunwoody overheard gossip in the library about Nelson Winston taking a job in Birmingham. Did you hear the same news? I'm trying to figure out why Nelson would want to leave town. He has a successful business here and was apparently well liked by most everyone." Except for whoever killed him, but I thought that a little insensitive to point out.

Daddy scratched his chin. "I do recall something of the sort."

"Do you remember who you heard it from?"

"Let me think. Let me think."

Ahead, I saw Dylan sitting on the stone wall that abutted the sidewalk in front of Mama's chapel. His long legs were stretched out, and his arms were folded across his chest.

It appeared as though he were waiting for someone.

Someone like me.

"I do believe it all began with Earl Pendergrass," my father finally said.

Earl was the local mail carrier, and I doubted anyone knew more about the goings-on in town than he.

"Apparently he mentioned to his daughter that Nelson had asked him about change-of-address forms."

Felicity Pendergrass was a reference librarian and a chatterbox. No doubt it was she who told Mr. Dunwoody of Nelson's impending move.

"Did he happen to say if anyone else requested change-of-address forms, as well? A female someone?"

Daddy's eyebrows lifted. "Not that I heard. You think he was leaving town with a woman?"

"It's the going theory. I can't verify it, though."

"Me, either." Daddy squeezed my hand before releasing it. "I don't suppose that helps much, does it?"

"It can't hurt to ask Earl if anyone else is planning to move," Daddy said.

"I suppose not."

"Now, Carly," he began. "I know you're the independent sort and all, but remember it's okay to ask for help once in a while."

My parents had always let me make my own choices. Sometimes they worked out; sometimes they didn't. "If I need someone to help me set my house on fire, I know who to call."

"You get your impudence from your mama."

"I know."

His eyes softened. "I think you have company." He nodded to Dylan, who came over to us and shook hands with my father.

"It's good to have you back in town, where you belong." Daddy shot me a look when he said this.

He'd never made it a secret that he thought Dylan and I should have kissed and made up a long time ago. It was the hopeless romantic in him.

Mama, on the other hand, had offered to burn his house down.

We had a thing for fire in my family, apparently.

Neither had happened—Dylan had packed up and left town, leaving me to lick my wounds in relative peace. Relative, because his mama still lived round these parts. Unfortunately.

"I agree," Dylan said, narrowing his eyes at me.

Daddy smiled, kissed my cheek, and said, "I better go make sure your mama's not getting into any more trouble."

"That's a full-time job," I said.

"Don't I know it?" he muttered.

Once Daddy was out of earshot, Dylan wasted no time in getting down to business. "What did John Richard want?"

I sat on the stone wall. "He wanted me to help get him a meeting with Aunt Marjie."

"Did you pull out your pitchfork?"

It was amazing how well he knew me. "No, but I thought about running home for it."

As he settled in next to me, his thigh brushed mine. I wiggled a little to the left, but he simply stretched his leg a little farther so it rested against my skin. I scooted a bit more.

"You're awfully fidgety," he said.

"Stop touching me, and I could sit still."

A smile lit his eyes. "Does my touching bother you?"

I glared. "You're aiming for a poke from that pitchfork, too. Now, what did you want to talk about? I have to get back to work."

"A little poking never bothered me much."

Jumping up, I said, "I'll see you later."

Being here with him in front of Mama's chapel was getting to me, bringing back bad memories. It had been here that our first wedding was to take place almost a year and a half ago.

My side of the chapel had been full of my friends and family.

Dylan and his family and friends were nowhere to be found. Because they were at a small church across town, waiting for me. Turned out his mama had changed the location of the wedding without telling the bride.

She'd won that battle. With no cell phones, we'd been powerless to figure out what was going on for a couple of hours. By then the hurt and anger had set in on both our sides. We'd had a huge fight, one that had taken months to forgive.

Then we'd tried to elope, running off to that chapel in Georgia. The chapel that had gone up in flames.

Much like our relationship.

He pulled me back down. "Settle down, Care Bear. I need to talk to you about your potions."

Crossing my arms, I frowned. "What about them?"

"Remember the bottle Nelson had in his hand in your shop?"

"The violet one?"

"Yep. The toxicology report came back on it. There was nothing in it but traces of bleach. Someone washed it clean as a whistle and wiped off any fingerprints, too. That person went to a fair amount of trouble to leave no trace of him- or herself."

"At some point that bottle belonged to a woman, but I don't know who or when." I filled him in on my color-coding system and how Delia had been selling used potion bottles.

He stuck his hands in his pockets and looked pensive as I spoke, as if he were processing every word. Finally, he said, "The tox report also came back on the potion bottle Coach had in his hand when he crashed into your porch."

I didn't like his tone. "What about it?"

"What did you put in it?"

"It was supposed to be a sleeping potion for Angelea, but when I sniffed it, there was nothing familiar about it. It smelled strange. Why're you asking?" I pressed.

The noise from Mama's party reached a fever pitch when she and Daddy started singing "Islands in the Stream." I was surprised she hadn't dressed him as Kenny Rogers in the first place, but I supposed that would have been a harder costume for Daddy to pull off.

Dylan nudged my elbow. "Let's go somewhere a bit quieter."

I eyed him. "You're not just trying to get me alone, are you?"

His eyes twinkled. "Why would I do that?"

Oh, he knew why.

Reluctantly, I stood up and headed toward the river. Dylan fell in step beside me as we strolled along the river walk. I tried to ignore how he kept brushing up against me, his body heat firing up my inner temperature faster than the scorching midday sun.

I gave up on avoiding contact, hoping he'd grow tired of trying to get my goat. So far that plan wasn't working so well. He was glued to my side.

The Darling River splashed and gurgled as we continued to walk in silence, putting distance between ourselves and the block party. It was a hot but gorgeous day, and couples were out by the dozens—most of them headed in the direction of my mama's chapel.

Once the noise quieted down, Dylan said, "There were traces of strychnine in Angelea's sleeping-potion bottle."

Stopping short, I searched his face for any sign of joking. He was dead serious. "Strychnine, the poison?"

"Along with whiskey remnants."

"But you said it was a diabetic reaction that caused the crash." My mind whirled. What little I knew of strychnine was enough to scare me silly. The poison was potent and almost always fatal.

"Fortunately, Coach didn't drink the potion. He still claims the bottle was empty when he found it in Angelea's car."

My eyes narrowed, and my tone hardened. "That wasn't a *potion* in that bottle. Stop saying so."

Dylan dragged a hand down his face and started walking again. "What exactly do you put in your sleeping potions?"

My dander was up, and as much as I wanted to be flippant, I kept thinking about *why* there was poison in the bottle. "Chamomile, lemon balm, valerian, and a little lily extract," I said, including Leilara origins in case that, too, had shown up in the report. "Certainly no whiskey or poison."

We'd reached the end of the river walk and turned, retracing our steps. A jogger zipped past, and I wiped dampness from my forehead.

"When did Angelea order the potion?" Dylan asked.

"I made it for her on Wednesday. She told me earlier today that she never drank any of it, so it should have been full when Coach found it while cleaning out her car. When I asked about it being empty when Coach found it, she got a little flustered and was being evasive. Angelea knows something about that potion she's not saying."

"I'll talk to her," he said.

We walked in silence for a few minutes before I said, "Look, I don't know what's going on here. Can we even be sure that the bottle Coach had in his hand was the same one I gave Angelea the other day? I mean, someone clearly planted the bottle found in Nelson's hand. Maybe someone planted the one in Angelea's car, too?"

"We can verify it was Angelea's, actually."

"How's that?"

"Fingerprints on the bottle. There were mine, yours, Coach's, and Angelea's."

"Oh." Well, I guess that settled that.

"There was also another set of prints on the bottle."

At the sound of his strange tone, I shaded my eyes as I looked at him. "Whose?"

"Nelson Winston's."

Dropping my hand, I squinted against the bright sun. I searched my brain for something to say, but I was too shocked to form any words.

Dylan, on the other hand, had no such trouble. "I also received the toxicology report from Nelson's autopsy this morning. Do you want to guess what killed him?"

Swallowing over a large lump in my throat, I said, "I'm guessing it wasn't a blow to his head."

"He died from acute strychnine poisoning. There was also alcohol in his system."

"Whiskey?"

Dylan nodded. "That poisoned potion killed Nelson Winston."

✎ Chapter Nineteen ✎

The Darling River churned—much like my stomach. I dragged my feet as Dylan and I walked along. His hands were in his pockets, his gun nestled against his body in its belt holster.

I said, "If the poison killed Nelson, then why was his head cracked open? Did that happen when he hit the ground?"

"Unlikely. The coroner found splinters in the wound. Most likely from a stick or a base—"

"Baseball bat?"

He confirmed this with a nod of his chin.

I knew who had access to baseball bats. Lots of them. Coach Floyd Butts.

"Nelson was still alive when hit, too."

"Dang," I whispered. Someone really had it in for him. "What now?"

"I have a few loose ends to look into before I bring Coach and Angelea in for questioning. At some point that bottle was in Nelson's hands. I want to know the circumstances."

"What kind of loose ends?"

"This and that," he said evasively, then let the silence linger a beat before drawing to a stop. Bracing his elbows on the safety rail, he stared at the water. "Before yesterday, when was the last time you saw Coach?"

I racked my brain. "I can't even recall a time recently. Maybe a few months ago at Déjà Brew."

"Did you exchange words?"

I leaned on the iron railing. "Nope. We went to great pains to avoid acknowledging each other."

"You're fairly good at that."

I had the grace to smile. "I was until recently."

"Probably safer for you now that you were forced to talk to me, what with the fire ants and all."

The water below us was flowing downstream, dragging a twig along for the ride. We weren't all that far from the bushes I dove behind to escape talking to him that one day. "Probably." I watched birds forage on the riverbanks before saying, "It's starting to look a lot like Coach might have been involved in Nelson's death, but I can't figure out a good motive why. It doesn't make sense, unless Coach had a fit of temper, but that doesn't seem likely. Poison means premeditation, right?"

"Figuring it out is my job." He tugged my arm and we started walking again. Bass thrummed right through me the closer we got to Mama's stage.

I glanced at him out of the corner of my eye. "I spoke with Bernice Morris this morning, and there's a chance that on the day he died Nelson received that handwriting analysis on Coach's checks," I said. "Maybe you overlooked it at his house. . . ."

One dark eyebrow lifted. "Care Bear."

"What?"

"Remember a few seconds ago when I reminded you about this being *my* job?"

"I have short-term memory problems."

"No, you don't."

"Okay, you're right. I don't. But like I told you earlier, I can't help it if I hear things around town." I waited a second before saying, "I tapped into Dudley Pritcherd's energy this morning while asking him about the embezzling. . . . I wanted to see if he was guilty of forging Coach's name on those checks, as Bernice Morris keeps suggesting."

Dylan let out a sigh. "And?"

"He's innocent."

"Could you have *misinterpreted* his energy?"

I wanted to punch him in the arm, but said, "I don't think so. He has a bad ulcer, so his focus was mostly on that, but he's not feeling the least bit guilty about that missing money."

Ahead, I spotted John Richard Baldwin looking at his watch, then glancing around suspiciously. What was he up to?

Dylan said, "It could be he's not feeling bad enough about it to have any guilt."

John Richard stole another look at his watch, then over both shoulders. He started walking quickly down the river walk, farther away from us.

"I don't think so. It was neutral energy." Curious to see what John Richard was doing, I picked up the pace.

"Why are you walking so fast?"

I grabbed his arm. "Come on."

"Are you trying to get me alone?"

"You wish. Look." I pointed at John Richard, who scurried along like he was up to no good.

"So?"

"He's acting funny."

"As funny as you?"

I pinched him.

"Assaulting an officer. For shame, Care Bear. I might have to handcuff you and bring you in for that."

My gaze shot up to his. Sparks flew. Heat flooded my cheeks at the thought of the things we used to do with his handcuffs.

Time stood still. The sun in his eyes made the green sparkle like wet grass. Or maybe that wetness was coming from my own eyes—I wasn't sure. For a split second, I wanted to tap into his energy and find out what he was truly feeling.

But I didn't dare. I'd been down that road once, and I still hadn't recovered.

My chest ached with the grief I'd been carrying around since we broke up. I'd done my best to shove the pain into places deep inside me so I didn't have to feel that sorrow every day. But here with him and that look in his eye, every muscle in my body ached.

I latched onto my locket and forced myself to look away. Just past the Snack Shack, John Richard slowed. I dragged Dylan down onto a bench and snuggled in close to him as John Richard looked around.

"I don't think he sees us," I said, peeking over Dylan's shoulder.

Dylan's hand came up and cupped my face. His thumb slid across my cheek.

My heart hammered as I once again looked into his eyes. "What're you doing?"

"I'm not sure." He leaned forward, his gaze intent on my lips.

His scent, his touch, his everything overwhelmed me. I jumped up just in time to dodge his kiss—and to see John Richard suddenly veer off the path.

I started after him when Dylan's grip on my arm stopped me short. "He's getting away," I said.

"Carly, we have to talk about—"

"We will." For some reason, his using my real name instead of Care Bear sliced right through me. "Later. Come on."

"Where?"

"We have to follow him."

"Why? Are your witchy senses acting up?"

They weren't, but I didn't want to admit I was just plain nosy, so I nodded.

Dylan narrowed his eyes but stood up and followed me. We hurried down the river walk and slowed at the spot John Richard had turned. It was a well-traveled dirt footpath through the woods that led up to the Ring.

Ordinarily, there'd be a handful of people on this trail, but it was empty and I figured everyone was at Mama's block party. She was still singing her heart out, her voice echoing among the dense trees. It was cooler but buggier under the leaf canopy. I swatted at gnats and tossed a look over my shoulder. Dylan was right behind me.

As I searched for any movement ahead on the trail, I tried to tamp down the ache in my chest, swallow the lump in my throat.

How could being with Dylan feel so right . . . and so wrong at the same time?

I wasn't sure. And I hated not knowing.

We were near the end of the trail, where it opened onto the sidewalk near the church, when Dylan's hand latched onto my shoulder, drawing me to a stop. "Dy—"

"Shhh," he whispered. "Listen."

I strained to hear anything other than my mama's voice and the rhythmic pulsing of my out-of-control heartbeat. Focusing intently, I finally picked up threads of angry male voices.

Dylan ducked ahead of me and grabbed hold of my hand as he passed, towing me along with him as he left the trail and plunged into the woods.

"I don't need an escort," I whispered.

"Don't want you to get lost." He smiled, and my heart nearly flopped to the mossy ground right then and there.

Dang. I needed to get a grip. I let him tug me along, from tree to tree. The raised voices grew louder and louder. I couldn't see who it was that arguing with John Richard.

"They're behind the church," I whispered. "But I can't see them or hear what they're saying. Can you?"

He shook his head and maneuvered us closer to get a better view. Trying to stay hidden, we ran from tree to tree like two characters in a cartoon.

"Get low," Dylan said, as we duckwalked to the next tree.

It was a narrow maple, and Dylan tugged me tight against him so neither of us stuck out.

"You're enjoying this, aren't you?" I whispered and squirmed as his arms wrapped tightly around me.

He didn't say a word but I swore I heard him smile.

"Failure is not an option, Mr. Baldwin," a voice said loudly.

I tipped my head.

"What?" Dylan asked.

"I know that voice," I said, my heartbeat kicking up a notch.

"Who is it?"

I wiggled out of his grasp, crouched, and made for the next tree, where I would hopefully have a good view behind the church. Behind me, twigs snapped as Dylan followed.

"Who is it?" he repeated as he leaned around me to get a look for himself.

His breath was hot on my neck and completely distracting. I pushed him back and peeked out behind a red oak. Sure enough, my ears hadn't deceived me.

Johnny Braxton had John Richard cornered. The poor lawyer looked side to side as if trying to gauge how best to escape. He wiped his brow and said something back to Johnny that I couldn't hear.

"What's he doing with Johnny Braxton?" Dylan asked.

I glanced back at Dylan. "Stop breathing in my ear like that."

Johnny Braxton started pacing, and some of the hair coloring he'd used had begun to drip down his cheeks. "You had one job to do!"

"Like what?" Dylan said, purposely aiming for my eustachian tube.

I shoved him and he fell back onto his rear.

Both Johnny and John Richard snapped their attention toward the woods. I dove on top of Dylan, pushing him flat to the ground. "Don't breathe," I whispered, hoping the tall scrub around us would block us from view.

"Bossy," he accused quietly.

And flustered, too. Having myself pressed against Dylan stem to stern was throwing my senses out of whack. My heart beat wildly against his sternum.

He reached up and pushed his fingers into my hair.

"Dylan," I started.

"Hush," he said, revealing a leaf that had been stuck to my head.

I leaned up, checking to see if either of the arguing men was going to investigate the noise in the woods.

Neither had budged.

I settled back into my spot.

"Carly," Dylan began.

"What?"

"For the love of God, stop wiggling like that."

Heat flooded my cheeks. I wanted to make a joke about whether that was his gun I was feeling, but I couldn't bring myself to do it.

I rolled off him.

We stared at each other for a long second before I couldn't stand the overwhelming emotion anymore. Dragging myself up, I crawled back to the tree.

Peeking around, I saw that Johnny and John Richard had gone.

"They left," I said, checking my hair for more leaves.

Dylan sat up. "Why were they arguing, do you think?"

I grabbed my locket and thought about what little I'd overheard. Pieces slid into place. About how John Richard had been hired by a mysterious client. And about how Johnny Braxton had made that elusive comment about owning more of the town . . .

"I think Johnny was the one who hired the fancy Birmingham law firm."

"He wants to buy Marjie's inn?"

I stood up. "That's my guess."

Dylan's fingertips brushed my calf. I jerked back.

"There was an ant on your leg," he said, smiling as he rose.

I'd had just about as much closeness to Dylan today as I could handle. "Why are you so calm about this?"

"About what?"

I gestured toward the church. "Them!"

He shrugged. "Should I care?"

Rolling my eyes, I said, "If Johnny Braxton hired that law firm, then he was probably the one who recommended Nelson Winston to them. And if Johnny is that mad at John Richard, imagine how mad he must have been when a local failed to get Marjie to sell. It could be what they were fighting over when Jessa saw them."

Dylan's eyes narrowed. "You don't seriously think Johnny had something to do with Nelson's death...."

As I met his gaze, I felt the wall that I'd built up around my heart when he left town starting to crumble. I thumbed a speck of dirt from his cheek and told it how I saw it. "I don't know what to think anymore."

≈ Chapter Twenty ≈

The locksmith was waiting for me when I arrived back at my shop. I made a joke about how he should have let himself in, but he didn't even crack a smile.

I tried not to take his sour puss personally.

As the locksmith set to work on the back door, it turned out he hadn't been the only one waiting for me to return. Delia paced outside, her cape flying out behind her with each sharp pivot. Every few seconds she threw a look into the shop, as if waging an inner debate about whether to come in.

While she warred with herself, I went about gathering supplies to make a few bottles of bath potions and sachets, a task normally done by Ainsley. But since I had no potions to create, these handmade items were good busywork. They weren't magical by any means, but they helped fill the shop with novelties that tourists loved. I also made and sold soaps, but did that at home so as to not stink everyone straight out of the shop with the lye scent.

As I worked, I couldn't help but think about Johnny

Braxton and his potential involvement in Nelson's death. I was also worried about how far he'd go to try to buy Marjie's inn. It was obvious he was determined—but he clearly didn't realize how stubborn Marjie could be.

If Johnny had killed Nelson, he'd done a scarily good job of planning it—though his attempt to frame me for the crime, getting Angelea's sleeping potion involved, was a bit convoluted.

All this time I'd been wondering why someone would choose *my* shop to leave Nelson in, but it made sense if Johnny wanted to cast suspicion on me—and my family. I snatched up a container of vanilla beans and the spice grinder. He probably planned to prey on us while we were in turmoil—and perhaps finagle Marjie to sell her inn during all the fuss.

Well, that plan never had a chance in hell.

When threatened, my family (both sides) closed ranks. We were nothing if not fighters—all of us.

Dylan didn't seem too convinced that Johnny had anything to do with the crime, but I had talked him into a having a conversation with the man. I wasn't convinced, either, but was just desperate for some kind of resolution. With any luck, Johnny would give a full confession and I could put this distressing chapter of my life behind me for good.

The whirr of an electric drill battled with the sound of the spice grinder as the locksmith removed the old lock on the back door and replaced it with three new dead bolts. I was hoping the triple deterrent would be enough to keep future murderers out of my shop. If I still had a shop after the rumors died down.

Starting to feel a pity party coming on, I threw myself into my work. The bath potions were sold in tall, colorful custom-made decanters that looked a lot like genie bottles. I set a purple-and-gold bottle on the walnut pedestal table along with various dried spices and scented essential oils and pulled up a stool.

Lavender was a favorite of my customers for its soothing scent and had many beneficial properties. I breathed in the sweet smell of the dried lavender sprigs. It was almost too overwhelming, but I'd worked with the strong scent for so long now it was just the thing to calm my nerves. It brought me back to more peaceful times, working alongside my Grammy Adelaide.

However, there was no time for reminiscing as the front door opened and Delia stuck her head inside. "Do you have a minute?"

I wasn't sure if her appearance meant she'd won or lost the war with herself. I glanced around the empty shop. "I don't know. I'm kind of swamped with customers."

"So I see." The corner of her lip quirked into a half smile as she scooted inside.

Boo stuck his head out of the basket hooked on her forearm and looked around. He was so adorable it made me want to get a puppy of my own, but I couldn't even imagine how Roly and Poly would react to that.

Probably not well.

Tucking a lock of pale blond hair behind her ear, Delia sidled up to the table. She not-so-casually drummed her long fingers on the countertop. Figuring she'd eventually get around to why she was here, I continued to work. I had a feeling her presence wasn't a social call, especially since we weren't exactly on the best of terms.

"It smells good in here," she said, placing her basket on the floor and sitting down on a spare stool. "Lavender?"

I nodded and added carrier oil to the decanter—it was

the base of the bath potion and would dilute any essential oils I added. To that I added the lavender essential oil, some dried ground lavender and vanilla beans, and a single drop of mint oil. I capped the bottle, gave it a good shake, then pulled the stopper to sniff the final product.

"Nice," Delia said. "A bit plebian but nice."

"Plebian?"

"You know, common."

"I know what it means."

"Then why'd you ask?"

"I wasn't asking. I was mocking."

Delia frowned. "This is what I get for trying to help you."

Boo hopped out of his basket and sniffed around as I set the bath potion aside. "Help me how?"

"Well, I took a nap a little while ago. . . ."

I lifted an eyebrow. "I bet you were exhausted after getting up early to sell my potion bottles at the white-elephant sale."

The locksmith turned on his drill again, cutting off whatever Delia was going to say. She stuck her thumbnail in her mouth and nibbled.

I grabbed a tag for the bath potion but found my hand was too shaky to write. Delia's presence had thrown me off-balance. "Why are you here, Delia?" I asked loudly, to be heard over the never-ending *whirrs*.

"I had another dream," she shouted.

"What now?" I asked, not sure I wanted to know.

Her face paled even more than normal, and she wouldn't look me in the eye. "I just . . . ah . . ."

"Just say it," I prodded.

With a firm shake of her head, she said, "I can't. It's too . . . disturbing." She bit her nail.

"You're making me nervous." The drill stopped, leaving the shop in silence. Thick tension hung in the air, and I felt sick to my stomach.

Boo sniffed my foot, and I reached down and picked him up. He licked my chin, and I wondered if Delia would notice if I kept him. He calmed me better than the lavender, and that was saying something.

She reached into her cape and drew out something closed within her fist. A long black leather necklace cord dangled from her hand and brushed the table. "Here," she said, pushing her fist toward me. Slowly, she unfurled her fingers, revealing a beautiful purple vial pendant with a sterling silver engraved stopper.

"What's in it?"

She finally looked at me, and I tried not to shiver from the look in her ice-blue eyes. "Is it a hex?" I asked.

"It's protection."

"You didn't answer my question."

She let the pendant dangle between us. "I think I did. Take it."

I set Boo down and reached out for the charm. The glass vial was stunning, and I immediately thought to add some to my collection of bottles—some of the potions I made would fill these small containers nicely. I pulled the stopper and brought it to my nose.

"I wouldn't do that if I were you," Delia warned. "One droplet of that stuff will make you temporarily blind."

I stared at the liquid sloshing inside. "What's the whole vial do?"

She shrugged. "I don't know, but I feel bad for the person who might find out."

I quickly shoved the stopper back in its place and held the necklace out to her. "I don't want this."

"Oh yes, you do. Trust me. Boo, come here." She patted her leg. "It's time to go."

I eyed her carefully. "No, really, I don't want it. I don't want anything to do with hexes."

She gathered up Boo and set him in his basket. Shifting off her stool, she adjusted her cape and looked at me with an expression that chilled me to the bone. "Carly, this is no time to stand on principles. Like I said, think of it as protection, not a hex."

"Take it," I said, still holding it out.

"Keep it. Just in case."

"No." I thrust my hand forward, the vial swinging between us like a pendulum.

The front door opened, and Emmylou Pritcherd hurried inside, wiping her brow. Oblivious to what she had just walked in on, she said brightly, "Whoo-ee, it's a scorcher out there! Hello, Delia!"

Ignoring the necklace and Emmylou, Delia said to me, "Do what you want with it, Carly. At least I know I tried." With a flourish of her cape, she rushed out the door.

Emmylou pushed a hand to her chest. "Was it something I said?"

"No." I stared at the vial, now resting in the palm of my hand.

"What's that you have?" Emmylou came toward me. "It's stunning."

Before she had a chance to examine the vial more closely, I closed my fist around it and walked over to the cash register counter. I pulled open a drawer and dropped the necklace inside, not sure how to get rid of it. A hex like that couldn't just be thrown away. "It's nothing."

She slid onto the stool Delia had just vacated. "Doesn't seem like nothing."

I was saved from having to say anything by the appearance of the locksmith. "Back door's done. Front will take just a minute."

He was a chatty fellow.

Emmylou watched him work and shook her head, *tsk*-ing. Before she could launch into all the woes that had befallen my shop, I said, "Let me get your potion started."

She smiled. "Please. I have big plans for tonight. Well, I hope to have big plans for tonight. I need to run Dudley over to the doctor first. I didn't have the slightest clue his stomach was feeling so poorly."

"Do you want me to make a potion for that instead?" I figured if she was going to slip him a potion, it might as well be one that would heal him.

She wrinkled her nose. "Can he take two at once?"

"Not a good idea," I said.

"Then no." She tossed a look at the locksmith. "Let's just go with the original one."

I nodded. The healer in me didn't want to go along with her, but I was also still feeling the sting of Dudley's rejection. He hadn't wanted one of my potions at all. . . .

Most likely, the doctor he was going to see would help his stomach. This other problem . . . I could take care of that.

I pushed aside my oils, spices, and bath-potion bottles and grabbed a jar and various supplies to make the impotence cure. Into the jar I mostly put ginseng water and a couple of other herbs to act as aphrodisiacs. As Emmylou watched, I swirled the mixture and funneled it into a potion bottle.

"Done," the locksmith said, packing up his tools. "You want me to bill you, or are you payin' now?"

"I'll write you a check."

We quickly settled up and he handed me new set of keys before walking out the door without so much as a "Good day."

"Cheerful guy," Emmylou said with a smile.

I couldn't argue that. "But he works cheaply and on a weekend, so I can't complain too much."

"How come you needed the locks changed? Because of the . . ." She pointed down the hallway.

I let out a breath. "Whoever left Nelson in here didn't break in. We think Ainsley's keys were used—she lost them last week."

"Oh no."

I jangled the new keys. "A little too late, but changing the locks gives me peace of mind."

"This whole situation is just crazy," she said. "Did you know that Dylan Jackson wants to interview Dudley and me? He left a message on our answering machine about it."

"You and Dudley? Why?" Were they the *loose ends* Dylan had been talking about earlier? Was this about the embezzlement? Because I'd already cleared Dudley's name about that.

"All because Nelson Winston's phone records showed he called our house the night he died." She wrung her hands.

What? "He called you? Why?"

"That's just it. We don't know. Dudley had talked to him earlier in the evening about something to do with the trial next week, but neither of us talked to him after suppertime. We did have a hang-up call that night. . . . It had to have been him. It's the only explanation. It just makes me feel ill thinking that he could have called us in his final hour. Maybe we could have done something. . . ."

If Nelson had been poisoned and not feeling well, he might have tried to call someone for help. Personally, I'd have dialed 911, but maybe he'd accidentally hit redial, which rang Emmylou's and Dudley's house. . . .

"I need to use your washroom, Carly. May I?"

She did look a little green. "Of course. I'll finish up your potion." As she wandered down the hallway, I stepped into the potion room and closed the door. I worked quickly, pulling the Leilara from its hiding spot. I added two drops of the magic tears to the potion, then hesitated before adding a third. Just to be sure. White tendrils swirled into the air, then dissipated—a feature of the Leilara that I'd never tire of watching.

I put the Leilara back where it belonged, boxed the potion bottle, and walked into the front of the shop just as the door burst open.

An angry Coach Floyd Butts filled the doorway. He pointed a finger at me. "You're just the witch I wanted to see."

❧ Chapter Twenty-one ❧

Making myself remain calm, I set the box on the counter and stepped behind the wooden cash register cabinet to put an obstacle between the two of us.

He seemed bigger, more muscled than I ever recalled seeing him. Yesterday when he crashed into my porch I'd been too flustered to notice anything but his injuries and the potion bottle in his hand. But I noticed now. His neck was almost as thick as one of the trees I'd hidden behind earlier.

I summoned some good old-fashioned Southern manners, as insincere as they might be. "Coach, you must be feeling better. You're certainly looking a sight better than the last time I saw you ... when you crashed your truck into my house and accused me of poisoning you. Are you here to apologize? If so, I accept."

Clearly, my manners needed some fine-tuning.

If the vein pulsing in his wide forehead was any indication, I may have pushed it a little too far.

"You!" he thundered, slamming the door behind him. I winced, fearing he was going to pop the stitches

along his forehead. I refused to appear intimidated, however, though my adrenaline suddenly shot through the
roof. My fight-or-flight response was screaming at me to
run. Instead I straightened as tall as I could and stared
him down. "What about me?"

He looked like a stereotypical jock, with his thick
neck, wide shoulders, and beefy arms. Dirty blond hair
stuck out from beneath red Alabama cap, and furious
dark blue eyes narrowed on me. Even at forty he still
had pimples marring his skin.

I had a potion that would work wonders for that, but
I didn't think now was a good time to mention it.

Slowly, he reached into his pocket and for a split second I worried he'd come armed. When he revealed what
he pulled out, I realized he had—in a way.

Armed with a potion bottle.

Meaty fingers held on to the faceted glass bottle. It
was such an incongruous pairing that I nearly laughed.

"What is this?" he demanded, shaking the bottle.

"It looks a lot like one of my potions."

He took another step toward me. "I'm in no mood for
your smart mouth, Carly Hartwell."

"Then I suggest you leave."

"Not until I know what this is."

"Why not ask Angelea?"

It was, after all, the stress potion I'd given to her earlier.

"She won't say." He took another step toward me, so
now he stood directly across from me, within arm's
reach. His bloodshot eyes narrowed, and I was beginning
to rethink my stick-it-out stance. Running seemed like a
perfectly good solution to this predicament. "Is this
some *potion*," he spat the word, "that will get her the

divorce she wants so badly? Are you helping her leave me? Tell me!" he thundered.

Steel laced my tone as I said, "I think it's time for you to go, Coach."

In one quick motion, he lunged across the counter, grabbing for my T-shirt.

"Get out!" I shouted as I jumped backward, out of his reach. I searched frantically for something to throw at him. The stapler, maybe. It was heavy enough to do some damage if I was closer to him.

But I didn't want to be that close. Not ever.

"Not until I get what I want." Menacingly, he scooted around the counter.

I went round to the other side, trying to stay one step ahead of him. His eyes burned with fury, and I feared that if he actually got his hands on me it wouldn't end well.

His behavior went beyond a fit of temper. It was . . . manic, and I immediately worried that he'd truly gone insane over the past few months and everyone had simply written it off as stress.

We circled the cabinet a few times, and I panicked, thinking that this standoff might never end. The stapler was starting to look like my only option.

"You deserve whatever happens to you," he snarled.

As I tried to think of something to say in response, he lunged again and latched onto my arm, his fingers digging into my skin. He squeezed hard, and I refused to let out the cry of pain I held in my throat. Just as my hand closed around the heavy stapler, the front door flew open.

"Let her go, Floyd!" Dylan shouted, stepping inside the shop.

Like a deer caught in headlights, Coach looked between Dylan and me, anger radiating off him in pulsing waves.

Dylan's hand settled on his gun. "Let her go!"

Slowly, Coach released his fingers.

"You okay?" Dylan asked me.

I didn't even have to look at my arm to know there were already marks there. My skin throbbed where each of his fingers had been.

"Why do you care about her?" Coach said, venom dripping from his words. "After the way she treated you? She ain't nothing but a—"

Dylan pulled his gun, effectively silencing the vitriol. "I suggest you shut up."

Coach sneered and suddenly reared back. He heaved the potion bottle he'd brought at the back door. With a deafening crack, the glass shattered, the potion splattering the walls.

Dylan leveled his gun as two uniformed deputies came running into the shop. "Cuff him and take him outside."

"Cuffs!" Coach thundered.

Dylan wore his "don't mess with me" look. Even though Coach was bigger and stronger, I had no doubt Dylan could take him down.

"Are you arresting him?" I asked.

Dylan said, "Absolutely. We'll start with assault and throw in criminal mischief for good measure."

"Assault!" Coach bellowed. "I barely touched her."

My throbbing arm suggested otherwise. Smiling sweetly at Coach, I said, "You deserve whatever happens to you. Bless your heart." I was pretty sure a few more vessels popped in his bloodshot eyes as the deputies led him outside.

Dylan took hold of my arm and examined the bruises forming on it. With a heated glance, he said, "Are you okay, Care Bear?"

For a second there, he looked like he wanted to kiss the injury to make it better. And, Lord help me, I would've let him. I shook off his hand and backed away. "Me? Fine. I could've handled him on my own."

"Sure you could have. You can put the stapler down now."

I dropped it on the counter, and my hand immediately ached from holding it so tightly. "How did you know I was in trouble? Were you just wandering by with deputies in tow and happen to glance in?"

"Got a call about a disturbance here."

"A call?"

"Yoo-hoo!" a shrill voice called. "Is it safe to come out now?"

"Emmylou!" I'd completely forgotten she was here.

She tiptoed down the hallway, trying to avoid shattered glass. "Whoo-eee! That was something! I hope you don't mind that I snuck into your break room and used the phone in there to call the sheriff. I didn't like the way Coach was talkin' to you."

"Do I mind? I could kiss you."

She fluffed her hair. "I do have that effect on people."

"Thank you, Emmylou," I said. "Without that call . . ."

She waved a hand. "I'm just glad Dylan got here in time, but I should be going now. My potion?" she asked, pulling a wallet out of her purse.

"On the house." I handed her the box.

"You're so sweet. Thank you!" She patted my arm before heading to the door.

As she walked out, Ainsley came strolling in. "What's

going on here? Why does Coach Butts have handcuffs on?" She had her hands on her hips, and her toe tapped the wood impatiently. Her gaze wandered to the hallway, where she spotted the broken glass. "Lordy be!"

I was wondering what she was doing here until I remembered my promise to take her to Rock Creek. It was just about time to go if we were going to get there before the pharmacy closed.

A curious couple wandered into the store, but Ainsley shooed them right back out. "We're closed on account of a crazy man lost his mind in here. Y'all come back to-morrow." She closed the door and flipped the lock.

Dylan said, "What did happen here?"

I gave them both a quick rundown. When I finished, I said, "I don't understand why he was so angry."

"Could be he's on steroids," Ainsley said. "I wouldn't doubt it, not with a neck the size of a wagon wheel."

It made sense. It was called 'roid rage for a reason. It also explained his bad complexion. Part of me felt sad that he was going to be locked up, but my sane self was rejoicing that he was going to be behind bars for a while.

Dylan ran a hand through his hair. "I wouldn't doubt it, either, but something sure set him off."

"The potion bottle." I flexed my fingers—they were still cramped. "He thought it might be a divorce potion." I explained Angelea's visit earlier and how I hadn't been able to help her.

Ainsley tsked and shook her head. "He's done lost his mind."

I nodded.

Dylan said, "And he's feeling threatened, which isn't a good combination."

"Threatened about what?" Ainsley asked.

I caught Dylan's look. "Nelson," I said.

"He's probably heard you've been snooping around town," Dylan asked. "If he's truly guilty of that embezzling, he might think you're getting close to proving it. Unlike Nelson, you don't hold attorney-client privilege with him. You can talk all you want—and perhaps he wants to shut you up."

If he thought that was possible, he didn't know me well at all. "I'm not snooping," I countered. "I just—"

Shaking his head, Dylan headed for the door. "Hear things. Yes, I know." He turned back and said, "Whatever has set him off, he's clearly snapped. It's a good thing he'll be in jail for a while, because in his demented mind, Carly, you're his number one enemy." He waved and walked out.

Ainsley looked around and then leveled an incredulous gaze at me and said, "You're racking up hot messes these days."

"Seems I've acquired a knack for it."

"Well," she said, smiling, "we all have our talents. I'll help you clean up the glass."

"Leave it. We need to get to Rock Creek. Cleanup can wait till tomorrow."

She nodded once, as if understanding that I just wanted to get out of the shop.

I grabbed the new set of keys and my pocketbook. As I headed for the door, I stopped and went back to the counter.

"You forget something?" Ainsley asked.

"Yep," I said, opening a drawer and pulling out the necklace Delia had given me. I slipped it into my pocket.

Just in case.

Chapter Twenty-two

Ainsley had insisted on driving my Jeep, which probably had more to do with my shaking hands than my penchant for driving too fast. She was a speed demon herself and liked to push my Wrangler to its limits on these back roads.

The radio had been cranked to a local country station Ainsley loved, and a dusty trail and flying pebbles lay in our wake as we made our way eastbound to Rock Creek. The silence between us was welcoming—Ainsley had known me so long that she knew when to push and when to back off and let me stew in my own thoughts.

I didn't want to talk about what had happened back at the shop, or what it might mean to Nelson's murder case. My mind was so jumbled with motives and suspects that I could barely think straight.

Ainsley glanced over at me and gave me her "it'll be okay or I'll make sure someone pays" smile and then started singing along to the radio. It was not, fortunately, a Dolly Parton song, as I'd had my fill for the day, despite how much I loved Dolly—and my mama.

Rock Creek was normally a fifteen-minute drive along a little-used, tree-lined, two-lane road, but Ainsley made it there in a little less than ten minutes. She slowed the Jeep dramatically as she entered town, switching from her closeted wild-child persona to that of a pastor's wife, despite the fact that she specifically came here because of the anonymity this town provided. It was doubtful we'd run into anyone we knew. The big city of Huntsville to the south of us was only a bit farther away and was the go-to place for most of Hitching Post when it came to shopping, doctors, restaurants, and cultural activities.

But Ainsley didn't like to take chances where Carter's reputation was concerned, so she put on her prim-and-proper face.

Which nearly made me laugh, considering why we were here.

Rock Creek was vastly different from postcard-perfect, picturesque Hitching Post. This was a tiny working-class town that didn't have the budget to gussy up public spaces, but it was clear the people of this town took pride in it. It was clean. And safe. Crime rates were low and there hadn't been a murder here for as long as I could remember. Hitching Post couldn't say the same.

Stores lined one main street and there were a few strip malls along the outskirts. Ainsley pulled my Jeep into a parking spot around the corner from Bixby's and grabbed her pocketbook. "Do you want to stay here?"

"I'll come. I need to pick up a few things." Roly and Poly needed kitty litter, and I was almost out of peanut butter, a staple in my pantry.

Bixby's was an old-fashioned pharmacy, and its smell always reminded me of my daddy's library. There was a hint of mustiness and dustiness in the air along with a charm that time hadn't been able to fade.

An older woman at the cash register was shelving cigarette packs as we walked in, and she smiled when she saw us. She didn't know our names, only our faces, but we'd been coming in once a month for a few years now.

As Ainsley headed to the pharmacy counter, I wrestled a buggy from its corral and set to shopping. The pharmacy was small, the aisles so narrow two people could barely stand side to side, and every space on the shelves was full of merchandise. I'd already put the kitty litter and cat food in the buggy when Ainsley found me in the peanut butter aisle.

She held up her bag, its receipt stapled to the top, and smiled. "Success. Safe for another month."

We'd been coming here for many years so she could anonymously buy her birth control pills under a fake name (for which she even had a license), and she paid cash, full price, as well. If she had her way, we would've taken her fake prescription (I didn't ask questions) down to Birmingham, but the four-hour round trip was too much to explain away.

I was fairly certain Carter knew what Ainsley was doing. Fairly.

Being a pastor's wife had placed her in a precarious situation, despite the fact that Carter's church held no negative positions on birth control. The people within the church, however, had many opinions on the subject, all of which Ainsley had to listen to at length. For her, this subterfuge was simply a matter of privacy—one that Ainsley took very seriously.

"Thank goodness," I joked, grabbing two jars of peanut butter from the shelf.

She gave me a playful nudge as I wheeled the buggy down the aisle. I'd turned down the next aisle to grab a new toothbrush and nearly hit the woman blocking the way.

"Sorry!" I cried. "I didn't see—" I went silent as I recognized the woman—and the item she held in her hand.

"Angelea?" Ainsley said, automatically shoving her bag behind her and into her pocketbook as if Coach's wife had X-ray vision. "What are you doing here and not at . . ." She trailed off when she saw what Angelea was holding.

Crimson that matched her hair flooded Angelea's face. "Hey. I, uh . . ."

My gaze didn't leave the blue box in her hand. A pregnancy test.

I immediately tapped into her energy to see if I could feel two, and was surprised that there was another energy present, strong and healthy. I hadn't picked up on it earlier, probably because I'd been so focused on Angelea's anxiety.

Anxiety that I now understood a whole lot better.

Angelea was pregnant. A little boy, if I was reading the energy correctly.

Yet she'd told me that Coach couldn't have children of his own. . . . My eyes flew open wide as the realization hit.

This wasn't Coach's baby.

Angelea watched me carefully, and she swallowed hard at my facial reaction. She had to know the conclusion I'd reached after our earlier conversation.

No wonder she was here at Bixby's—she'd come for the same reason as Ainsley. Anonymity. Except, unfortunately for her, we'd run into her—almost literally.

Her gaze darted around as she dropped the pregnancy test into the basket on her arm. "I, uh, should go. I best get home and get supper on the table before Floyd notices how long I've been gone."

Ainsley said, "Home? You didn't hear what happ—Ow! Carly!"

I'd stomped on her foot. If Angelea hadn't heard that Coach had been arrested for assaulting me, I didn't want her hearing it from us.

"Happened?" Angelea said, color still high in her cheeks. "What happened?"

Ainsley coughed and said, "Happened? Nothing happened."

"But you said . . ." Angelea frowned.

"So," Ainsley said, deflecting. "You think you're pregnant? That would be wonderful!"

It was my turn to cough. I wasn't sure how wondrous Angelea deemed this monumental event.

Angelea looked like she wanted to melt into the 1950s linoleum. "Yes, it would be," she murmured. "I should go. If you two could . . ." She wiggled her hand so that we'd move aside.

Ainsley stepped back just as someone said, "Well, I'll be! What are y'all doing here?" Behind Angelea, Emmylou Pritcherd came flouncing down the aisle, her own pharmacy bag in hand. "It's like a regular Hitching Post reunion in here."

Her gaze went from face to face and finally to Angelea's basket, where that bright blue box practically transmitted look-at-me waves like a homing beacon.

"Oh!" Emmylou said, covering her mouth with her hand.

I tried to cut off any comments by saying, "What are you doing here, Emmylou?"

She held up her pharmacy bag. "Just picking up some

medicine for Dudley's stomach." To Ainsley and Ange-lea, she said, "He's been feeling puny lately. The doctor said it was an ulcer."

"I'm surprised you didn't go to Huntsville," I said, as Angelea shifted nervously on her feet.

"Dudley's cousin works at the clinic here in Rock Creek. We always come here. Why are y'all here?"

"Carly needed kitty litter," Ainsley blurted. Then added, "The Hitching Post market was out." She shrugged.

"Did y'all come together?" Emmylou asked, her gaze once again on that blue box.

"No," Angelea said, "and I was just leaving. I need to get home."

Ainsley and I parted to let her squeeze through, but she faced a new obstacle: Dudley.

"Darlin'! What are you doing in here?" Emmylou said. "You were supposed to wait in the car."

He cleared his throat as he glanced from Angelea to the item in her basket. It may as well have been ticking like a bomb set to explode. "I came to see what was tak-ing so long." His eyebrows dipped, his cheeks colored, and he couldn't take his gaze off that pregnancy test. "What are all y'all doing?"

I wondered at his strange reaction. Was it possible he had been having an affair with Angelea? Emmylou had hinted that Coach's wife wasn't over Dudley. . . . I didn't even dare look at Emmylou, afraid of what her expres-sion might be. "Shopping," I said cheerfully as though there weren't tension as thick as glue.

"Kitty litter," Ainsley mumbled.

"But we're finished now," I said, giving Angelea a nudge.

"Right," she said. "I have to go." Giving a little wave,

she hurried down the next aisle, headed for the cash register.

"I have to get back, too," Ainsley said.

"Me, too," I added, though I had nowhere in particular to go. I finally glanced at Emmylou. Her eyes were blank, and there was a bright smile on her lips. I had a feeling she was holding in an emotional hissy fit, but I definitely didn't want to read her energy to find out for sure.

Ainsley gave me a push to get going, and said, "I hope you're feeling better soon, Dudley." He murmured his thanks, and as we headed to the register, she leaned into me and said, "That was weird, right?"

"Right," I said.

At the counter, Angelea was still paying. We got in line behind her as the clerk said, "Do you want to pay cash, Mrs. Butts, or add it to your husband's account?"

Two things struck me at once. One was that Angelea came here often enough to be known by name (which meant that Ainsley was going to start dragging me back to Birmingham), and the other was that this was the kind of place that still ran tabs. That was amazing in this day and age.

She glanced over her shoulder at me. "The tab, thanks."

The clerk slid a slip of paper and pen to Angelea. "Just sign here."

As I watched Angelea sign her husband's name, a small pit formed in my stomach. How often did she sign Coach's name? If it was a lot, she could probably produce a good replication. She slid the paper back, said a few more words to the clerk, grabbed her bag, and headed for the door.

I had to act quickly before she walked out. I casually

(yet loudly) said to Ainsley, "How about this Nelson Winston business? Did you hear that Nelson had a hand-writing analysis done for the upcoming trial? The report was sent to his house just a couple of days ago. . . . The police haven't found it yet, but I heard they were going to be searching his house until dark tonight."

Angelea paused a step before walking out the door.

The clerk looked at me like I'd grown two heads, and Ainsley gave me an eye roll. "Subtle," she said.

I loaded my items on the counter. "I had to do some-thing," I whispered.

"Something, like what?" Ainsley asked. "I can't for the life of me figure out what you're up to."

"Laying a trap," I said as I paid and gathered my items.

"For?"

As we walked out into the warm evening, I said, "An-gelea, of course. I bet she signs her husband's name real well. She could be our embezzler."

"Could be," Ainsley said. "But what if she bites? What's the next step?"

"To stake out Nelson's house, of course. If she's guilty of the embezzlement, she'll want to know what that re-port says. Do you want to go on the stakeout with me?" I set my bags into the back of the Jeep.

"As much fun as that sounds, I don't think I can. It's family night tonight. But you'll fill me in?"

"Definitely."

As we climbed into the Jeep, I spotted Dudley and Emmylou coming out of the pharmacy. Emmylou still wore that same bright smile, and Dudley looked more ill than ever.

Again, I wondered about the father of Angelea's baby.

And if Coach had any idea that his wife was carrying someone else's child . . .

Because if he did know and had gone into a jealous rage, that might explain how the sleep potion I'd given Angelea had come to be poisoned.

It had been meant for Angelea—to kill her.

But that still didn't explain how Nelson had ended up drinking the potion.

ᴔ Chapter Twenty-three ᴔ

The phone was ringing as I walked into the house after dropping off Ainsley. I set my bags on the counter and grabbed up the receiver.

"It's Dylan," he said.

The tone of his voice set me immediately on edge. "What's wrong?"

"Coach escaped from the jail."

My stomach plummeted. "He what?"

"He went ballistic when he found out that his getting arrested again would revoke his original bail and send him back to jail until his trial. He overpowered one of the guards and took off. We have men looking for him, but I wanted to let you know right away."

My hands began to sweat. I knew why Dylan had called—he feared that Coach would come after me again.

I feared the same thing.

I was also afraid he'd go after Angelea. "You need to send someone to warn Angelea as well."

"Warn her why?"

"I think she was the one the poisoned potion was meant for."

"Because it was in the bottle she bought?"

"No," I said. "Because she's pregnant with someone else's baby."

There was a long pause on his side of the line before he said, "You'd better explain."

I told him about Angelea's and my conversation earlier, what had happened at the pharmacy, and how I'd read Angelea's energy and confirmed her pregnancy.

"Is it possible the baby is Coach's?" he asked.

"Angelea told me that he couldn't have children because of a complication of his diabetes."

"But maybe that diagnosis is wrong. After all, she did get pregnant once before."

Right after high school graduation, which was why she and Coach married in the first place. "Supposedly. Don't you remember the rumors that she faked that pregnancy to trap him? Plus, she told me it had been many months since she and Coach . . ." My face heated. "You know. The baby's energy is only that of a one- or two-month-old fetus."

"I'll go see Angelea myself about the coach situation. You may want to spend the night at your parents' place."

"And put them in danger? I don't think so."

"Don't be stubborn about this, Carly. Coach is dangerous."

As if I needed the reminder. "I'll find somewhere to go."

"Do it soon, Care Bear. I'll be in touch."

I hung up, my nerves on edge. Where on earth was I going to go? I didn't want to put anyone I knew in danger, but I also couldn't stay here.

As I headed upstairs to pack a bag there was a knock

on the back door. I froze, momentarily scared that Coach had come knocking, but then I realized how ridiculous that was. I spun and went back into the kitchen. I swished aside the curtain and was very surprised to see the woman standing on my back steps.

The look on her face was more sad than menacing, so I cautiously opened the door. "Miz Morris? What're you doing here?" I kept my tone firm and used my body to block the doorway so she couldn't force her way inside. I hoped she hadn't come here to do her brother's dirty work.

"I heard what happened earlier, between Floyd and you, and I wanted to make sure you were okay. It's not like Floyd to be so . . ." She shook her head. "He's not himself these days."

I grabbed onto my locket, letting it warm in my palm. I assumed she hadn't heard about the jailbreak yet, and she probably hadn't considered that he might have tried to kill his wife. "I'm fine, thank you."

"And I wanted to give you this," she said, holding out her hand, palm up. A silver key rested against pale skin.

"What's that?"

"The key to Nelson's house."

"I don't understand."

"I don't really expect you to." She looked off to the distance, then refocused on me. "I worry with Floyd's arrest this afternoon that the police will stop looking for any other suspects in Nelson's death and pin the murder on Floyd."

"Why would they do that?" I asked.

"Because it's the easy thing to do," she sneered. Beady eyes narrowed on me. "You made me an offer this morning. I'd like to take you up on it. I'd understand if you have no desire to prove Floyd is innocent, but, as you said, if he is innocent, someone else is getting away with embezzlement . . . and murder. Nelson kept all his important files and papers at home, hidden under the floorboard in his bedroom. They're locked in a safe, so you'll have to figure out how to get it open. I didn't tell the police because . . ."

I could easily follow her train of thought. "What if it turns out that Coach is guilty of one crime or the other. Or both?"

Her lips pursed. "My first inclination is to protect him, but if he's truly guilty, then I suppose he has to face those consequences."

I wondered if his altercation with me this afternoon had changed her opinion of her brother, because as of this morning, she had been steadfast in her belief of his innocence. "Why not tell the police now? Why give this to me?"

"I'm afraid that if you find that handwriting report and it proves that it wasn't Floyd's signature on those checks, then they'll hide the evidence to wrap up this case."

"Dylan Jackson is as honest as honest can be," I said. "He'd never bend the law like that."

"Maybe. Maybe not. I'm not trusting many these days. Take it," she said, holding out the key.

"Why don't you go yourself?"

Suddenly tears filled her eyes. "I can't go in there, knowing what happened to him. . . . I have to go. Maybe it was a mistake coming here. I just didn't know where else to turn." She spun to leave.

I stepped outside. "Give me the key."

Wordlessly, she handed it to me and then walked quickly away. I watched her go for a few minutes before going back into the house.

I stared at the key I held.

It could possibly be the key to solving this whole case.

Or, my cynical side warned, it could be the key to setting a trap for me.

I'd have to be careful.

Very careful.

I called my parents to let them know what was going on,
then packed a bag, dropped Roly and Poly off at Mr.
Dunwoody's (he'd graciously agreed to keep them for
me), and headed for the Ring. My housing options were
limited, but I finally decided where I'd be safest.

But first, a stop a Déjà Brew, then the market.

I needed provisions.

The bell on the door jangled when I entered, and
when Jessa looked up her eyes flew open wide. She
rushed right over to me and wrapped me in a hug.

"I heard what happened earlier." She held me at arm's
length. "You okay, darlin'?"

"I'm fine. Just a little bruised."

She shook her head. "I'd never have thought it of
Coach. He's done lost his mind." She settled me in a
chair. "Coffee?"

I nodded. "And some treats to go. Lots of them."

Bribery never hurt anyone, and I planned to use the
goodies to help my cause. I wasn't entirely sure that I'd
be welcomed at the place I wanted to stay tonight.

The news that Coach had broken out of jail obviously
hadn't hit town yet, as Jessa hadn't pumped me for information, and there was no hum beneath the usual chatter.
I, however, was very aware. My leg jiggled nervously, and
I moved my seat to face the door. As I adjusted, I felt a

pinch in my pocket from the charm Delia had given to me earlier.

I was at odds with myself for not having thrown it away.

A hex was a hex, and I'd vowed never to use them.

But protection was protection, and with Coach out of jail, I couldn't be too careful.

If push came to shove, I wasn't sure I'd be able to use it. And if that was the case, the hex was more dangerous to me carrying it around than not. Because it gave me a false sense of security.

From behind the counter, Jessa gathered up treats and said, "Talk is going around town that Coach might have had something to do with Nelson's death, after all. I personally don't believe it. But do you think that's true?"

"I don't know, Jessa. I honestly don't know what to think."

Her eyebrows dipped. "It makes no sense to me if it was him. And why kill Nelson in *your* shop? Surely not because of a ten-year-old grudge."

I shrugged. I really didn't know. Nothing made sense.

"I haven't been hearing too much else. Nothing about any girlfriend Nelson may have had. And no one with any beefs against him, either."

I was starting to get a headache. "My coffee, Jessa?"

"Oh! Coming right up, darlin'."

The bells rang out on the door, and I nearly jumped out of my skin. Caleb Montgomery rushed in, his gaze landing on me immediately. He dragged a hand over his dark hair and let out a breath.

"I've been looking all over for you." Worry filled his blue eyes as he sat across from me.

"You found me." I fidgeted, unable to sit still with the way my nerves were acting up.

He leaned in. "You heard about Coach?"

I nodded.

"You need somewhere to stay? I have that cabin in the woods...."

"Thanks," I said, "but I think I have a place here in town."

"Where?"

I told him.

He leaned back and laughed. "You're serious?"

"No one will think to look for me there. Especially Coach. He's not the brightest bulb."

"Don't underestimate him, Carly."

No, I shouldn't. I'd done that before, and I hated to think of that outcome if Emmylou and Dylan hadn't been around. I'm not sure at all that my stapler would have done a bit of good against his hard head.

"Why not get a hotel room out of town?" he asked.

"I have something to do tonight."

"Like what? You shouldn't be out and about with Coach on the loose."

I bit my nail. "Can I ask you a legal question?"

Rolling his eyes, he said, "Dear Lord, Carly. What are you planning?"

"Is it considered breaking and entering if you have a key?"

He thumbed a crumb from the Formica tabletop. "Do you have permission to enter the house?"

"By the owner?"

"Of course. Who else?"

"No, not the owner, seeing as he's dead."

Caleb held up a hand. "I don't want to hear any more."

"Does that mean you don't want to come with me tonight?"

"To break into Nelson's house? No. I'd like to keep my law license, thank you."

"Is it breaking in, though? I have a key."

"Yes, it's breaking in if he didn't give you permission!"

Jessa appeared and set a big bag down on the table, along with a to-go cup of coffee, its lid askew. She squeezed Caleb's shoulder and said, "Your usual?"

He shook his head. "Actually, I can't stay."

She wiggled her eyebrows. "Hot date?"

"A blind date," he said. "So I don't know about hot."

"You should let me set you up," I said.

"No," he answered, standing up.

I looked up at Jessa. "He knows I'll have him married with babies in no time."

He shuddered.

Jessa laughed. "There are worse things."

"Death, maybe," he said. "Listen, Carly, if your plans don't work out for tonight, call me, okay?"

"Yes, sir." I gave him a salute.

He scowled and walked out.

"Do you have a hot date, too?" Jessa asked. "With Dylan?"

"No," I said, pulling money from my wallet. "And what was with sending him over to my place?"

She smiled slyly. "You're not the only one who can matchmake around here, Carly Hartwell."

"You're wasting your time."

"We'll see about that. We'll just see about that."

❦ Chapter Twenty-four ❧

The house I stood in front of was tucked into a clearing surrounded by dark woods on all sides. The home itself, though, looked the picture of quaint mountain living. It was small one-story post-and-beam home with a steep-pitched roof dotted with skylights. It had a large stone chimney on one side and a screened porch on the other, and flowering shrubs and plants filled the front garden with color. The late-day sun added an extra golden glow everywhere I looked.

I could hear the rushing water of the Darling River behind the house as I parked Bessie Blue in front of a small black SUV and grabbed the bags out of the basket on the front of the bike. I hitched my overnight bag onto my shoulder, followed a stone path to the front door, and knocked.

Yapping filled the air as an icy blue eye peeked out the front door's sidelight. I thought I saw that eye roll just before the door swung open.

"What are you doing here?" Delia asked, scowling.

She wore long black lounge pants and a black tank

top, and I was beginning to wonder if she owned anything of color. Her locket swung slightly and she took hold of it, wrapping her long, slim fingers around the silver orb.

Boo bounded outside and danced around my feet. At least one of them liked me. "I thought it was time I got to know my cousin a little bit better." I held up a bag. "I brought fixin's for supper. Steak and potatoes and corn on the cob. I'll cook. And Jessa sent cake for dessert."

She leaned against the doorframe as I bent to pet Boo's head. "What are you *really* doing here?" she asked.

I straightened. "Coach Butts attacked me earlier and was arrested, but he broke out of jail about an hour ago. I need somewhere safe to stay tonight in case he comes after me again, and I can't imagine he—or anyone—would think to look for me here. Can I stay the night?"

As she bit a nail, she searched my face.

I was beginning to wonder if she was about to slam the door on me when she said, "What kind of cake?"

"Triple chocolate fudge."

She held open the door. "Come on in."

Cautiously I followed her inside, Boo hot on my heels. Delia closed the door and took the food bags from my hands.

I found myself frozen in place, staring. The house was much bigger than it appeared from the outside. Like most post and beams, a popular design in this area, it was an open layout, with the living room blending into the kitchen, a small dining room, and a sun porch. A short hallway disappeared off to my left and probably led to one or two bedrooms and a bath.

The space was cool, light, and bright. The skylights let in plenty of sunshine, and most everything within the house, except the wooden floor and the beams, was crisp white. It was stunning. Absolutely beautiful in its serenity and peacefulness.

"What's wrong with you? Why are you just standing there?" Delia asked. "You have supper to make."

"It's nothing. You just keep surprising me, that's all. Next thing I know, you're going to tell me that you don't even have a broomstick that flies."

"Flying broomsticks are so last century, Carly. Get with it."

"I don't know how I'm going to get over this. I thought for sure you lived in a dark, Dracula-type castle and slept in a coffin."

There was a hint of a smile on her face as she said, "You haven't seen my bedroom yet."

I thought I knew her well, but clearly I didn't know her at all. "Well, there's plenty of time for that. Except I do need to go out later." I was banking on Angelea Butts breaking into Nelson's house after dark. If she had already gone there, I was going to be sorely put out.

She set the bags onto a pale granite countertop in the kitchen. "Well, that makes two of us who're surprised. You're not exactly someone I'd ever thought to find on my doorstep."

I swallowed what little pride I had and said, "Thanks for taking me in."

She unpacked the bags. "Don't make more out of it than it is. I was hungry. No human I know can resist Jessa's triple chocolate fudge cake."

I was about to make a crack regarding my doubts about Delia being human, but in light of her opening her home to me, I held my tongue. A small miracle. I helped her unpack groceries. "Your house is gorgeous."

I bet she didn't have critters chewing *her* wiring.

"Thanks. Where do you have to go tonight?"

"I could tell you," I said, "but then you might be charged as an accessory or coconspirator or something if I get caught. It probably wouldn't make me a very good houseguest if I got you arrested."

Her eyes narrowed. "You're serious?"

I nodded.

"Is this about Coach Butts? Are you going to burn down his house?"

I set my jaw. "No, I am not going to burn down his house."

"You don't need to take that tone. It's not like you haven't done it before. I heard about that one chapel you burned down."

"That was an accident!"

"If you say so." She set the steak in a glass dish and sprinkled the meat with seasonings. "Do you want to cook this inside or out on the barbecue?"

"Out," I growled.

She smiled sweetly. "I'll fire up the coals."

I watched her walk through the sunroom and out a set of patio doors that led to a deck on the back of the house. Through large kitchen windows that overlooked the river, I could see Delia fussing with a bag of charcoal. I glanced down at Boo. "How do you live with her?"

He wagged his tiny tail.

As I wrapped potatoes and ears of corn in foil, I was wondering how I was going to make it through the night here. I hadn't quite considered that coming here posed its own dangers. Delia's and my whole relationship was a Pandora's box that was better off kept closed. Tightly. The cause of our family's split lay between the two of us.

It was a lot of weight for us to shoulder, and until now we'd done our best to ignore it and go our separate ways. But over the past couple of days I'd seen more of Delia than I had in years.

And I couldn't help but wonder what our relationship would be like if she had been born first. Would we be the best of friends? Would I have chosen to make hexes?

The hex she'd given me still sat snug in my pocket. Now was the perfect time to give it back to her, but every time I thought about doing so, I could see Coach's face. And murder in his eyes.

Delia came back inside and said, "It'll be a few minutes till it's ready."

I tipped my head. "Why did you come see me yesterday morning? Why warn me about the danger I was in? We barely know each other. Why do you care?"

"Why are you here?" she countered, her ice-blue eyes softening. She scooped up Boo. "We're family, Carly. Families should take care of their own, even if they don't like each other much."

I traced a vein in the granite with my fingertip. "I don't *not* like you," I said begrudgingly. "I just don't really know you."

"And what you do know of me you don't like."

Well, there was that. "I could say the same of you."

"True. Yours is a difficult shadow to live in. Plus, you have everything, and I . . . Well. My mama has run off to be with a crazy man, and I own a business based on the misfortune of others."

I was about to argue, but I suddenly realized what she said about living in my shadow was probably true. "But at least you never burned down a chapel. Accidentally."

From a cupboard she pulled a bottle of wine. "Or poked Patricia Davis Jackson with a pitchfork."

"She deserved it."

"I have no doubt of that." She poured two glasses and pushed one my way. "She's come to see me more than once to buy a hex to put on you."

My jaw dropped. "She has? What did you do?"

Delia smiled and held up her glass in a toast. "Sold her one, of course. Money is money." Then after a second, she added, "A placebo. Family is family after all."

Family *was* family. I wasn't sure we could ever be friends, but it might be time to close ranks between us. I held up my glass. "To getting to know my cousin better?"

After a long second, she nodded. "To getting to know my cousin better."

Supper had long been eaten, the dessert plates licked clean, and the dishes washed and put away when I decided it was time to head over to Nelson's. The sun was about to set and it would be fully dark within an hour. I expected Angelea to show up not long after.

Even though I didn't want to go alone, I had my witchy senses to guide me, and if I felt like I was in any kind of danger, I wouldn't take any chances.

My mama hadn't raised a fool.

Delia said, "Are you sure you're not planning to burn down Coach Butts's house? You're acting awful antsy."

I dug through my pocketbook, looking for the key Bernice had given me. I could've sworn I put it in here. "I'm sure."

Boo was nestled in the corner of the couch, flat on his back with his tiny paws in the air. He snored softly, and I suddenly wanted to stay home and get a good night's sleep.

I dumped my bag upside down and shook it.

"You should probably clean that thing out once in a while."

"It's my portable office," I said, sorting through receipts and written reminders I'd never followed up on.

"What are you looking for?"

I stood up and searched my pockets, finding only the hex Delia had given me. "A key. I didn't drop it around here, did I?"

She helped me look around. "A key to what?"

I brushed my hair off my face and let out a breath. "Nelson's house. I'm going to break in and wait for Angelea Butts to show up to find the handwriting analysis Nelson ordered for Coach's trial that will supposedly show Coach is innocent. Bernice Morris gave me a key, but now I can't find it."

Delia held up a hand, palm out. "One, why would Angelea want the analysis, and how do you know she'll be there tonight? Two, why would Miz Morris give you a key? Three, is it breaking in if you have a key? And four, how were you planning to get to Nelson's?"

I lifted my index finger. "Because I suspect that she might be the real embezzler, and I laid a trap when I saw her earlier." I added my middle finger next to my index. "Because she wants me to prove that Coach is innocent." I lifted my ring finger as I made my third point. "According to Caleb Montgomery, it is." And finally lifted my pinky as I said, "I'll ride my bike over. But now all that planning has gone to waste since I lost the key. Maybe I dropped it at Jessa's. Can I use your phone to call over there?"

"No need for that." Delia walked over to a kitchen drawer, yanked it open, and pulled out a set of keys. "I still have a key to Nelson's house; he gives them to all his girlfriends. And I'll drive us over there. Your girly bike is not made for the hill he lives on."

I let the "girly" comment slide. "Us?"

"Yes. You shouldn't go alone. I'm not sure I trust Bernice Morris's intentions."

I couldn't argue with her reasoning. I'd been worried about the same thing.

"Plus," Delia added, "I know where Nelson keeps his important papers and the combination to the safe."

My jaw dropped. "You do?"

She shrugged. "Unless he changed the combo. But even then, I have a way with locks."

I really didn't want to know how she'd stumbled upon that talent.

She grabbed her cape and two flashlights, and jangled the keys as she headed for the door. "Are you coming?"

She left me with little choice. "Okay, but breaking and entering and possibly getting ourselves arrested wasn't quite the way I thought we'd get to know each other."

"Carly, we've never been a normal family."

Truer words had never been spoken.

❧ Chapter Twenty-five ❧

Nelson didn't live all that far from Delia's, maybe two miles as the crow flies, but the road was steep and laced with switchbacks. Thanks to the sheer drop into the ravine on my right, I nervously held my locket as we climbed upward. I couldn't help but wonder why there weren't guardrails lining this whole road and was suddenly grateful for my money-pit, critter-infested house in town.

Delia had been right—my bike never would have made it up here. Even if it had, my lungs wouldn't have. I never realized how far up this hill Nelson lived.

"There's a logging road just past Nelson's house. We'll park there, out of sight," Delia said.

Darkness had fallen. Clouds covered the moon and stars, making the night black as tar. Delia's high beams cut through the worst of it, but the light against the trees cast eerie shadows across the road.

My witchy senses were twitching, and I was beginning to rethink this plan. "We should go back."

"But we're almost there. It's just around this bend."

"I have a bad feeling."

She glanced over at me. "How bad?"

I was surprised she understood my feelings meant real trouble, until I remembered her dreams.

No, our family was far from normal.

"On a scale of one to ten, a four and a half."

"That's not *too* bad."

"It's bad enough that we should turn around."

She slowed as we drove past a house, a gorgeous multilevel post and beam perched high above the river. Security lights lit the wraparound porch and driveway, but all the immense windows were as black as the night sky. "That's Nelson's dream house. He handpicked every beam that went into that place."

It was a showstopper, and clearly he'd invested a lot of money in it. Which made me wonder again why he wanted that job in Birmingham so badly. The big city was too far to commute to every day—he wouldn't have been able to live here.

His motivation had to be something big.

I ruled out money—he clearly had enough and had never seemed the greedy type.

Was someone blackmailing him to leave town? Who? And why? Something to do with the trial?

Love, maybe? Did his mysterious girlfriend live in Birmingham?

There were frustratingly few answers.

Delia drove onward, and about a quarter mile down the road she turned left onto a gravel road and parked the car. "Do we stay or do we go?"

I could see Nelson's lights through the trees. Just knowing that there could be answers to some of my questions inside his house lured me toward it. Those lights . . . they beckoned.

Yet my witchy senses were still tingling. Danger was in the air. But not enough to keep me from Nelson's safe. "We go."

We kept to the tree line and headed toward his porch, two moths drawn to the light. I just hoped we weren't being lured to our deaths.

I shook that thought from my mind. This was no time to be thinking like that.

Humidity sat heavily in the still air, punctuated by the cries of owls in the distance, the snapping of twigs, and the incessant chirping of nighttime bugs. But every once in a while, all would go silent. Deathly quiet. Exhaling could be heard several feet away.

Chills swept up my arms and down my back. Keeping a hand on my locket, I moved a little closer to Delia, who led us along the dark street. She clearly knew her way around the property well and moved surely and quickly.

Wooden stairs creaked as we stepped onto Nelson's front porch. Delia slipped the key into the front doorknob, and the tumblers turned easily, clicking loudly as they released.

The door opened soundlessly.

We rushed inside and closed it, both of us pressing our bodies against the wood as if expecting the door to fly open behind us.

The glow of the outdoor lights spilled in through the windows. We stood in the great room, which had definitely been furnished with a man's tastes in mind. Large, sleek leather sofas, armchairs done in solid fabrics, heavy wooden tables. No knickknacks or clutter.

Dylan had said the place had been ransacked, but there was no evidence here of that. Everything was neat and tidy in its place.

There was an utter stillness in the house, and it brought immediately to mind a line from "'Twas the Night Before Christmas."

Not a creature was stirring.

Not even us.

I hardly dared breathe. My back was pressed flat against the oak door, and Delia gripped the doorknob so tightly her knuckles had turned white.

The good news was that my witchy senses hadn't jumped off the scale. There was still a sense of danger in the air, but I felt relatively sure that threat wasn't in this house.

"Where's the safe?" I whispered. "We might as well crack that open while we're waiting for Angelea."

"Do you really think she's going to show up?" Delia finally released the doorknob. "You couldn't have been more obvious at the pharmacy."

I'd told her all about my trap over supper. "Honestly, I'm not sure. I don't think Angelea would suspect I'd bait her, because we're friendly, and she isn't known for her smarts, either."

"But if she is the embezzler, then she's smarter than anyone has given her credit for, isn't she? She's had half the town thinking her husband was guilty. Why would she let him take the fall? Do you think he knows she's the guilty one?"

"I have a feeling Coach doesn't know half of what his wife is up to." I hadn't told Delia about Angelea's baby. She'd certainly been catting around, and I couldn't help but imagine Dudley as the baby's father. He had been acting guilty earlier.

It was a shocking revelation. Dudley had always seemed so devoted to Emmylou. But maybe I was wrong.

I hoped I was wrong.

For Emmylou's sake.

"Where's the safe?" I asked.

"His bedroom. Upstairs."

I started for the steps and noticed Delia hung back. There was a strange look on her face that had me worried. "Are you okay?"

"I'm . . . it's just . . ."

Ah. It must be very difficult for her to be in this house. I kept forgetting that she'd had an attachment to Nelson, and suddenly I was angry with him for dumping her. Obviously she had been quite smitten with him. "I can get the safe and bring it down here to you. Just tell me where it is."

She shook her head and wisps of white-blond hair flew all about. "You can't. It's built into the floorboards. I'll be fine." She took a tentative step forward.

"Do you want me to hold your hand?" I offered.

"Don't be ridiculous."

I smiled. It was nice to hear a little fire in her voice. We crept up the steps. At the top, a long open hallway, like a catwalk, led to the master bedroom to the left, and a short hallway to the right led to guest rooms.

We tiptoed along the catwalk, and I hoped we couldn't be seen through the windows. There were dozens of them, floor to cathedral ceiling, and all resembled big black (square) holes. Of course, to be seen, someone other than raccoons would have to be outside. Which was unlikely, considering we hadn't seen another person since we'd turned onto the street leading up to Nelson's. His house was as private as private could get without being gated. The only other people who came up this way were loggers and hunters—and neither would be out this time of night.

Of course, Angelea could be out there ... waiting to break in. If she saw us, she might turn tail and run, which would defeat the whole purpose of this night.

Figuring out what was in Nelson's safe was only a bonus.

"It stinks to high heaven up here," Delia said, flicking on the flashlight as we entered the master bedroom.

It did.

Delia drew up her cape to cover her nose. "What is that? Oh!" she cried as she swept the beam of light over the room.

It was the scent of sickness. Nelson had clearly been violently ill.

From the poison in the potion bottle.

I covered my nose and mouth with my hand and forced myself not to breathe through my nose.

Tears filled Delia's eyes. "What happened to him? Why does his room look like this? He's a neat freak."

Beyond the evidence of sickness, the room was a mess. Drawers upended, clothes and papers everywhere.

"Nelson was poisoned," I said softly. "And Dylan said someone broke in and trashed the place."

"I don't understand," she mumbled. "His head ..."

"I don't understand, either. Apparently someone bopped him to make it look like he died that way."

Dazed, she shook her head.

I said, "Where's the safe?" I had to keep her focused on why we were in this room. The sooner we could get out of here, the better.

She walked over to a corner of the room, crouched down, and pressed on a knot in the pine floorboard. A section of planks popped up. She pulled those out of the way and aimed the flashlight downward.

Well, I'll be. A large safe was nestled under the floor, the combination spinner facing upward. She leaned downward and spun the dial this way and that. After a second, the door released.

I dropped down next to her as she opened the safe's door wide. She reached in and slowly started pulling out items. Cash rolled in bundles, many files, and a small black ring box. She stared at that last item for a long second before cracking the box open. A large diamond ring was snug inside a velvet layer.

Delia swallowed hard and stared at the ring.

I clicked on my flashlight and held it between my chin and collarbone as I flipped through the files, looking for anything that resembled a handwriting analysis. I didn't have to look far.

"It's here," I said.

"What?"

"The report."

"Oh."

I leaned over and pried the jewelry box out of her hand and slammed the lid closed.

"Who do you think he was going to give it to?"

I could see the heartbreak in her eyes, hear it in her voice. "We may never know. But I do know he wasn't the right man for you."

"And just how do you know that?" she snapped.

I shrugged. "He let you go."

Her jaw jutted. "He'd clearly lost his mind."

"Undoubtedly."

After a second, she said, "What's the report say?"

"It's from some fancy forensic handwriting expert." I

skimmed the page. " 'Blah, blah, blah, based on the samples sent, blah, blah, it has been determined that the samples do not match.' "

"What's that mean?"

I flipped through the rest of the report. "I think it means that Coach didn't sign those checks."

"Does that mean Angelea did?" Delia asked.

Just as the words left her mouth, light swept across the room. We inched our way to the window and looked out. A car had pulled into the driveway. The driver stepped out of the car and looked around.

Angelea Butts.

"I'm guessing yes," I said.

I quickly folded the report and tucked it into my shirt. We stuffed everything else back into the safe and replaced the floorboards.

Delia glanced at me. "We need to hide."

"Not in here." It was undoubtedly where Angelea was going to look. Plus, it reeked.

"Across the hall. Come on." She grabbed my hand and yanked.

"I thought you didn't want to hold my hand."

"Hush!"

We were on our way out the bedroom door when the clouds shifted and moonlight spilled into the room, and glinted off an object on the nightstand. I wiggled my hand free.

"What are you doing?" Delia asked.

"Just a sec." I tiptoed over to the bed and aimed the flashlight downward. I didn't dare pick up the object, but I knew immediately what it was.

A lavender-colored stopper to one of my potion bottles.

It was the stopper to the sleeping potion bottle I'd given Angelea. . . .

With fresh eyes and a new understanding, I looked around the room. It suddenly dawned on me that the place hadn't been ransacked at all—instead it looked like someone had come in and cleared their stuff out in a hurry.

Someone like Angelea. Bits and pieces were finally starting to make sense in my head.

"Carly, come on. She's coming." Delia walked over and grabbed my arm again, dragging me out.

We were on the catwalk when Angelea's shadow fell across the front windows. We'd just made it to the other side when we heard the key in the lock.

Delia froze and I bumped into her. "What?" I asked.

"She has a key."

I barely had time to register that before the front door swung open and Angelea slipped inside. Delia and I scurried into the hallway bathroom.

My chest was pounding.

Angelea had a key.

What Delia had said earlier at her house came back to me: "I still have a key to Nelson's house; he gives them to all his girlfriends."

Angelea and Nelson. This reinforced the conclusion I'd just come to. They had been a couple.

I glanced at Delia.

Her mind must have been spinning in the same direction, because she lurched forward. "Oh, hell, no."

I grabbed her arm and pulled her back down, but she wriggled free and charged toward the stairs. I reached for her foot, and she went sprawling on the landing.

"Let me go!" she cried.

From downstairs, Angelea yelled, "Who's up there?"

Delia had just squirmed her way loose when the front door flew open, and Dylan Jackson strode in and cut on the lights.

His eyes went from Angelea at the foot of the stairs to Delia frozen midway down the steps, and me flat on my belly at the top. His gaze narrowed on me.

My witchy feeling went from bad to worse.

Much worse.

Chapter Twenty-six

Delia and I sat on the bottom step, nibbling our nails, while Angelea fidgeted in an armchair across the room. Dylan paced the length between us.

He kept shaking his head and muttering under his breath, and I was fairly sure I didn't want to know what he was saying.

I was still shaking *my* head about how he'd ended up here. Apparently Dylan had been worried about not being able to reach me, and he'd contacted Caleb, who'd ratted me out without a second thought. There would be payback. Soon.

"Tell me again about this trap you set?" Dylan said to me.

I'd already told him twice about seeing Angelea in the pharmacy and realizing she could probably sign Coach's name better than he could himself. I ran through it again, and didn't miss the fire in Angelea's eyes as she looked at me.

"I reckon Carly's supposition was right," Delia said,

spitting her own fire, "since Angelea broke in here, looking for that handwriting report."

I'd already turned the report over to Dylan.

"I didn't break in," Angelea said smugly. "I have a key. Nelson gave it to me."

In a flash, Delia came off the step in a lunge, and I grabbed her arm and pulled her back down.

Angelea smiled a satisfied grin; she was verbally staking her claim on Nelson on purpose to get under Delia's skin. It was the equivalent of saying, "Nyah, nyah. I won and you lost." It made me want to yank her hair out by the roots in support of my cousin.

Her little quest to prove she was the fairest in the land had a catch, though. A big one. "Why did Nelson give you a key, Angelea?" I asked.

I already knew, but Dylan had failed to ask her as of yet.

She glanced at Dylan and her smile faltered. "Because of the trial . . ."

Even Dylan rolled his eyes at her lie. He said, "And why'd you come here tonight?"

She tucked a strand of her red hair behind her ear. "I, ah, was driving by and saw someone moving around in here."

I never realized how good a liar she was. Until now. I'd had enough. I'd pieced together a lot since I'd been sitting on this step, but I needed Angelea to confirm some details and clear up some hazy spots.

"Here's the real deal," I said to Dylan, then glanced at Delia, feeling a pang for her. I didn't quite know where we stood in our relationship, but I knew I didn't want to hurt her any more than she already was. "Maybe you should wait outside."

"I'll stay," she said stubbornly.

"You're not going to like what I have to say."

Delia pursed her lips. "I'll stay."

"Can *I* go now?" Angelea asked.

"No," Delia, Dylan, and I said in unison. She huffed and crossed her arms over her chest.

Dylan said, "Go ahead, Carly. Say your piece."

"Angelea has a key because she was seeing Nelson."

Delia threw me a disgusted look. "You mean 'sleeping with.'"

"I was trying to be tactful," I said.

"This here is no time for tact, Carly. Call it like you see it. She's a tramp."

This time it was Angelea who came out of her chair and lunged at Delia. Dylan grabbed her and guided her back to her seat.

"Anyway," I said loudly, "they had a relationship. For a few months now, at least. They were planning to run off with each other to Birmingham." I bluffed about that part—it was pure conjecture on my part (well, on Caleb's part, really), but when Angelea didn't argue, I figured I'd guessed right.

Tears filled Angelea's eyes but didn't spill over. She whispered, "We loved each other," and it was probably the only honest thing she'd uttered all night.

"But then," I went on, "a couple of things happened. One is that Nelson couldn't quite tie down the job he wanted in Birmingham. It was Johnny Braxton who'd recommended him to that fancy law firm, right, Angelea?"

She nodded. "But your aunt wouldn't sell her inn to Nelson. He was going to keep trying, but then . . ." Biting her lip, she fell silent.

"Then," I filled in, "Nelson got the handwriting analysis that proved Coach was innocent. Most likely, he came to the same conclusion I did about Angelea, and broke up with her."

"That's not how it happened." Angelea sniffled. She glanced at Dylan. "I'm not saying I did take that money, but *if* I had, I might not want to start a new relationship with a lie and might have confessed to Nelson."

By phrasing it that way, she had all but just confessed to us that she *had* taken the money.

"After he already figured out it was her," Delia mumbled, setting her elbow on her knee and her jaw in her hand.

"Why take the money in the first place?" I asked.

Her red hair stuck out wildly. "If I had, it would have been to escape this town and get away from Floyd once and for all."

"But you'd let him take the blame?" Delia asked.

Angelea stiffened. "Don't judge till you've walked a mile in my shoes." She stared out the window. "I was all set to pack my bags and leave town when Nelson took Floyd's case. I fell for him hard." She sniffled. "We planned to get married. Until he got that damn hand-writing report. We had a big fight, and he said he needed some time to think."

I glanced at Delia out of the corner of my eye and wondered if she, too, was thinking of the engagement ring upstairs. I said, "Johnny Braxton and Nelson had a big argument the day he died. Nelson told Johnny he was no longer interested in the Birmingham job.... I'm guessing that's because being with Angelea was the only reason he wanted to move away ... and he was no longer interested in being with her."

Delia said hopefully, "So she killed him! A woman scorned."

"Nooo," I said.

Delia tried again. "Killed him because she didn't want to go to prison?"

"Nooo," I said.

"Killed him for—"

"I didn't kill him," Angelea interrupted loudly. "We talked about it. He promised he wouldn't turn me in. He planned to clear Floyd's name in court and return the money anonymously. All the fuss would have been forgotten in a couple of weeks. He loved me! He would have come back to me eventually. Especially when he found out about—"

"What?" Dylan asked, dragging a hand down his face.

"About the baby," I said. "Angelea's pregnant with Nelson's baby."

Delia's eyes flew open wide and her whole body stiffened.

Angelea glared at me.

"What?" I asked. "Do you deny it?"

She went back to staring out the window. "Does it matter now? Nelson is gone. Someone killed him. . . ."

"You?" Delia asked.

Angelea whipped her head around. "I told you it wasn't me!"

"Well," I said. "Maybe not on purpose . . ."

"What's that supposed to mean?" Angelea snapped.

"I'm curious myself," Dylan said.

"Correct me if I'm wrong," I said to Angelea. "But you probably spent a lot of time here, right?"

She nodded.

"Probably kept some of your belongings here, right?" I prodded.

"Some."

I looked at Dylan. "I don't think this place was ransacked by someone looking for something. It was trashed by Angelea. She found out Nelson had died and rushed over here and collected all her belongings before someone realized that she was Nelson's girlfriend. She was in a hurry and made a mess. Right, Angelea?"

She nodded.

"Where are you going with this?" Dylan asked me.

"One of the items she collected was the sleeping potion I made her. Coach doesn't like her getting potions, so she once told me that she hides them in her car and at her friends' houses. In this case, I think the sleeping potion was here. The stopper is still upstairs."

"So?" Angelea said, her brow wrinkling.

Dylan's eyes widened with understanding.

"For some reason, the night Nelson died," I said, "he drank that potion."

"He doesn't really believe in the whole potion thing, but he hadn't been sleeping well, so he decided to try it," Angelea said, looking between me and Dylan. "Why does it matter?"

Ah, this explained why she was flustered in my shop earlier. She knew exactly why the potion bottle Coach found had been empty, but she couldn't tell me why without giving up her double life with Nelson.

Dylan said, "That potion was poisoned. It's what killed him."

Angelea gasped and covered her mouth with her hand. "That's not . . . That's not possible."

"Had you drunk any of that potion yet?" Dylan asked her.

She shook her head. "No . . . The day I got it is the day I realized I might be pregnant. I didn't want to take it just in case it wasn't safe for the baby. I was waiting to tell Nelson until I knew for sure, but then that handwriting report came in, we had a big fight, and then he . . . he died." Tears spilled down her cheeks.

Delia said, "So, was someone trying to kill Nelson . . . or Angelea?"

I'd been debating the same thing. "I think Angelea was the intended victim."

Delia stood up. "I think I'll wait outside now, before I say something I might regret later. I'll get the car and meet you out front, Carly."

I nodded and watched her walk out.

Dylan crouched in front of Angelea's chair. "Is there any chance that Coach found out about your affair with Nelson?"

"I don't think so," she mumbled, her eyes glazed. "He would have confronted me about it. He has no filter lately. He did go ballistic when I asked for a divorce last week." Her nose wrinkled and fresh tears filled her eyes. "Do you think Floyd tried to kill me because of that?"

"I don't know," Dylan said. "It's possible. If he knew you wanted out of the relationship, he might have wanted it to be on his terms."

His deadly terms. I shuddered at the thought. He could have tampered with the potion before she brought it to Nelson's. She suspected someone had been following her. . . . If Coach had seen her going into my shop for the sleeping potion, he might have hatched his evil plan then and there. It also explained why Nelson's body had been found in my shop—because Coach hated me and blamed me for his troubles.

I bit my nail. But it certainly didn't explain how Coach knew Nelson had drunk the poisoned potion or why Nelson had also been hit in the head with a bat . . . or how Coach got Nelson's body into my shop.

Or—and this was my biggest question—why Coach had accused me of poisoning him after he crashed into my porch if he was the one to put the poison in the bottle in the first place. Was he simply trying to frame me? Was it his delusions at work?

I sighed. I supposed those were questions for Dylan to ask Coach . . . when he found him.

"Let's call it a night," Dylan said. "You both need to lie low, though. Coach is still running free, and if what we're guessing is true, then he might have it out for both of you."

I glanced at Angelea. "Do you have somewhere safe to stay tonight?" I wasn't about to offer up Delia's place, but I wanted to make sure she was out of harm's way.

She nodded. "A friend's house in Rock Creek."

"I'll follow you there," Dylan said, "to make sure you get there safely."

"Thanks," she mumbled.

Dylan ushered us outside, and Angelea climbed into her little hatchback. Delia's SUV idled on the side of the road, and I started toward it before I felt a hand on my arm, pulling me back.

Dylan's eyes were in shadow as I turned to him, his fingers hot on my skin. "Be careful," he said.

I tugged my arm out of his grasp. I said, "I will be."

He sidestepped a bit and light fell across his eyes. The raw emotion I saw there nearly knocked me to my knees.

Cupping my face, he said, "I'm not sure I could bear losing you for good."

Tears suddenly stung my eyes. I wanted to yell that I wasn't his for the losing, but my chest ached so badly that I could barely whisper anything at all. "I'll be careful."

And as I walked to Delia's car, I wasn't sure whether I was talking about staying safe from Coach or protecting my heart from Dylan.

Chapter Twenty-seven

"What was that about?" Delia asked as soon as I slid into the passenger's seat.

"What was what?"

"The way Dylan was looking at you. The way you were looking at him."

I glanced out the window. Dylan was getting into his sheriff's cruiser. "I don't know what you're talking about."

She slipped the car into drive, and Angelea pulled out behind us as we started down the steep hill. "If you say so."

"I say so."

Flipping on her high beams, she said softly, "Do you really think the baby is Nelson's and not Coach's?"

The bright light made the road a bit less scary, but not by much. In the side-view mirror, I noted that Dylan had pulled out behind Angelea. It was quite the little parade we had going on. Dylan's voice was ringing in my head, and I fought to silence it. "I think so." I told her about how supposedly Coach wasn't able to have kids, and how she and Coach hadn't had much of a marriage recently.

"But there's still a chance the baby might be Coach's?"

"I suppose."

Her silhouette bobbed as she nodded. "Good."

"Is it?" I asked.

"Isn't it?" she countered, frowning as she adjusted her rearview mirror.

"Call me crazy, but I'd much prefer a little Nelson running around than another Coach."

She bit her lip. "I suppose you're right, but it just . . . The thought of it . . ."

"I know," I said. And I did. I'd often lain awake at night, torturing myself by imagining a time when Dylan would find someone else, get married, and have kids. It had been like a searing-hot knife to my heart. I'd been lucky—my dark flights of fancy had not become reality. Delia's had.

I'm not sure I could bear losing you for good.

Delia glanced into her mirror again and frowned.

"What's wrong?" I asked, peeking back.

"Angelea is following a little too close for my liking."

She was. In fact, she continued to speed up. "What's she doing?"

There was a hint of panic in Delia's voice as she said, "I don't know." She pressed on the gas, but going fast on this road, with the sharp curves and no guard rail, was a death wish. "Is she crazy?"

I peeked back again. The lights on Angelea's car were too bright to see inside the vehicle, to catch a glimpse of her frame of mind. "I'd tap into her energy, but I'm afraid all I'd pick up is yours."

"Try!"

I let down my guard and immediately felt pure panic and desperation come over me. "I think she's scared."

"Then why doesn't she slow down?" Delia cried as we rounded a corner, tires squealing.

The lights atop Dylan's car came on, and flashes of blue and red colored the night. I saw him try to speed up next to Angelea, but the road was too narrow, and the drop-off on the other side too terrifying to contemplate.

"Is there anywhere to pull over?" I asked, fear taking root in the pit of my stomach.

Her hands gripped the steering wheel. "Not here. Down a little farther there's a scenic overlook."

Shadows fell across our path as we flew down the road. I looked back and wished I hadn't. "She's going to hit us! Go faster!"

"I can't!" Delia took another corner, and I watched in horror as Angelea veered off toward the cliff, only to swerve back onto the road.

"I don't think she can stop." My heart raced, and I found myself holding my breath with each curve we encountered. "She almost went off the edge just then."

"What do you mean, can't stop? Why wouldn't she be able to stop? Do you see any smoke? Did she burn out her brake line?"

I could think of only a few reasons and none of them were good. "There's no smoke."

Dylan followed closely behind Angelea, practically on her bumper.

"Hold on!" Delia cried, taking another corner. Tires and brakes screeched loudly.

I grabbed onto the door handle as the wheels on the driver's side came off the ground for a brief second before hitting the pavement with a loud thud.

Glancing back, I saw Angelea's car fishtail before she

gained control of it again. But as we lurched downhill, her car gained speed.

"She's going to hit us!" I yelled.

Suddenly, we jerked forward as Angelea's car banged into the back of us, and I knocked my head on the windshield. The crunch of metal on metal split the air. Delia swerved hard right and braked, but the force of Angelea's momentum kept us going forward.

Dylan managed to get the nose of his car next to the rear of Angelea's, like a bookend. I could hear the *bang, bang, bang* of her car hitting his as we careened down the road.

Angelea's car came loose from our bumper and swerved right toward the woods before veering back onto the road.

"Oh no," Delia said.

"What?" Then I saw. The steepest part of the road. A tight turn where going more than ten miles an hour would be dangerous.

I swallowed hard.

Delia said, "Brace yourself." She braked hard and steered right, hugging the trees.

Angelea's hatchback rammed into us with a jarring crunch, pushing the SUV, and I all could think about was that little baby. . . .

Jerking the wheel, Delia somehow managed to keep us on the road. We'd just made it around the corner when Angelea's car tore loose from ours and hurtled to the right, into the woods.

Delia slammed on the brakes. I reached for the door handle and watched in horror as Angelea's car hit a rock and flipped over with a gut-wrenching crunch of metal and glass. It skidded into a stand of trees, where it finally came to a stop on its top, its headlights beaming into woods that would never, ever look the same to me.

My legs buckled when they hit the ground, but I grabbed on to the door to keep from falling. Sirens bellowed in the distance, and I realized that Dylan must have radioed for help as soon as he realized there was a problem. He angled his car so his headlights lit the crash scene, and I saw him now, running toward the hissing car.

I followed him, stumbling along. Delia reached out and grabbed my arm to steady me, and I flinched, not even knowing she'd been beside me. I glanced at her and saw a dazed look in her eye—one I'm sure she saw in my own.

Dylan knelt on the ground, and I could hear him shouting into the car but couldn't make out his words.

Dark smoke poured from the engine. My breath caught as the car shifted and sparked. Flames burst out from the hood.

Unconscious, Angelea hung upside down, supported by her seat belt. Blood gushed from a wound on her head. Flames crackled.

Dylan said, "We've got to get her out of here. The seat belt . . . I can't reach the release." He tried to shimmy inside, but the space was too narrow for his frame. "I need my knife from my car."

Delia said, "I'll get it." She sprinted off.

There was another pop and more flames shot out.

The sirens closed in.

I dropped next to Dylan. "I'll go in."

"No."

The flames were working their way into the cabin of the car, creeping along the dashboard. Thick smoke clogged my throat, stung my eyes. "There's no time! Grab hold of her."

I glanced in the car, trying to figure out how to go about this, and realized the best way was to approach from the other side.

I quickly ran around the car, pulled my locket over my head, and tossed it a good distance away. If I ever lost it inside that car . . . I didn't even want to think about it.

I fell to my knees, slid onto my belly, and worked my way through the broken passenger's window.

Emotions slammed into me. Mostly fear.

It was probably my own.

Heat blasted my face; flames licked my skin. I had limited visibility, so I reached out to feel for the seat-belt release button. My fingers brushed Angelea's hand, and I couldn't help the shudder that rippled through my body at how lifeless she had felt.

Metal scraped my skin as I pushed my way in a little farther. I followed the seat belt on Angelea's lap to the release and pushed for all I was worth. The belt gave way, and Angelea immediately dropped down. Dylan had hold of her upper body, but her legs had knocked me into the dashboard.

I yelped at the heat and jerked backward, trying to back out. I felt hands on my feet, then my knees, tugging.

Wincing against the pain, I worked my way out, and as soon as I was free took a deep breath of air. Before I knew what was happening, I was being pulled—dragged, really.

The car burst into a big ball of flames, the explosion busting out the rest of the windows. A blistering heat cloud flashed over me. The hands were there again, pulling me backward, toward the street. Toward safety. And, finally, to the ground.

Shaking, I sat and wiped the soot from my eyes.

Emotions pummeled me. Anxiety, fear, love. *Love*? I reached for my locket, then remembered that I'd tossed it aside. Panic rose in me as I realized the heat from the car would surely melt the silver. I went to stand up to find it, but a hand tugged me back down, and in my palm my locket appeared.

I looked at the person sitting next to me. The person who'd saved me.

Delia closed my fingers around my locket. "Hold it tight."

Slowly, I nodded and sank back down next to her. I looked around and saw Dylan yards away, hovering over Angelea's body.

"He got her out in time," Delia said. "Thanks to you."

A sheriff's cruiser swerved to a stop, followed closely by an ambulance and a fire truck. More help, certainly, was on the way.

Dylan looked up, searching the area until he found me. He held my gaze.

Love.

An EMT knelt next to him, and he broke eye contact.

Delia gave me a nudge. "I know exactly what he was thinking just then."

"What's that?" I said thickly.

Her teeth flashed as she smiled. "He was thinking that if you thought your hair looked bad before, you should see it now." She wiggled her eyebrows like Groucho Marx.

I threw my head back and laughed. I laughed until I cried.

Then I just cried.

Chapter Twenty-eight

It turned out that Delia hadn't needed to share her guest room with me. I'd spent the night in the emergency room at Pape Medical Center in Huntsville, with my mama, daddy, and aunts Hazel and Eunice hovering over me like a bunch of mama hens protecting their chick. Marjie had declined to come, on account that she hated hospitals. I didn't blame her one bit. If I'd had a choice, I wouldn't have been there, either.

I'd been released just after dawn, and my aunts were driving me home. We'd already dropped off Delia, and it had been quite the production explaining why she'd been with me in the first place.

I was fine. A few bumps, scrapes, and cuts were all. Nothing a little salve and a potion or two couldn't take care of.

Unlike Angelea.

She was in the ICU, clinging to life. So far the baby was clinging, too, but the doctors didn't have high hopes that either would survive much longer.

Aunt Hazel swerved into my driveway and slammed

on the brakes. I had a flashback to the night before and gave myself a mental shake.

Aunt Eunice chided her sister for her reckless driving, which started an argument that could probably be heard into the next county about who was the better driver. Wincing, I shoved open the back door, yelled, "Thank you for the ride!" and slammed the door closed.

They were still arguing as I climbed the back steps. I, unfortunately, caught my reflection in the glass of the back door. Delia hadn't been kidding about my hair. My freckled face was scraped and red from the heat of the fire, and soot clung to the skin on my neck, the roots of my hair.

I needed a long, hot bath. A good soaking that would hopefully dissolve the bad memories along with all the dirt.

My aunts peeled out of the driveway, their bickering carrying on the wind.

I reached up above the doorjamb for the spare key and slid it into the lock. I slipped inside the house, hoping that Coach was long gone out of town and not sticking around for more retribution.

Just in case, I took my pitchfork from the broom closet and suddenly realized how quiet it was in the house. Mr. Dunwoody still had Roly and Poly, but this quiet went beyond that. Then it hit me. There was no hum coming from the fridge, no whir from the ceiling fan.

I cut on the lights, only for them to remain dark.

My power was out again.

I grabbed the phone, and it, too, was dead.

The critters in the wall had declared war, and I was ready to wave a white flag. It had been one of those weeks.

With a heavy feeling of dread, I realized my plan for a hot bath was out the window. I couldn't stay here. I'd pack some clothes and head . . .

Where?

I was still in the same sinking boat I'd been in the day before. With Coach on the loose no one was safe.

I'd just have to go back to Delia's. Resolutely, I trudged toward the stairs and stopped dead in my tracks once I stepped foot in the living room.

"Can I shoot him?" my aunt Marjie asked.

My gaze whipped to Coach Butts, who cowered in the corner near the front door.

Marjie was perched on the edge of the couch, her shotgun aimed squarely at Coach's chest. By the panicked look in his eye, they'd been here for some time.

"I saw him sneaking round your house in the wee hours and caught him breaking in. I should've shot him on the spot, but I wanted to make sure you wouldn't mind the mess beforehand. Can I shoot him?"

Coach's eyes went wide. Sweat dripped down the sides of his face and darkened the fabric of his shirt. "She's crazy!"

He was a fine one to talk about crazy.

Marjie cocked the gun. "What did I tell you about using that word?"

"Call the police!" Coach cried, tears streaming from his eyes.

I shrugged. "Can't. Phone's dead."

Marjie chuckled. "Ain't that a shame? Can I shoot him now?"

"Let me think a second." On one hand, he deserved what he had coming to him. On the other, I'd just painted the wall. I tapped my fingers on the pitchfork. As I inwardly debated, I heard a door slam. I peeked out the window. "Dylan's here."

"Dang it all," Marjie grumped. "Ain't no way he's going to let me shoot him."

"You might be surprised," I said. "After what happened last night."

"How're you feeling?" Marjie asked. "You look a sight."

"I'm okay."

"What happened last night?" Coach asked.

I threw him a dirty look. To Marjie, I said, "If he tries anything, shoot first; ask questions later. I've got more paint, so don't worry none about the mess. I'm going out to talk to Dylan."

Marjie's eyes brightened, and Coach kept saying, "What happened?"

I met Dylan on the back steps. He winced when he saw me.

"That good, huh?" I said, sitting down, propping the pitchfork on the railing.

He sat next to me. "Could be worse."

That I knew. "Any word on Angelea?"

"What's with the pitchfork?" he asked, eyeing it warily.

A ruckus rose from within the house. "Help! Help!" Coach yelled.

Dylan stiffened. "Who's that?"

"Coach Butts."

"What?"

Crows flitted from tree to tree. "Marjie's got her gun on him. Apparently he broke in here sometime during the night, and she's had him cornered since. She's itchin' to shoot. Can we let her? Pretty please?"

"As much as I love it when you look at me like that, no. Why didn't she call for help?"

"My phone's dead again. The power's off, too."

He cursed under his breath.

"Tell me about it. I was planning on a long, hot bath." His eyes darkened, and I felt a blush rising up my neck.

"Does she have him under control?"

"Oh yeah. He's crying like a baby. Angelea? How is she?" I reminded him before I could do or say something I'd regret.

"Same," he said.

"Did you find out why her brakes didn't work?"

"Someone cut the brake line. There was a little fluid on her driveway—she probably lost the rest on the way up to Nelson's."

"Wouldn't she have realized her brakes were going?"

"Maybe. It's an older car, so she might have thought it was just being temperamental. We might never know."

"Help! Help!" Coach yelled again.

I was surprised Marjie was showing such restraint. Me? I'd probably have shot him already.

"I'll radio for backup," he said, walking to his truck.

"I think Marjie's the only backup you need."

"Your family is . . . interesting."

"I know."

He made the call on his truck's radio, then came back over to the step and held out a hand to help me up. With me on the step, we stood eye to eye. Reaching out, he brushed a strand of hair behind my ear and let his fingers trail down my neck. My heart began thumping hard against my ribs.

"You scared the life out of me last night."

Love.

"I was careful," I whispered.

He leaned in, his gaze intent on my lips. Heaven help me, but I knew I couldn't resist. His lips had barely brushed mine when a shotgun blast split the air.

Dylan said, "Stay here!"

Like hell.

I followed him inside.

Coach lay in the fetal position on the floor, crying buckets of tears.

Marjie beamed from the couch. "It was just a wee little warning shot."

Buckshot dotted my wall like some sort of abstract art piece.

Dylan quickly cuffed Coach, and it was only a minute more before a sheriff's car screamed into my driveway. Two beefy deputies rushed into the house and dragged Coach away.

"Miz Marjie," Dylan said, shaking his head.

Patting his cheek, she said, "Someone's got to keep the law around here." She winked at me and headed for the back door.

"I've got to get to the jail," Dylan said. "But after that, I can come back and fix your power proper."

"Like last time?"

He smiled. "Proper enough until Jasper comes back. What'll you do in the meantime?"

"Find a bathtub that has hot water. Then go to work. It'll help take my mind off things. Plus, there are bound to be a lot of customers today, mostly looking for gossip, but they'll buy potions while they're there. I can use the business. Especially since I have a costly electrical repair ahead of me."

"Don't forget about the drywall work, courtesy of Marjie."

I glanced at him, thinking about what might have happened if Marjie had come seen me in the hospital. "Thank goodness for Aunt Marjie."

He nodded. "I should go. You need a ride anywhere?"

"No. I'll probably bother one of my aunts or Delia for a tub."

Dylan looked off into the distance, then back at me. "Coach won't be bothering you anymore."

"Promise?" I asked him. I glanced out the window. My witchy senses were still acting up, and I didn't know why.

He cupped my face with his hand. "Promise."

"I'm going to hold you to that, Dylan Jackson."

His expression turned somber and his voice dropped to a whisper. "I take my promises seriously, Care Bear. I don't ever break them. You, of all people, should know that."

I recalled him once promising to love me forever. . . .

Oh.

Love.

"Sometimes I forget," I murmured, my heart aching for all we had lost.

He nudged my chin, then started for the back door. "Then it's my job to help you remember. Isn't it?"

After a second, I said, "I guess so."

He pulled open the door. "I look forward to it."

As I watched him drive off, I couldn't help but think that I was looking forward to it, too.

Very much so.

≫ Chapter Twenty-nine ≪

There was nothing quite like the restorative power of hot water. It was Mr. Dunwoody who'd loaned me the use of his guest bath when I went to collect the cats. I'd taken a hot shower first to wash away the grime, then soaked my sore bones for an hour, having to refill the claw-foot tub twice to keep the water steaming hot.

I'd taken my time blow-drying my hair and dabbing on a little makeup to cover the worst of the bruises on my face, but had to use a bandage to cover the cut on my forehead. I changed into clean clothes, putting on my favorite green sundress to brighten my mood, and figured I'd burn the outfit I'd been wearing the day before.

There was one thing I kept from the outfit, however.

The vial pendant and necklace that had been in my pocket. For lack of a better place to put it before giving it back to Delia, it now hung around my neck, the vial tucked under the ruffled neckline of my dress.

Roly and Poly had been so spoiled at Mr. Dunwoody's that at first they didn't seem to want to leave with me. Then I reminded them about all the critters in the walls of our house they needed to catch, and they *really* didn't want to leave.

Finally, I'd bundled them into their carrier, thanked Mr. Dunwoody profusely, and forcibly taken the kitties home. Ordinarily, I'd bring them to the shop with me, but there was the issue of broken glass that I still had to clean up. I didn't want to risk their paws being cut.

They were home now, sniffing around the living room as if they knew strange people had been inside the house. I, on the other hand, knew there had been strange people in the house, so I was on my way to Déjà Brew for my morning cup of coffee.

If there had ever been a morning I needed caffeine, today was the day.

It was a little past eight when I walked into the coffee shop, the bells on the door chiming loudly. Jessa took one look at me, *tsk*ed, and came around the counter to give me a hug.

"She was in a car wreck last night," she said to the four customers in the shop, who all collectively *tsk*ed and blessed my heart.

Jessa smelled of vanilla and hugged me like Olive Debbs hugged her father's leg. I wriggled free and took a seat at the counter. "I'm okay."

She kept shaking her head, and not a hair in her rat's-nest bun jiggled a bit. "I couldn't believe it when I heard the news this morning. Coffee?"

"Please," I begged.

"And Angelea? Any news?"

"As far as I know she's still in the ICU."

"Good heavenly days!" She kept on *tsk*ing as she held the coffee carafe over a cardboard cup. I reached over to grab the lid so she didn't have to fuss with it. "And Coach?"

"Back in jail," I said.

She set down the carafe. "I heard Angelea was having an affair with Nelson and that's why Coach killed him and tried to kill her."

News traveled fast. I reached for the cup. "It's not that cut-and-dried. There's still some investigating to do."

It had probably been a mistake to come here, I realized. There was too much talk. Too much gossip. In light of that, it might be a mistake to open the shop today, too. The business would get by. . . .

I'd go clean up the glass, then decide. Technically, I didn't open till eleven on Sundays, so I had time to figure out if I was ready to face the public.

The front door flew open, the bells nearly flying off their string. I spun around to find Ainsley in the doorway, gasping for breath. "Hell's bells!" she cried when she spotted me, then slapped a hand over her mouth.

The coffee shop customers were getting quite the show this morning.

Ainsley gave a big smile and scooted to the counter. She took my face in her hands and examined each and every abrasion up close and personal. "Why didn't you call me?"

She gave me such a stern, motherly look that I almost called her ma'am when I said, "It was late. Then it was too early. Then my phone was dead. Sorry."

In a rush, she said, "I heard the news about the crash at church and ran straight to your house. Then you weren't there, but then I saw Mr. Dunwoody . . . so at least I knew you were alive. I'm never going to hear the end of it from Carter about running out the way I did."

"He'll understand," Jessa said, propping her elbows on the counter. "He knows how much you care for Carly."

"Eventually, maybe." Ainsley sat down and drew in a deep breath. "Can I get one of those, Jessa?" She motioned to the coffee. "To go. Now that I know Carly is alive, I need to get back to the church. I left the Clingons unsupervised, and that's never a smart thing to do. I'll come by the shop this afternoon and get the full scoop."

Jessa slid a coffee cup and lid across the counter. I slipped off the stool and pulled a five-dollar bill from my pocket, but Jessa waved it away. "On the house today. Oh, and I found this after you left last night, under the chair you were sitting in." She pulled a silver key out of her apron and handed it to me. "I tried to call you about it but no one answered."

It was the key Bernice had given me. "Thanks, Jessa. I was looking for that."

Affectionately, she patted my cheek. "Stop in this afternoon, Carly. Odell's making your favorite cookies, on account that you didn't die last night. Chocolate macaroons. "

"I'll try." I wasn't making any promises, though it was sweet of Odell to be thinking of me.

The bells on the door rang out as Ainsley and I stepped outside. She looked at me long and hard. "Do you need me to stay with you?"

"I'll be fine."

"You sure?"

"I'm sure."

"You wouldn't be lying to me, now, would you, Carly Hartwell?"

"Maybe a little."

"I'll be by straight after services." She squeezed my hand and marched off across the picnic green, passing Dudley and Emmylou on the way.

Dudley was busy with his metal detector, and Emmy-lou looked to be lecturing him on how to go about it.

I smiled; some things never changed.

While other things would never be the same.

As I unlocked the shop and went inside, I couldn't help but think about Bernice Morris. She'd asked for my help in proving Coach's innocence in the embezzlement case, and I'd actually done that. But in doing so, it had revealed him to be a killer.

I still had those questions about how Coach had known Nelson drank the potion—and how he'd gotten him into my shop. . . . I hoped Dylan was getting those answers at this very moment, because they were the only puzzle pieces that didn't fit nice and neat and proper.

What a mess. A hot mess, as Ainsley would say.

I set my coffee cup on the counter and wondered if I should give Bernice a call. I actually picked up the phone, only to set it down again. There were no words I could offer that would set her at ease. Or at peace.

Her brother was going to jail for a long time.

I rubbed my temples and glanced down the hallway at the shards of glass littering the floor. Cleaning up would keep my hands busy, if not my mind.

I had started toward the supply closet when I heard a knock at the front door. I spun and found Delia peeking in. I waved her inside.

Boo was nestled in the crook of her arm. "I brought your bike back. I might have to get myself one. Boo loved riding in the basket."

"A matching bike?" I asked.

"Don't be ridiculous. Blue is not my color."

"Well, I'm sure you can find one with a skull motif."

"If not," she said, "I have a stencil and can design my own."

I laughed. "I should have known."

"I have something for you. Here, take Boo." He licked my fingers.

"What's she up to?" I said to him, as she dashed out the door.

He wagged his tail.

"You're seriously too cute for your own good," I said, rubbing his ears.

Delia was back a second later, a broomstick in her hand. "Here. It's one of my favorites from my shop."

Tentatively, I reached out. The stick was gorgeous, a dark wood that had been carved into a spiral. The broom head was thick and lush and expertly woven. "It's gorgeous. Does it fly?"

Rolling her eyes, she said, "I already told you about that. But I thought no proper witch should be without one."

I wrapped my fingers around the handle. "Thank you."

There was a softness in her eyes as she said, "I should get going and open my shop."

"Wait a sec." I pulled the vial off my neck. "I need to give this back to you."

"I told you, it's yours." She gathered up Boo.

"I can't keep it."

"You're going to have to, because I'm not taking it back."

I sighed. "You're stubborn."

"It's a Bell family trait. I'll see you later." She pulled open the door.

"Delia?"

She looked back at me, a question in her eyes.

"I wanted to say thanks. You know, for what you did last night. I owe you."

Her eyes twinkled. "Enough to share the Leilara secret with me?"

"No."

She shrugged. "You can't blame a witch for trying."

As soon as she stepped out, Caleb Montgomery came in, throwing a look over his shoulder as Delia walked away.

"What was she doing here?" he asked.

"What, no 'How're you, Carly?' or 'I'm so happy you're alive, Carly'?" I *tsk*ed, sounding very much like Jessa as I set the vial pendant on the counter next to the cash register.

He folded his arms. "Of course I'm happy you're alive. Don't be ridiculous."

The phrase had me thinking about Delia. And him. Delia and him. *Hmm*. The matchmaker in me was at work.

"But really," he said. "What was she doing here?"

"Bringing back my bike. It was at her house. I'm sure you already heard what happened."

Caleb gazed at me, his eyes softening. "You could have been killed."

I appreciated that he didn't fawn all over me. I'd had my fill of smothering. "But I wasn't. Mostly thanks to Delia."

Tossing a look out the window, he said, "I don't trust her."

Okay, setting them up wasn't going to be easy. . . .

"Don't tell me you do," he added.

I shrugged. I didn't trust her. At all. Not yet. "I want to."

"Be careful what you wish for, Carly."

I rolled my eyes. "Is that why you came here? To lecture me?"

"Yes. And now my job is done." He kissed my cheek and headed for the door.

"Wait! How was your hot date?"

"Lukewarm."

"Good."

"What?"

I cleared my throat. "I said, 'That's not good.'"

He eyed me warily. "Eh. Another girl will come along."

I threw a loofah at him. "Get out of here before I sic Marjie on you."

Laughing, he ducked out.

Before the door could even close, a hand reached out held it open. For being closed, I sure was busy.

A bolt of surprise went through me as the man stepped into the shop. "What are you doing here?"

Johnny Braxton said, "I need your help."

❧ Chapter Thirty ❧

"If you're here about my mama . . . ," I started saying.

"I'm not."

"Or to confess that you're the one trying to buy my aunt Marjie's inn, I already know."

His eyebrows rose a bit at that.

"I saw you talking to John Richard Baldwin yesterday, and Angelea Butts also confirmed that you're the one who recommended Nelson to that law firm in Birmingham. You weren't happy when he quit that job, and that's why you two were fighting the other day."

He closed the door behind him. "You've been busy sticking your nose where it don't belong. And it shows, by the looks of you."

I gingerly touched the bandage on my forehead. "You don't know the half of it."

"I've heard most of it. Coach Butts in jail. Angelea near to dying."

I didn't want to go through it all again. "Why are you here? What's this about you needing help?"

I allowed myself to read Johnny's energy, because if

he was here to cause trouble, I wasn't in the mood. I let my defenses down and felt only neutral energy coming from him. Nothing bad; nothing good. Though his heart . . . I eyed his big barrel chest.

"Why are you looking at me like that?" he asked, stepping up to the counter, his boots clicking on the floor.

"Have you been having chest pains? Maybe it feels like indigestion?"

His hand went to his sternum. "No."

I rolled my eyes at his obvious lie. "Your arteries are clogged. You need to see a doctor. Sooner rather than later." My potions wouldn't be able to clear that much of a blockage.

"How do you know that?"

Sassily, I said, "I'm a witch, remember? Now, why're you here? I know it's not for medical advice."

He studied me, but not in the way he had the other night at the river walk, with a threat in his eyes. This time he looked at me more like I was a bug under a magnifying glass.

I truly didn't appreciate it, either.

I stood firm. "Mr. Braxton? Why are you here?"

He snapped to. "I've been thinking about what you said the other day."

"What did I say?" Dang if I could remember.

"About me finding a woman. It's time."

My mouth dropped open, and I snapped it closed. "You're serious?"

"As a heart attack."

"Interesting choice of words, considering your arteries . . ."

"You're not very subtle, Miss Carly."

"No one ever said I was, Mr. Braxton."

Looking around the shop, he said, "I'm in the market for one of your love potions."

I nearly laughed. "Maybe my matchmaking services might come in handy first."

"No need. I already have my sights set on the perfect woman."

I wasn't sure if I was happy for him or scared for her. "Who?"

He shook his head. "Not telling."

Probably so I couldn't warn her. "My love potions have contingencies," I said, explaining about the Backbone Effect.

"Sounds fishy to me that you can't guarantee the results. What kind of establishment are you running here?"

I set my jaw. "Do you want the potion or not?"

He wavered for only a second. "I'll take it."

I grabbed a red potion bottle from the wall and set to making the magical formula. Johnny watched me like a hawk through the pass-through.

"What are you doing in there?" he asked.

"Working."

I thought I saw his lip twitch. Or maybe it was a hallucination from bumping my head too hard last night.

I quickly wrapped the bottle, set the room back to rights, and set the boxed potion on the counter. "A little goes a long way. The directions are on the tag."

Handing over his credit card, he said, "I'll let you know how it goes."

As I ran the card through the machine, I thought I detected a derisive undertone to his comment. But when I glanced at him, there was no facial expression or look in his eye to substantiate what I thought I'd heard.

"Sign here," I said, sliding the paper over to him.

Chuckling, he said, "With prices like that, I think I'm in the wrong business."

I slid the potion box into a bag and forced a smile. I probably looked a little like the Big Bad Wolf when he first met Little Red Riding Hood. "Have yourself a good day, Mr. Braxton. You might want to consider walking really slowly home. Keeping your pulse low."

His hand went again to his sternum, and he frowned at me before turning around and striding out the door like a bull on a charge to prove some sort of point.

He can't say I didn't warn him.

I turned the Closed sign to Open, seeing as how no one was paying a lick of attention to it anyway, and set to cleaning up the broken glass at the end of the hallway.

From the supply closet I grabbed a broom (not my fancy new one), a dustpan, and a paper sack. I kept my gaze averted from the break room while I swept up shards of glass. I'd start the major renovation in there as soon as possible.

My mind was abuzz as I worked, flitting between Johnny Braxton and his mystery woman and everything else that had gone on in the past few days. As I bent to swish the pile of glass into the metal dustpan, I couldn't help but peek inside the break room.

It took no effort at all to conjure the image of Nelson on the floor in there, and though the floor had been scrubbed clean I could easily picture the pool of blood and exactly where it had been.

The glass made a beautiful tinkling noise as I dropped it into the sack. I sat on my haunches, staring into the little room and reflecting on why Coach had put him in there, reflecting on how he'd lost his mind. He probably had a good shot at an insanity defense, which kind of terrified me, thinking he might one day be let out, free to come after me again.

Standing, I shoved the broom into the tightest corners and dragged it backward. The cracks in the old wooden floorboards were being stubborn about releasing the tiny shards of glass. I set the broom aside and pulled the vacuum from the supply closet, attached the soft brush, and took great pleasure in hearing the bits of glass being sucked through the tube.

I was just about done when I spotted something glistening in the crack between the wooden floor and the baseboard. I ran the vacuum hose over it several times, but the object wouldn't budge.

Bending down for a closer look, I saw it wasn't a piece of glass at all. It was something shinier. Sterling or white gold or platinum. I shut down the vacuum and went in search of something long enough to poke the object out of its spot.

I snatched two pens from the cup next to the cash register and went to work on the shiny trinket. Poking this way and that, I tried to pry it out, but it was having none of it.

Sitting back, I tried to imagine what it was. Maybe something my grandma Adelaide had lost decades ago?

Excitement flowed through me at the prospect, almost making me forget about my troubles over the past couple of days. I had to free the bauble.

Inspiration struck while I stared in the supply closet. There was an old chisel in there, left over from who knew when. I grabbed that and the hammer. If the shiny bit wouldn't come out with the baseboard on . . . I'd just take the baseboard off.

I stuck the chisel into the crack between the baseboard and the wall, wedged it just so, and banged it with my hammer.

I eyed the result. Not so good. I'd lifted the hammer to bang it again when I heard the front door of the shop open.

"Carly?"

I glanced over my shoulder. "Hey, Dudley."

He came down the hallway and knelt next to me. "What're you doing?"

"A rescue attempt of an unknown shiny object." At his blank look, I clarified. "Something's stuck in the crack down there, and I want to get it out. Did you need something?"

"A healing potion."

I leaned back. His face was pale, his eyes troubled. I tapped into his energy and my stomach ached something fierce. "The doctor's treatment not working on your ulcer?"

"Not yet at least."

I nodded. "Give me a sec to get this thing out, and I'll make something for you. You'll be feeling better in no time."

"I, uh . . ." His cheeks flamed. "I'm sorry, Carly. For what I said the other day. I didn't mean any harm. I let the gossip go to my head."

"I should say sorry, too. For a day or so there I thought you might have had an affair with Angelea Butts. I'm sorry I misjudged your character."

"It's okay. I'm sure I looked guilty as sin. It's been difficult keeping the news of Nelson's and her relationship a secret."

"You knew?" I asked.

He nodded. "From the beginning. They'd both talk to me about it but swore me to secrecy."

"Did you know Angelea was the true embezzler?"

"No. If I'd known, I would have spoken up. Coach, well, he's not perfect by any means, as you well know, but he didn't deserve the hell he's been put through by being arrested, then finding out his wife wanted a divorce and had taken up with his lawyer. . . ."

Coach was a big jerk, but Dudley had a point. A lot of Coach's troubles had been brought on by someone else. Angelea. It didn't excuse his reactions, by any means, but it did make them slightly more understandable.

Not that I was going to forgive him anytime soon . . .

"Do you need some help?" Dudley asked, motioning to the bauble.

"Sure." I wedged the chisel behind the baseboard, shoving it down as far as it would go with the hammer. Then I leaned back, using the chisel as a lever.

Dudley grabbed the baseboard and pulled. A loud cracking noise filled the air and the board popped loose, sending him backward.

He laughed as he sat up and dusted himself off. I zeroed in on the shiny bit, which popped right out of the crevice with a little encouragement from the end of a pen.

I pulled it out and set it in the palm of my hand. It was a ring. A wedding band.

"That looks like . . . ," Dudley began, then fell silent.

I checked the inscription.

4-ever & 4-always

It didn't just look like Emmylou's wedding ring. It *was* her ring.

But what was it doing in my shop?

Chapter Thirty-one

W e were still sitting and staring at the platinum orb when the front door opened.

"Yoo-hoo!" Emmylou yelled. "What're y'all doing back there?"

I glanced at Dudley. His face wore no expression at all.

Mine, I was sure, looked confused as all get-out. She'd lost the ring on Friday afternoon ... or had she? I thought back long and hard to Friday morning, when I ran into her outside Mr. Dunwoody's house. Closing my eyes, I tried to recall if she'd been wearing her ring when she tucked her hair behind her ear.

She hadn't been. Her finger had been bare.

Which meant she had already lost her ring *before* her picnic later that day with Dudley.

She'd staged the whole scene of her ring flying off, probably using that tin ring I'd found on the picnic green as a decoy.

I could think of only one reason why she'd want Dudley to think she'd lost her ring that day and not before. ...

Because she'd lost the ring in my shop. When she left Nelson's body in here.

Puzzle pieces tumbled into my head, fitting neatly in place. It hadn't been Coach at all. . . . It had been Emmylou. *Emmylou!*

Swallowing hard, I stood up and wobbled a little, knocked off-balance by my thoughts. "Just cleaning up the mess Coach made yesterday. Dudley was kind enough to lend a hand."

Emmylou sashayed into the shop. "I couldn't believe the news when I heard it this morning. Is Angelea going to be okay?" Her voice dropped. "The baby?"

The ring grew warm in my palm as I squeezed it tightly. Dudley followed behind me and stepped up next to Emmylou, a dazed look in his eyes. My guess was he had come to the same conclusion I had.

"Nelson's baby, you mean," I said, watching her closely.

Her eyes flew open wide. "Nelson's?" she squeaked.

"Whose did you think it was?" I asked.

Sharply plucked eyebrows drew downward. "I-I'm not sure. I heard Coach couldn't have children, but I thought it some sort of miracle. . . ."

"You didn't know Angelea was having an affair with Nelson for months now? Dudley knew. He's been keeping their secret."

Emmylou's gaze flashed to her husband. Her face had gone as pale as his. "Of course I didn't know."

"No," I said, "because you thought Angelea and *Dudley* were having an affair, didn't you?"

I was slowly putting more pieces together. Emmylou had been worried about Dudley not loving her because of his performance problems and automatically jumped to the conclusion that he was having an affair. She had snapped, just as Coach had. Except she was smarter and more calculating.

Emmylou straightened. "What's all this about?"

I set the ring on the counter, where it spun in small circles before coming to a stop. "We found your ring while we were cleaning up the glass."

Her head snapped between Dudley and me.

I went on the offensive, hoping that if I talked fast enough, I could encourage her to make a confession. "You poisoned the potion I gave Angelea, but you didn't count on her suspecting she was pregnant and not drinking it. She left it at Nelson's, and when he couldn't sleep, he drank it. And when he was sick and dying, he called your house for help. You answered that call, didn't you, Emmylou? It wasn't a hang-up at all, was it?"

As if in a trance, she nodded. "He said he'd had some of Angelea's potion. . . ."

"You didn't think to question *why* he had Angelea's potion?"

She shook her head. "I wasn't thinking clearly. Nelson was in such pain."

Dudley gripped the counter.

I prodded. "So you went over there?"

"Dudley was asleep. I snuck out to . . ."

Oh, dear Lord. "To put him out of his misery?"

She nodded. "I had to. I'm not cruel, you know."

I wanted to laugh at the absurdity of that statement but managed to keep my cool.

"I knew he couldn't survive the poison," she said. "I managed to get him into my truck and . . ."

"You hit him on the head with a baseball bat," I supplied. No wonder her van had been so clean. And I bet she hadn't been looking for her contact lens the afternoon Ainsley and I saw her on all fours. She'd been looking for her ring. It also explained why she'd snuck back into my shop after the police had been here: She was still looking. Clearly, she didn't know for certain where she had lost it.

"I didn't want him to suffer," Emmylou explained.

My temper was rising. "Why did you put him in my shop? How'd you get *into* my shop? Where did that potion bottle in his hand come from?"

"Ainsley's keys. I stole them from her purse when she came in to check the menu for her boys' party."

"Wait a sec. That was before Nelson died. . . ."

"You're not very bright, are you, Carly?"

I'd been called many things, but stupid was never one of them.

"Emmylou," Dudley said.

She shot him a look. "Shut up, Dudley. I planned all along to put the body in your shop, Carly. Although I thought it would be Angelea's body. I'd seen her in here, getting her potion, and I couldn't abide the sight of her anymore. She had to go, and I knew just the way to do it. A way that would get at the both of you. I've been watching her as much as possible, just waiting for her to take the potion. . . ."

So Angelea hadn't been paranoid about someone watching her. I was surprised that Emmylou had never caught Angelea with Nelson. If only she had . . . maybe this whole situation would have been avoided.

If only.

"Emmy," Dudley said again, reaching out to her.

"Shut! Up!" she snapped, shaking off his hand.

Her gaze narrowed on me, and I'd never noticed the

hint of crazy in her eyes before. *Why haven't my witchy senses picked up on that?* I wondered.

"I had that violet potion bottle a while now," Emmylou said, "and I didn't plan on using it, but in my rush to get Nelson out of his house, I forgot to take the poisoned potion with me. I didn't dare go back for it—I wanted to minimize my presence in his house because of forensics and all. I'd been careful handling the poisoned potion, so I knew my prints weren't on it, and by using the bottle I had at home I still got my message about you across."

She sounded proud. Smug. My temper was rising. I wanted to cry out that the potion hadn't been poisoned—it was simply poison in the bottle. She'd left it behind at Nelson's, and Angelea, in a rushed attempt to cover her tracks at his house, had unwittingly put the murder weapon in the car, where her husband later found it . . . and ironically accused me of using it to poison him. It was quite the tangled web.

"If I hadn't been so flustered by it all," Emmylou said, "I would have put some strychnine in the potion bottle Nelson was found with." She shook her head as though chastising herself. "It was a crazy night. I wasn't thinking straight." Her eyes glazed a little as she added, "I had trouble getting Nelson in here—I ended up having to use my dolly from the truck to get him inside, and it was near impossible not to drip any blood, too. I had to wrap dish towels around his head, and he kind of looked like a mummy and that freaked me out a little. And then I realized I lost my ring somewhere, but I didn't know where. . . ." She gave her head a little shake, as though trying to break the creepy trance she'd been in.

Dudley and I stared at her in horror. No, she definitely was not thinking straight.

I pressed for more information. "What message was it that you wanted to send to me, Emmylou? What did I ever do to you?" I asked.

Sharply, she said, "This whole mess with Dudley is *your* fault."

Oh, hell, no, as Delia would say. "Mine? How so?"

"Your stupid potions. They don't work. You only say they do."

"They do when they're used properly," I said. "And why keep coming back for them if you don't think they work?"

"To keep up the charade. It might have looked suspicious if I suddenly stopped coming by. None of the potions you gave me worked." She stamped her foot. "Especially not your love potion! Dudley was supposed to love and honor me always."

"But I did, Emmy," Dudley said softly.

Her eyes narrowed, then widened. She shook her head. "No . . . You cheated. You got her pregnant!"

"I didn't," he insisted.

She'd woven a story in her head that she could no longer keep straight. It was obvious she couldn't grasp that she'd been wrong about the cheating. Because if she was wrong, all her actions had no reasoning behind them.

"So, what?" I asked. "You left a dying Nelson in your food truck and went home to get an empty potion bottle? Just for a little misguided revenge? That's plain sick."

"Don't you judge me, Carly Hartwell!" Her eyes blazed with fury.

"Oh," I said snidely, "I'm judging. You're touched in the head." I banged my hand on the counter like a judge's gavel. "Guilty! And you cut Angelea's brake line, didn't you?" I accused.

Color flooded her cheeks. "How dare she chase after

my husband? And then she gets pregnant with Dudley's baby, too? Oh, hell, no. That should have been *my* baby! I couldn't allow it. The poisoned potion didn't work out the way I'd planned, but I thought for sure the cut brake line would." She jabbed a finger at me. "I should have known you'd mess that up for me somehow!"

"It is Nelson's baby," Dudley said loudly.

But she wasn't listening. There was a distant look in her eyes as tears fell down her face. "My baby!"

She'd attempted to kill Angelea and her unborn child and instead unwittingly killed Nelson. All because of some psychotic attachment to Dudley.

I'd heard enough. I picked up the phone.

"What are you doing?" Emmylou cried.

"Calling the police."

"No, no, no!" She looked around and her gaze landed on the countertop. She snatched the vial pendant Delia had given me and ripped out the stopper. "Put the phone down. I don't know what's in here, but I know it's bad. I saw the way you reacted when Delia gave it to you. Put the phone down!"

I put it down as she waved the vial back and forth.

"C'mon, Dudley, we're leaving."

Dudley shook his head.

"Come on!" she shouted.

"No, Emmylou."

He'd picked a fine time to stand up to her. "Maybe you should go," I prodded him.

He looked at me like I'd grown two heads. He didn't realize that this wasn't going to end well unless he left with her. Then I could call the police.

I eyed the stapler, but Emmylou was pacing, and I didn't have good aim.

Outside the window, I saw John Richard Baldwin walk by. He glanced in, saw me, and waved.

I didn't know how to react. I didn't want him coming in, so I gave a friendly wave as if nothing out of the ordinary was going on in here.

Unfortunately, he took my wave as an invitation and pushed open the door.

Emmylou raged at him. "Get out! Get out! Get out!"

He stood frozen, just like he'd been in Aunt Marjie's yard.

When he didn't move Emmylou doused him with the hex, and he started screaming. "My eyes! My eyes!"

Dudley lunged for his wife, and she threw the hex on him as well. He dropped to his knees. "I can't see! I'm blind!"

She immediately fell next to him, telling him she was sorry. I quickly picked up the phone and dialed 9-1-1, leaving the phone off the hook so the dispatcher could trace the call.

John Richard stumbled over both of them, and they all ended up in a pig pile on the floor. I quickly grabbed the broom Delia had given me and pressed the handle into Emmylou's back.

"Don't move or I'll shoot!" I yelled.

Everyone froze. John Richard's whimpering filled the air. I reached down and grabbed the vial pendant from Emmylou's fist and let out a breath. It was empty.

Emmylou cried, "Dudley? Dudley? Where are you?" And I realized she must have gotten some of the hex on herself as well.

"I'm here," he said dully.

"Don't leave me," she cried. "Don't ever leave me."

～ Chapter Thirty-two ～

It had been nearly a week since the showdown with Emmylou in my shop. Mr. Dunwoody's forecast this morning had been cloudy with a chance of many weddings, which wasn't much of a stretch. It was a beautiful May evening, and the town was busy with tourists here for weekend weddings. Mama's chapel was booked solid through till Sunday night, and I hoped that meant she wouldn't have time for any more impromptu concerts.

Mr. Dunwoody's forecast last week had sadly proven true not just for one couple but for two; Coach and Angelea and Emmylou and Dudley. Coach had been cleared of the embezzlement and murder charges but would go to trial for my assault, breaking out of jail, breaking and entering, and a host of other crimes he'd committed against me. It would be a long time before he was free again, and I hoped he'd get some psychological help while he was locked up. He'd filed divorce papers from jail. I'd heard through the town grapevine that Bernice Morris had put her house up for sale and planned to use the proceeds to hire Coach a new lawyer. She was currently staying with a cousin just north of here in Tennessee.

The blindness from the hex splashed on John Richard, Emmylou, and Dudley had worn off within a couple of hours. Which was just about how long it took for Dudley to initiate plans for the dissolution of his marriage, but I wasn't sure Emmylou was even aware of that fact. She was currently in a psych ward being evaluated for an insanity plea after being charged with murder.

Dudley had been spending an awful lot of time at the hospital, too. But not to see Emmylou. He'd been visiting with Angelea, who was awake and out of the ICU but not completely out of the woods. Her baby, miraculously, was doing well. The doctors had gone from guarded to cautiously optimistic.

I didn't want to speculate on Dudley's motives, but I couldn't help but wonder if Emmylou hadn't been all that wrong about Dudley's feelings for Angelea. . . .

Mysteriously, the missing twenty thousand dollars had been returned to the baseball league sometime during the week, and I suspected Dudley had a hand in helping Angelea anonymously return the money. Last I heard, everyone, including Dylan, was willing to pretend the whole embezzling incident never happened.

John Richard Baldwin had been fired from the fancy Birmingham firm. Much to everyone's surprise, he'd moved to Hitching Post, and was in the process of setting up his own firm.

He claimed that he liked it here. Why, after what he'd been through, no one could quite decipher.

Birdsong filled the night air as I rode Bessie Blue home. Roly and Poly sat in the basket, with their eyes to the sky, as if hoping one of the birds would fall right on their paws.

I had to laugh at the thought, since they wouldn't know what to do with the poor creature if one did fall. The critters in my house had been evicted, thanks not to my two feline friends but to a local exterminator, who'd thankfully used humane traps to locate the generations of mice that had taken up residence behind my walls.

Jasper, my electrician, had taken pity on me and charged me a pittance for redoing all the electrical work in the house. Ordinarily, I wouldn't have accepted such a gift, but I'd had a hell of a week, and his generosity had nearly brought me to tears.

Streetlamps threw light across the cobblestones as I turned onto my road. It wasn't all that late, just a little after eight, but I'd closed up my shop an hour early.

Business was back to normal, better even than before, but being in the shop was harder than I thought. The comfort it used to bring me was gone. Ainsley kept telling me that it would eventually return if I just had faith. I chose to believe her, mostly because she threatened me with a switch if I didn't. And, well, the thought of closing the shop didn't sit well with me, either.

Down the road, I saw the shell of my new front porch taking shape. My daddy had pulled some strings with the local insurance company so work could begin right off. Sometimes it paid to live in a small town.

As I drove past Marjie's, I heard a laugh and slowed to a stop. I blinked a few times to make sure my eyes weren't deceiving me, but no . . . Marjie was sitting on her front porch with Johnny Braxton.

And she was laughing. Hand to God, she was.

"Evening, Miss Carly," Johnny said, raising his glass to me. He smiled wickedly and patted his shirt pocket before lifting a red potion bottle up just enough for me to see.

The lying dog had used the potion I'd given him on my aunt Marjie.

"Evening," I said through clenched teeth.

"Beautiful night," he said, "isn't it?"

Marjie smiled at me (actually smiled!), and said, "Get along with you now, Carly. Can't you see I'm entertaining?"

Roly and Poly looked back at me as if to ask why I'd stopped. I rather wished I hadn't, but as I pedaled toward home, I couldn't help but smile myself.

And wonder what game my aunt was playing.

Because I knew there had been nothing in that potion bottle but a little rose water.

My mama hadn't raised a fool.

I'd known better than to trust Johnny Braxton. I figured he deserved whatever Aunt Marjie had planned for him, but I wondered if she knew he was using her.

Eunice and Hazel were bickering as I rode past, and as I turned into my driveway, I wasn't the least bit surprised to see Dylan's truck parked there. He'd been round all week, fixing stuff in the yard, helping with the cleanup of the old porch and the construction of the new one. But currently he was nowhere to be found.

I plucked Roly and Poly from the basket and brought them into the house. As soon as I walked through the back door, they wriggled free and took off. "Dylan?" I called.

"In here," he said from the living room.

I found him cleaning a putty knife. He'd just finished spackling all the buckshot holes in the wall. "Did you break in here?"

"I *entered*. I still have my key."

I narrowed my eyes. "I'm going to need that back."

"I think I lost it."

"I'll change the locks."

"You might want to hold off on that. I'm coming back tomorrow with supplies to fix the air-conditioning."

Dang. He had me there. I'd do just about anything for air-conditioning heading into the summer. "Fine. I'll change the locks next week."

"It's a plan, then." He set down a putty knife, covered the spackle jar, and walked over to me. "I also brought over a generator. Just in case. It's a spare that was collecting dust at the lake house, so don't argue. I put it in the garage."

He stood close. So close. I closed my eyes and was brought back to a different time when I could wrap my arms around him and hold him as long as I wanted. I wished with all my might that we were in that place again, but I knew that wishing wouldn't make it so. "What do you want?"

"I want a lot of things," he said, watching me intently. "But for now a thank-you would be nice."

"What else?" I wanted to hear. I wanted the words. I wanted to know if we could somehow piece *us* back together again.

He moved in even closer. Skin touching skin. Heartbeat against heartbeat.

"I wouldn't turn down a kiss."

My pulse thrummed in my throat as I leaned up to brush my lips against his. A tiny kiss. A tease. A memory, really . . .

He'd just wrapped his arms around me, holding me tightly, when a horn blasted from outside. A loud *aaaooooga*.

"What is that?" he asked, his breath hot against my neck.

"Delia's new bike horn." I wriggled free of his arms and looked out the window. Delia had parked her new bike (black with hot pink skulls) next to mine. She pulled Boo out of the basket and headed for the back door.

"What's she doing here?" he asked.

I smiled. "We're going to pop popcorn and watch chick flicks. Want to stay?"

He looked into my eyes. "With you? More than anything. With both of you? No, thanks." He gathered up a few supplies and pulled open the front door. "But I'll be back tomorrow, Carly."

I watched him go, and heaven help me, I was already looking forward to seeing him again.

Boo came charging in on the hunt for Roly and Poly, and Delia tipped her head when she saw me. "You have the strangest look on your face. What're you thinking about?"

I laughed. "Cleaning out my underwear drawer."

"And people think I'm the strange one in the family."

"That's because you are."

She smiled and threw a rag at me. "Are you going to give him another chance?" she asked, nodding to Dylan as he backed out of the driveway.

"We'll see," I said.

But even as the words came out of my mouth, I knew this wasn't about giving Dylan another chance.

It was about giving myself one. I was a healing witch. It might just be time to heal my own heart.

It wasn't going to be easy.

I latched onto my locket, felt the warmth in my palm. But I was up for the challenge.

Read on for a sneak peek at the next novel
in Heather Blake's Wishcraft Mystery series,

The Goodbye Witch

Coming in spring 2014 from Obsidian

"Do you think I can get away with murder?"

The back door slammed, punctuating the startling question as Starla Sullivan rushed into the kitchen of As You Wish, my aunt Ve's personal concierge business, which doubled as our home. Or, more appropriate, the old Victorian house that doubled as a business.

Soap bubbles slid off my fingers as I set down the pot I'd been washing. Early-afternoon sunlight streamed in through the window over the sink as I dried my hands with a dish towel and studied Starla carefully. Typically I'd laugh off such a question. Murder? Impossible. She was the most even-keeled, joy-filled witch I knew. But panic clouded her usually sparkling blue eyes, and a touch of fear slid down my spine.

"Maybe," I said honestly. Since moving to the Enchanted Village last June, I'd learned a thing or two about homicides—I'd helped solve several local cases. There were ways to get away with murder if you planned carefully enough. I'd picked up a few tips and tricks to evade the police—but couldn't imagine ever implementing the knowledge. I wasn't usually the murderous type, either, unless my family and friends were threatened. Then, look out. The mama bear in me wouldn't back down. As I watched Starla pace nervously, I had the uneasy feeling this was one of those times for her. "Why? Who do we need to kill?"

Holding on to a thread of hope that she was simply venting and hadn't really turned homicidal, I'd purposefully kept my voice unnaturally light. My dog, Missy, formally known as Miss Demeanor, looked up from her bed near the mud room door and cocked her head as though understanding the seriousness of this conversation.

"*We*, Darcy?" Tears brimmed at the base of her light lashes.

"Obviously I'm not letting you do it alone. If you deem that someone needs to go, then I trust your instincts. *Patooey*. I spit on that person, and that's saying something, because you know I hate spitting."

Sunbeams fell across Starla's face, making her look more angelic than usual, despite her sudden affinity for homicide. A quivering smile spread over her lips and lit her from the inside out. Then a passing cloud blocked the sun, her smile faltered, the tears fell, and she suddenly threw herself into my arms and started sobbing.

A lump lodged itself squarely in my throat as I held her closely like I used to do with my younger sister, Harper. Because I was the only mother figure Harper had ever known—our mom died the day she was born—she'd never minded crying on my shoulder. Until she hit her teen years. And those were years we would both rather forget. She was now twenty-three and was well past her aversion to affection.

As I soothed, I noticed that Starla's skin felt chilled,

probably a remnant of the icy air outside. January in the Enchanted Village, a themed neighborhood of Salem, Massachusetts, was about as cold as anyplace I'd ever experienced. The village had already received more than a foot of snow this month alone, and it was only two weeks into the new year.

"Oh, Starla, what's wrong?" I whispered, rubbing her back as she trembled beneath my hand. "Did Vince do something?"

Vincent Paxton was Starla's boyfriend, and someone I didn't quite trust. Not yet. Maybe not ever. He was a Seeker, a mortal who longed to become a Crafter—a witch, like Starla and me. Specifically, we were Wishcrafters, witches who could grant wishes, though technically she was a CrossCrafter, a hybrid witch. She was part Wishcrafter (her predominate Craft) and part Bakecrafter (she had zero skills in the kitchen), which was the complete opposite of her twin brother, Evan, who owned the only bakery in the village.

There were many things I didn't like about Vince, including his past history as a murder suspect with questionable morals, and only a few things I did. One was how much he obviously cared about Starla. But if he had hurt her . . .

"It's not Vince." Sniffling, she backed away from me. As fast as she could wipe them away, more tears filled her blue eyes.

"Then, what?" I asked, an ache growing in my stomach.

Right now I wished with all my heart that I could take away the obvious pain Starla was feeling. But one of the frustrating rules of being a Wishcrafter was that we wouldn't grant our own wishes.

Her voice cracked as she said, "He's back."

"Who's back?" I suddenly wished my aunt Ve was around in case Starla needed additional moral support. Plus, I had no doubt she'd help us hide a body if need be. But she was out of town for the day on an As You Wish assignment.

Starla began pacing again, her boots hitting the wood floor with the force of her anxiety. With each pivot, her blond ponytail swung out behind her, slashing the air. "Kyle. Kyle's back."

I knew of only one Kyle in her life, and simply hearing the name come from her lips was enough to make my blood run cold. "Your ex-husband, Kyle?" I said in a hushed breath. "Are you sure?"

"I'm fairly sure. I was wrapping up my afternoon rounds on the village green when I saw him near the ice-skating oval. One minute I'm snapping shots of a toddler wobbling on the ice, and the next I'm feeling my world disintegrate beneath my feet."

Starla owned Hocus Pocus Photography and was often out and about in the square taking pictures of tourists, mementos the visitors could purchase on their way out of the village.

"Could it have been someone who looks like him?" I asked. "Maybe his twin brother?"

Kyle and Liam Chadwick were fraternal twins, but looked very similar. Kyle's whole family—his mom, dad, and two brothers—still lived in the village. They owned Wickedly Creative, an art studio just beyond the square. It was excruciatingly awkward when Starla bumped into one of them.

"No, it wasn't Liam. It was Kyle. I'd know him anywhere. I took pictures of him just to be sure—and to show the police. He's back."

"Let me see the pictures." I'd seen Kyle Chadwick's face often enough on the Wanted poster in the village police station to know what he looked like.

Her hand fluttered to her chest, where her camera usually hung. But it wasn't there.

"My camera!" she cried. "I was so freaked-out at seeing him that my legs went weak. I had to sit down for a second, and I must have left it on a bench near the skating rink. I have to go back and get it."

"Let me call Harper. She can get there faster than you." That, and I was starting to realize I needed reinforcements. If it was Kyle . . . this was big news. Big, dangerous news. "Hold on a sec."

Nodding, tears spilled down Starla's face. I quickly ducked into the As You Wish office, closed the door a bit, and dialed my sister at her bookshop, which was just across the street from the ice rink.

"Spellbound, this is Harper."

"It's me," I whispered into the phone.

"What's wrong, Darcy?"

She knew me too well, picking up on my anxiety from only two little words. "It's Starla. She left her camera on a bench near the ice-skating rink—can you go get it?"

"Why'd she leave it? What's going on?"

There was no point in trying to be deceptive with Harper. She would get the information out of me eventually. "She accidentally left it there when she saw Kyle Chadwick."

There was a beat of silence before she said, "Kyle Chadwick?"

"Yes. Well, she thinks it's him." I explained the situation.

"For the love . . . ," Harper muttered. "Did she call the police?"

The office was its normal mess—a source of contention between Aunt Ve and me. Today the clutter only added to my stress level. I pulled my long ponytail forward over my shoulder and fussed with the dark strands of my hair. "I don't think so. Not yet. I'll see if she did."

"If she hasn't, you should."

Harper was right. The sooner the police were involved with this, the better. "Can you get the camera? It'll be nice to have confirmation that Kyle is in the village when the police get here."

"I'm on it." She hung up.

Setting the phone onto its dock, I let out a long sigh. Chill bumps covered my skin, and I noticed my hands were shaking as I walked back into the kitchen.

Starla had quit pacing and now sat on a kitchen stool with my aunt's Himalayan, Tilda, curled in her lap. Tilda seemed to have a sixth sense for when people were upset. Despite her persnickety disposition, she almost always set aside her normal crankiness to offer comfort. This time was no different.

I often wondered whether Tilda was a familiar, a Crafter who took on the form of an animal after death, but if she was one, she wasn't letting on. Other familiars I knew, such as my close mouse friend, Pepe, and Archie, the scarlet macaw who lived next door, had no trouble speaking to me. If Tilda was a familiar, she was giving me the silent treatment.

Pulling up the stool next to her, I said, "Did you call the police, Starla?"

She buried her face in Tilda's fur. "I didn't. I snapped the pictures of him, then kind of froze. I started shaking. I don't remember much after that—only running here." Tears swam in her eyes. "Maybe it wasn't him. Maybe I'm making a fuss out of nothing. Maybe my mind is playing tricks on me. It is almost the anniversary of when he was arrested, and it's been on my mind."

Maybe. But I wanted to be sure—for her sake.

It didn't escape my notice, either, that she referred to the upcoming anniversary as when he had been *arrested*. But it was a couple of days from being two years since Kyle Chadwick had tried to strangle her, leaving her for dead.

My hands curled into fists as I said, "We should call Nick."

Nick Sawyer wasn't only the village's police chief. He was also . . . mine. My boyfriend, a term that seemed childish but was technically appropriate. We'd been dating since summertime. We'd had our ups and downs, but right now we were in a good place.

"Only Nick for now, okay?" she said, putting her hand on my arm. "I don't want . . ."

I reached out and held her hand. "What?"

"It's just that when he was arrested . . . there was so much scrutiny."

"That makes sense. He was charged with a horrible crime."

"Not only scrutiny of him, Darcy. Of me. People didn't want to believe me about what happened. . . . I don't want to go through that again. At least not until I'm sure that the man at the rink was really him. The pictures will prove it."

"I'll call Nick's cell phone, not the police station," I said soothingly.

"Okay."

I dialed, but Nick didn't answer. I left a message for him to come over as soon as he could, that it was important.

"I can't stop shaking," Starla said, absently watching her hand tremble.

I couldn't blame her. It had to have been such a shock to see her ex-husband. A man she'd once loved with all her heart.

A man who'd tried to kill her.

Tilda's purrs filled the air as Starla asked, "Why would he come back?"

"I don't know." According to Aunt Ve, one of the best gossipers in the whole village, Kyle had jumped bail and disappeared after being charged with Starla's attempted murder. No one had seen hide nor hair of him in two years. He was still a fugitive.

I'd lived in the village for less than a year, so I had never met the man, but I hated him with every drop of blood in my body, as did everyone who loved Starla. Why would he risk surfacing in a place where people knew him so well? It didn't make sense. I hoped that she'd been mistaken. That he wasn't here in the village. But I doubted she would have had such a visceral reaction if she wasn't certain.

The back door swung open and Harper hurried inside, a camera in hand and her cheeks bright red. Whether the color came from the freezing temperatures or from her agitation, I wasn't sure. She tugged a stocking cap off her head, leaving her pixie-cut light brown hair sticking up in static-filled tufts.

Setting the camera on the counter, she went over and hugged Starla, who might be my best friend but had quickly become like family to all of us. She was practically another sister to Harper, another niece to Aunt Ve.

Missy came off her bed and barked. She probably felt the tension in the air and didn't like it much. I scooped her up and held her close. Her heart beat furiously against my hand. Probably a lot like the way my heart beat against the dog's spine.

Harper and I hadn't known a thing about Kyle Chadwick until a month ago, when Starla opened up to us, telling us her fateful story of love gone wrong. According to Ve, Starla didn't talk much about her tumultuous marriage, telling people only that she was divorced and that it most certainly hadn't been amicable.

That had been the understatement of a lifetime.

It was a miracle she was sitting there.

There was a tap at the back door, and Nick stuck his head inside. "Darcy? You called?"

Missy squirmed, and I set her down. She bounded over to the door as I waved him inside. He bent down to rub Missy's ears before coming into the kitchen.

All it took was one look at our faces before his dark eyes shifted from those of a curious boyfriend to those of a hardened policeman. "What's going on?"

Standing close to him, I felt the warmth of his body and moved a little closer. I cared for him more than I had ever dared to admit. I was working up my nerve to confess those three little words, even within the silence of my own head. It had been a long time since I'd said them to a man—my ex-husband had been the last, and we'd been divorced for more than two years now. But even as lousy a husband as Troy had been, he was a saint compared to Kyle Chadwick.

Starla related what she'd seen on the green, and fresh

tears filled her eyes. "He was exactly the same as he was two years ago—maybe a little thinner, but the same crew cut, the same square face, the same piercing eyes. I always thought that if he came back he'd wear a disguise. Change his hair color, grow a beard. But no. He was just . . . him. And he was watching me."

I shivered.

Harper shuddered.

Nick dragged a hand through his dark hair. He knew the history of Kyle Chadwick, the village's most notorious fugitive. "Starla, are you sure it was him?"

"The longer I sit here, the more I doubt myself. But I took pictures. They'll prove it one way or the other." She pushed the camera toward him. "You know what he looks like, right? From his mug shot and the Wanted posters?"

Fortunately, Kyle was not a Wishcrafter—or else his photos would be nothing but bright starbursts. He was a Manicrafter, a witch with magic hands. And he was a sociopath.

"I'd know his face anywhere." Nick drew in a deep breath as he reached for the camera and flicked the power switch. He hit the button to review the photos and clicked and clicked and finally looked up at Starla.

"What?" she asked, lifting off the stool at his strange expression. "It's him. Isn't it him?"

"How many pictures did you take this afternoon?" he asked.

"Of just Kyle or everyone?"

"Everyone."

"Hundreds. I was wrapping up my afternoon rounds when I saw him."

Nick's brown eyes were flat and unreadable as he

turned the camera around. "Then it looks as though someone might have tampered with your camera."

"What do you mean?" She grabbed for the Nikon and let out a little cry.

I leaned over her shoulder as she continued to click a button, despite the message on the review screen.

FOLDER CONTAINS NO IMAGES

There was no photo of Kyle.
There were no photos at all.
They'd all been deleted.

Also available from

Heather Blake

IT TAKES A WITCH
A Wishcraft Mystery

Darcy Merriweather has just discovered she hails from a
long line of Wishcrafters—witches with the power to cast
spells by making a wish. She's come to Enchanted Village
to learn her trade—but instead finds herself in the middle
of a murder investigation...

"Magic and murder...what could be better? It's exactly
the book you've been wishing for!"
—National bestselling author Casey Daniels

Available wherever books are sold or at
penguin.com

facebook.com/TheCrimeSceneBooks

OM0102

Also available from

Heather Blake

A WITCH BEFORE DYING
A Wishcraft Mystery

When Darcy Merriweather, Salem's newest resident wishcrafter, is hired by Elodie Keaton to clean up her missing mother's disorderly home, she's shocked to find something disturbing beneath the piles of old newspapers and knickknacks—Patrice Keaton's body.

Now it's up to Darcy to investigate Patrice's death. Was it a crime of passion, or were Patrice's troubles caused by the Anicula, a powerful wish-granting amulet that had long been in her possession? Darcy has to not only find the killer, but also the Anicula—before the powerful wish fulfillment charm falls into the wrong hands…

"An enchanting and thoroughly likable sleuth."
—*New York Times* bestselling author Denise Swanson

Available wherever books are sold or at
penguin.com

facebook.com/TheCrimeSceneBooks

Also available from

Heather Blake

THE GOOD, THE BAD, AND THE WITCHY
A Wishcraft Mystery

When magical florist Harriette Harkette decides to throw
a lavish eightieth birthday party for herself, she hires
Darcy and her aunt Ve's personal concierge service, As You
Wish, to plan the soiree. But turning eighty isn't all
Harriette is celebrating—she's recently created the
midnight black Witching Hour rose, the first all-natural
black rose. Darcy works hard on planning an extravagant
celebration, but when a cake delivery boy is found dead,
the celebration is cut short. Now his ghost has imprinted
on Darcy; meaning they're bonded until she can untangle
the thicket surrounding his murder—and discover what it
has to do with the V

"An enchanting and tho
—*New York Times* bestselli

Available wherever b
penguir

facebook.com/TheC